12-19

THE GREY SISTERS

THE

GREY

SISTERS

JO TREGGIARI

PENGUIN TEEN
an imprint of Penguin Random House Canada Young Readers,
a Penguin Random House Company

First published 2019

1 2 3 4 5 6 7 8 9 10

Manufactured in Canada

Library and Archives Canada Cataloguing in Publication

Title: The Grey sisters / Jo Treggiari.
Names: Treggiari, Jo, author.
Identifiers: Canadiana (print) 20190058870 | Canadiana (ebook) 20190061049 |
ISBN 9780735262980 (hardcover) | ISBN 9780735262997 (EPUB)
Classification: LCC PS8639.R433 G79 2019 | DDC jC813/.6—dc23

Library of Congress Control Number: 2019932591

www.penguinrandomhouse.ca

Penguin
Random House
PENGUIN TEEN CANADA

For Silvia Rajagopalan.

And all my sisters,
be they blood, soul, or heart.

We all originated from the same place. Northern Europe mostly. Immigrants fleeing persecution, war, or famine. But within a couple of generations we became mountain folk or valley folk. It was as simple as that. Those of our ancestors less fortunate settled in Pembroke Cross, an irregular rectangle of poor soil backed up against the hard skirts of the Grey Sisters mountain, hemmed in by the vast forests of pine, maple, and birch, and isolated from those who farmed and fished the lush pasturelands and rich streams of Abbotsford and its cousin to the east, Feltzen Corners. At the entryway to Abbotsford, three fine wooden churches, Baptist, Lutheran, and Presbyterian, stood sentinel and guarded the souls of all who lived there. The gateway to Pembroke Cross was marked by tar-paper shacks, screaming babies, and the husks of broken-down machinery.

Although the rocky heights were inhospitable, there was a pride in surviving them. People were chewed up and spat out, broken on the granite walls. Seeds washed away in the floods and there was barely any grazing. Goats thrived eating weeds and thistles, but the coyotes, mountain lions, and bears picked them off one by one.

And yet we endured. In spite of the mountain. Because of the mountain—those three soaring peaks that swallowed the sky and soaked the earth in their black shadow.

There was something pure at the wild heart of it that ran through our veins even when families fractured and moved away. The mountain was our touchstone, our true North. The snows came and went, the sun rose and fell, and there was the sense that even if the world failed, the mountain would continue. Eternal.

—*In the Shadow of the Grey Sisters: The Townships of Pembroke Cross, Feltzen Corners, and Abbotsford, A Personal History*, Earl Lumsden, 1982

ONE

-*Kat*-

IT WAS NOTHING REALLY. Her ears closed up and then she felt a discomforting pressure like a rough, heavy hand on the top of her head. She tried swallowing repeatedly to equalize the pressure in her ears and then rummaged in her bag for some gum. She didn't find any. Instead, she discovered Floppy Monkey stuffed down at the bottom with a spare pair of thick woolen socks.

D must have snuck him into the bag and kept Floppy Giraffe with her. They were ancient stuffed toys knitted for them at birth by their Nonna. They normally lived on the bookshelf, but not when the girls were sick or one of them was traveling solo. Kat smiled to herself. He was almost as good as having her twin sister sitting right there beside her, and she wished she could cuddle with him unnoticed for a minute but that was unlikely. She touched her fingertip to her lips, pressed a kiss onto his poor worn head, and hid him away again.

It was a small plane, and the twenty-eight kids and two teachers filled it completely. That was half of the tenth grade; the other half were building houses for low-income families, but she'd done that in grade nine and quickly realized that she wasn't compatible with power tools.

Next to her, Jonathan interrupted the contemplation of his heavy book and swept his gaze around the crowded airplane. "G-force," he said, staring at her with his amber eyes. His heavy-framed glasses magnified them hugely. It was unsettling, like looking at a praying mantis close up. Funny how, even though he and his just-eleven-months-older sister, Spider, shared an undeniable family resemblance—same eyes and brows, same strong features and dark hair—Jonathan hadn't grown into his face and body yet. It was as if he was wearing a skin suit a few sizes too big and it made him ungainly and awkward. Spider was the opposite of that, sure and graceful in her movements. "You know, gravity."

Kat grunted. He was always saying weird things and then not explaining them. This time though, he continued. "But are we going up or down? Roller coaster?" He moved his hand in a wave motion and pursed his lips.

She had no answer, nor could she be sure he was even talking to her. More like *at* her. Spider always said Jonathan was on his own trip, and barely noticed other people. He even referred to them as *humans* for chrissakes, as if he were from outer space or something. And being so smart, he'd gone straight from eighth grade into tenth—*their* grade. It was something he never let any of them forget.

Still, they'd all grown up together on the same cul-de-sac and Kat got him, or at least more than most.

"Is your seat belt on?" he asked, poking at her upper arm.

She lifted the corner of her shirt to show him and returned her attention to the thick notebook open on her lap. It was her idea book, stuffed full of images and clippings. Everything and everyone she drew inspiration from. At the moment, she was totally in love with Mexican floral embroidery and Yayoi Kusama's crazy polka dots. Sometimes when she was snuggled under the covers in her bed, she saw flowers and butterflies imprinted on everything. A glorious world of movement and color.

The plane dipped, propelling her stomach into her neck.

Two rows up, she could see the back of Henry Chen's tousled head, John Brewster's hand high-fiving him. The noise of chatter washed over her, transforming the cabin into an even smaller space.

Surely they must be getting close? She estimated they were somewhere near Spectacle Lakes. Her Nonna had told her that they were so blue they were like a slice of heaven.

She was sitting right above the wing, though, so she didn't have much chance of any kind of view. She wished her sister were with her, distracting her with a joke, but D and Spider had both managed to contract chicken pox shortly before the school trip. In the middle of the first month of school, no less! Kat didn't know whether to be happy she wasn't sick or mad because for the first time ever the two of them hadn't shared an illness. She opened her mouth wide and tried swallowing again. No go. Her head felt crammed with fluffy cotton wool.

The flight attendant—there was only one on this minuscule flying machine, a woman with a fixed, white-toothed smile and strawberry-blonde hair in a high ponytail—began to collect the lunch trays even though some people were still eating. Henry tried to hold onto his half-consumed ham and cheese sandwich but the attendant gently wrested it from his hands.

Almost simultaneously, an announcement crackled over the intercom. "This is your captain, Jim Davies. We're making an unscheduled landing. We'll be on the ground in twenty minutes."

Kat checked her belt again. Jonathan was sitting straight up, his neck extended like a meerkat spotting danger.

The plane gave a lurch and immediately a *ping* sounded through the cabin. Then the overhead lights dimmed and went out.

"*Merde*," Jonathan muttered, pushing his glasses up his nose. "That's the 'something is wrong' ping."

"How can you tell which ping it is?" Kat said, trying to control her irritation.

"Clearly it's different."

"And?" Kat said. "We're just getting ready to land, like the captain said. At another airport. There's probably weather or something. The mountains are known for it. There's that big range around here." She watched the attendant slowly and methodically checking that everyone's seats were upright.

She fiddled with her seatbelt again, cinched it tighter, angry that Jonathan was making her anxious.

Jonathan had read the safety card, of course. He'd counted the rows to the exits and relayed all this information to Kat even though she'd begged him to shut up. If Mrs. Rojas, their English teacher, hadn't forced her to sit beside him, she'd have been closer to the front of the plane. Maybe across the aisle from Lindsay and Maria, who were heavily involved in the drama department and wanted her to help design the costumes for this year's production of *Our Town*. That would have been a positive distraction. She couldn't remember any of what Jonathan had said now. Her brain didn't seem to be working. The buzz of conversation had ceased and instead people were staring out the windows. All Kat could see was a massive cloud-bank like a snow hill, and the back of everyone's heads. She looked up instead at the attendant; the woman had paused near them, her hand lightly resting on the back of Kat's seat. She didn't seem too worried, judging by her body language. Kat's eyes dipped to her name tag: ANNIE WILBUR. *Annie Wilbur is wearing a dull-orange knee-length A-line skirt, and an autumnal-patterned short-sleeved blouse with mud-brown brogues,* said the critical voice in Kat's head. She wondered what it would be like to have no say in what you wore to work. Could you accessorize? Change the length? Mix up the colors?

"Is something wrong?" she asked the attendant.

"No, no," she said. "Just a little hiccup."

Jonathan took a deep breath beside her and let it out audibly. Annie gave them a quick smile and moved up the aisle. Jonathan breathed again, loudly, as if he was meditating or something.

"What are you doing?" Kat asked.

"I think the air's getting thin. And can you smell that? Is it smoke?"

"Don't be an idiot," she snapped. "Look at Annie. She's perfectly calm."

"Who the hell is Annie?"

"Forget it." Was he right? Her sinuses were feeling clogged, like a constrictive band across the bridge of her nose. Suddenly, it was as if the cabin walls were closing in on them. The air was being sucked away.

"What do you think is going on?" she asked Jonathan.

"Could be a few different scenarios. I'm trying to calculate the odds at the moment. It's an interesting hypothesis."

"It's not a puzzle," she snapped.

"Yes it is. It's a puzzle with laws and various outcomes."

She glowered at him and he stared back until finally she closed her eyes. His expression had been curious but completely disinterested in her and what she was asking. "Can't read cues," Spider was always reminding her. "He's off in his own world, and it's more exciting than anything you can offer."

She tried to get comfortable in the seat but it was hard against her spine. She tried to will her mind elsewhere. Into the middle of her imaginary field of wild blooms, luna moths, and swallowtail butterflies. At home with D and Mamma and Nonna. Safely landed. But she couldn't relax. And then the sense of pressure against her body again. This time well on the other side of bearable. Crushing. Her head felt as if it were swelling up, bobbing from her shoulders by a thin cord.

"Ladies and gentlemen," came the announcement. "This is your captain. We have to make an emergency landing. Please remain in your seats and listen for instructions."

Jonathan whistled softly.

Mrs. Rojas bobbed up quickly. "Just do what you're told, kids, and everything will be fine." Her voice, squeaky like an unoiled gate, hitched at the end of the sentence as if she was asking a question.

Sound rose like a wave. An excited clamor, a few screams.

"It is smoke. It is smoke," Jonathan said. Kat grabbed his hand without thinking about it. It was rougher than she expected, so different from Spider's smooth, soft grasp. His was calloused, and his grip was crushing. He still bit his nails, all the way down, fingers like chewed-up nubs. Did D realize what was happening right now? This exact moment?

D hadn't known when Kat fell off her bike and fractured her arm. Kat had been oblivious when Sally Beaumont and her crew jumped D in the girl's bathroom in fifth grade and smashed her face in the sink.

Could she call Mamma? Was there time? Where had she put her phone? She couldn't seem to make a decision. Nothing felt real except for the cold, weirdly powdery hand gripping hers. She'd never get to hold Spider's hand again. Never discover if it meant anything at all.

"Clouds," someone said. "So many clouds."

Across the aisle, Sally Beaumont was rocking and crying. Tears dripping from her fingers with wet splats onto the vinyl seat. Shit, she was going to die in Sally's company. What if they ended up spending eternity together? This was not how it was supposed to be.

Her head continued to swell, filling up with helium, lifting from her body.

The oxygen masks dropped.

She could barely hear a sound, but all the faces around her looked calm. No one was screaming anymore. Everyone sat quietly now, complacent, except for Jonathan, who was pinching her arm savagely and yelling at her to *wake up, Kat!* And then he was pushing the plastic cup over her mouth and nose. His own face resembled something animal-ish—a pig, or elephant.

"Wing's on fire," he yelled, but his voice was so muffled she wasn't sure. The plane banked hard and she watched her hand-embroidered bag sail down the aisle, hitting Annie Wilbur —whose smile had been sunny until now, who'd given her extra snack mix—square on the nose and breaking it. She saw blood explode like a water balloon and then Annie was flat on her back, her toes pointing in Kat's direction. Those really were some ugly shoes.

Jonathan yelled and tugged at her, pointing—"The emergency exit!"—but Kat was looking up.

It was *snowing*. Bits of stuff in the air swirling around. Dirty snow. The plane was rocking from side to side, shuddering with a high metallic whine. Her vision was whiting out. She felt cold, then warm. It was so bright, like sun blazing on the ice. Diamonds! And then the dark swooped in, black wings closing around her head.

TWO

— D —

IT WAS THE LAST WEEK of eleventh grade and D's brain was officially numb. She blamed mathematics. A subject demanding an all-consuming focus. Well, also the fact that she was coming up on her second solid week of final exams and to end with trigonometry (which was definitely not her favorite subject) seemed monstrously unfair and God she was so tired she wasn't sure she could remember which end of a pencil was right. On the way from her car to the school entrance she'd narrowly missed beaning herself against a lamppost, and over breakfast her mother had asked her three times, or maybe more, judging by her irritated expression, if D could pick up some soy milk after school. D couldn't recall what answer she'd given, come to think of it. She'd buoyed herself up with the thought of sleeping for a few days when it was all over and done with, but that wasn't much of a prize. Sleep meant dreams. The bad ones that wrapped themselves around her mouth and nose like clotted smoke until she jolted awake, catapulting herself to the open window to breathe cool air and count down from one hundred. Or the good ones—even worse—so real, so tender that they broke her heart all over again.

A couple of classmates had approached her as she sat against her locker mouthing mathematical formulas, but an angry glare had warded them off. She couldn't engage in frivolous conversation. Not until this exam was done. But still she should have known, should have paid attention.

"D!"

D looked up and saw Min hurrying toward her. Min was totally impervious to D's stern eyebrows.

"What? I've got fifteen minutes. I think I can get to this chapter." She fumbled, dropped a sheaf of scrawled notes on the floor.

"Where's your phone? Did you hear? They were talking about it in the office," Min said.

"Please tell me Mr. Johansen decided to grade us solely on attendance and our willingness to copy neatly from the black-board?" Mr. Johansen was all about directing their attention away from electronic devices.

"Huh?"

"Math bubble. Trapped. Might die. Can't breathe."

"D," said Min, sounding unlike herself. It was the note in her voice, halfway between freaked out and in tears, that hooked D's attention.

And it was then she realized that the upper halls of Campbellton High were full like they never were, with people huddled in groups talking excitedly. It seemed as if the entirety of the grade-eleven class was squeezed into this small area, and her heart twinged because normally they were all spread so thin, classrooms cavernous and sports teams restricted to the junior years.

"Phone," Min said again, and D handed it over. Min googled a word or two and then tapped on the first entry. She sank down next to D, pressing against her, and held the phone steady.

It opened to the local news site. The photo was dark because the room was dark, and maybe, D thought, this was a photo that should not have been taken. A haggard woman sitting up in a hospital bed, her limbs barely making a ripple in the sheets, and a sloppy wool hat covering most of her head. Her eyes were startled, one thin hand upraised as if to defend herself. *Flight 394 Crash Survivor Wakes from Coma!* blared the headline. *A Miracle!* A miracle was what the newspapers had called it nearly two years ago when she was found after the crash, badly injured but alive. D didn't believe in miracles.

"Is that . . . ?" she mumbled. Her tongue felt curiously thick. The blood was pounding in her ears.

"Annie Wilbur, the flight attendant."

"No, it can't be." D swiped the screen, enlarging the photo. Her fingers were shaking so badly they hardly seemed like part of her.

"Spider," she croaked.

"Of course! I should have . . ." Min squeezed her shoulder. "It's a shock. Stupid me. I'll get her right now."

"She was grabbing a smoothie."

Min nodded and raced off in the direction of the cafeteria.

What did it mean? Staring at the photo wasn't helping. She wasn't sure her mouth could even form words.

When Spider arrived, breathless, all D could do was point dumbly at the corner of the photograph. At the brown lumpy thing tucked against Annie's pillow.

"Is that?" A range of emotions flickered across Spider's face. D recognized pain followed by grief before her friend's eyes shuttered.

D nodded with difficulty.

"Floppy Monkey." Last time she'd seen him, she'd been shoving him into her sister's bag.

THREE

– D –

IN D'S MIND, the trip was straightforward and easy. They'd leave early in the morning, drive most of the day, and arrive at the crash site in the late afternoon. A to B. In reality, they left late—closer to ten than seven, courtesy of Spider—and hit the freeway right around the height of the mid-morning congestion. Stop and go. Inching through traffic. Just getting to the roundabout had worn D's nerves to shreds, and after only two hours of driving, she could already feel the tension in her lower back.

She relaxed her grip on the steering wheel, darting a venomous glance at Spider, who snored in the seat beside her. It's the journey, her therapist, Doctor Octavian, would have reminded her, but no, not for D. If she could have, she'd have clicked her heels to get there in an instant. This trip was all about the destination for her. Standing on that ground, breathing the air, seeing it with her own eyes. The place where her sister had died.

Ever since the Annie Wilbur story had broken, she'd felt a compulsion to go, and Doctor Octavian had been fully supportive. She'd half thought the therapist would advise against it, but instead the doctor had smiled and leaned forward, hands clasped, notebook laid aside for once. "I know it's hard," she'd said, "but if you can get open, if you can emotionally experience the event, grasp the reality of it, it might stimulate the return of healthy emotion. Then you can move on from there."

Her mother had been somewhat less enthusiastic. D could have said to her, "I can't see any future. I don't know who I am. Sometimes I have to lie down because it's all so overwhelming I can't make sense of it, and then I begin to dissolve." But instead, she'd shaken her head and pulled herself regretfully from her mother's embrace, kissed her cheeks, and said, "The job at the gallery doesn't start until next month. I'm going. This is for me, Mamma." Making decisions like this gave her a sense of control that she hadn't felt for so long.

"I wrote her a letter," she said into the drowsy silence.

"What?" Min raised her head from the pillow she'd made from their backpacks and sat up. Her cheeks were pale and she had that quirk in her voice that D was certain meant she was feeling nauseous. "Who?"

D felt a rush of love. Min knew she'd get sick on this trip, and yet still she'd come.

"Annie Wilbur," she said, turning down the true-crime podcast they were listening to. "The day after. Almost two weeks ago. I don't expect her to answer. I'm not sure if that would be a good thing. I just wanted her to know Kat's name and a little bit about her."

Min wrinkled her brow and then spoke tentatively. "She's a link."

"Yeah. Or maybe a bridge." D wasn't sure what to do with that information, but just knowing there was someone still in the world who had been right there, had intersected with Kat, meant something.

The cars ahead of her on the dual highway slowed, red brake lights glowing. D looked up ahead but could see no reason for it. Something in the road maybe? Deer? She flipped the visor down. The day had started grey but they were now driving into the sun. Mamma's photo clipped inside smiled back at her. She and Kat took after their mother—brown eyes under straight black brows, olive skin, long fingers and toes—and not after their tall, blond Norwegian father. Their parents had split two years after they'd been born. D didn't blame him. He had a new family now, lived in Florida, and still sent a card every birthday without fail.

"Where we at, Minalicious?" She and Spider amused themselves by giving Min various nicknames. She could check the GPS but it was easier just to ask Min, who'd been acting as map navigator ever since noon, when they'd driven beyond D's limited knowledge. Basically her usual route was school, mall, downtown, home—short jaunts she could probably drive blindfolded.

"It's this next exit, going north," Min said. "And after that, it's a straight shot for at least a couple of hours."

D took it. Time ticked on. Spider snored, her face soft and vulnerable. Min curled up in the back, just the top of her blue-and-black-dyed head showing from the nest of her folded arms. The podcast ended, and a new one began. The sameness of the road, the strip malls and fast-food pit stops, lulled D into an almost trancelike state. Min gave her directions when necessary, she took the various exits and turns, the roads got smaller, and her butt got steadily more numb.

A siren blasted from the podcast. D hurriedly turned it down, but beside her Spider stretched and yawned, wiping the sleep from her eyes as she peered around.

"Where the heck are we?"

Min waved her hand limply from the back seat, indicating the single-track road and the impenetrable trees on either side of them. "Hello, wilderness," she said.

"I have to go to the bathroom," Spider announced, sitting up straighter.

"You'll have to hold it," said D, gritting her teeth as the front right wheel hit a pothole. "I'm not pulling over on a blind curve."

She-Ra's transmission was vibrating and groaning. She-Ra, so named because Spider mockingly called her a Princess of Power. The country roads were worse than D had expected, and she wondered now whether she should have taken the old VW in for a full overhaul rather than trusting in the extra cans of oil she'd brought along.

Luckily they hadn't had to pass any big trucks, but she'd been tensing her muscles for the last twenty miles in preparation. Eyeballing the road, it didn't seem possible for two vehicles to go head to head without stripping paint. And she knew that their route was going to continue to climb, narrowing roads winding through forests until they hit the foothills, and then the mountain. That was roughly where they were heading. The Grey Sisters—a jagged three-peaked colossus. On the map, the few dots designating small towns were scattered below it like spilled peppercorns. The main three lay roughly in an obtuse triangle, with microscopic Pembroke Cross the closest to the crash site.

"I might have to puke," Spider said. "The five-bean chili I had for dinner last night is not being kind."

Min groaned and rolled down her window. "Don't say *chili* and don't say *puke*, dammit."

"I believe that if you let yourself pu—vomit, you feel better afterward," Spider said. "We could all pu—regurgitate together. Like sisters. Or mother birds."

"Shut up, Spider," D hissed, shooting her the sternest look she could muster. Spider closed her eyes again and rested her head against the window.

Spider was like a sister to D, and she loved her in all those complexities, but their bond was also something that tortured her in a weird way. Because it was Spider and Kat who had truly been the best of friends, always whispering and laughing together. And even though they both tried their hardest, D and Spider were not that to each other. They were second-best, but linked together always by shared grief. And this last year Spider had seemed shut off even to her. Most of the time, D didn't have a clue where she was or who she was with. Sometimes, Doctor Octavian had said, tragedy can bring people closer, but sometimes it rips them apart.

If nothing else, D thought, at least this trip meant they were spending time together.

FOUR

– Ariel –

WE'RE HUDDLED IN THE WATERY SHADOWS thrown by the eaves of the round, flat roof. A few candles flicker inside the hall, but the rest of the compound is still in darkness and the fog shrouds the mountain. This is why Big Daddy calls our home the fortress of Avalon. From what he's told us, during his regular lessons interwoven with tales of bravery and battle, Avalon was a magical island wreathed in mist, holy and hidden from the eyes of most people. It bred warriors. That's what he said. And that's what we are. So few of us now, but he says that makes us even more special.

Soon, the mommies will wake to get the fires going and the big pots of porridge cooking. The cows—what we call those women who aren't spoken for and not yet with child—will feed the babies and make a start on the washing. Other community members will head out to the potato fields or the woods to hunt, or to the sheds to fix machinery that always seems to be breaking down or rusting out.

We've each got an apple and a handful of moldy nuts from the very bottom of the winter bins. I checked mine over already. Half of them have insect-bored holes. I'll crack them and find dust and a curled-up maggot. Diana doesn't mind eating them.

She says it's protein, no different from meat, but I can't see it like that.

Hannah yawns hugely, showing yellow teeth. "Think it'll rain?"

I don't bother answering. Of course it will. There will be choking fog and a creeping damp and more likely than not a thunderstorm or two. The rocks will be slick with wet and the mud will churn its way free of the mountain. Water I can handle.

My muscles feel tight, but in a good way. Like butterflies are trapped under my skin. I just want to get moving, shake off this coldness.

It's barely dawn, but that's part of the trial. "No one will ever attack in the bright of day," Big Daddy told us. "They'll come like thieves in the night with no honor. And they'll steal your lives before you even have time to catch your breath."

We need to learn how to operate on little sleep and in all conditions. Plus, the hike up the mountain will take us the better part of the day if we keep to the pace I'm aiming to set. Best to make camp when we can still see what we're doing. The unknown dark is dangerous. That's one of his many cautions. Big Daddy's Rules. You might call them our laws. All of us who live here learn from him.

He's up of course, running his eyes over our gear, although it's the bare essentials. Water bottles, heavier clothing than usual—all of us have a thick flannel shirt—our knives and coils of thin rope. "You need to think on your feet. Never let your guard down. Steer clear of strangers."

Big Daddy swings his arm out toward the valley. We follow the wide half circle with our eyes. Not that we can make out much. The trees are so dense that even at midday the sunlight hardly makes it down to the ground, and the fog lies over the top of them like a white blanket. Clouds too fat and heavy to float in the sky. We know who he means when he says strangers. The lowland folk and beyond. All of the outside world.

He brings his hands together. I see the blue tattoos on his muscular forearms wriggle as if the snakes inked there are truly alive. He's told us the story plenty of times. How when he was a kid—maybe four or five years old—his mother, Nana Rachel, who froze to death in the bad winter a few years back, went to wake him and right there, alongside him, was the limp body of a snake, one of the poison-filled kind. He'd strangled it before it could bite him and then gone back to sleep. It was a sign, she said, that he was special. That he was put on Earth to fight back the evil that thrived everywhere. Arthur—named for the once and future king.

"Why do they hate us?" Faith asks, her voice barely more than a whisper. She knows. She's heard the taunts in the school hallways, felt the yellow spit against her cheeks, the sly pinches.

Diana makes a rude noise. "Because we show them how they are lacking. Isn't that right, Daddy? Leaders of change are always feared and hated at first."

Sometimes she's so eager to repeat everything Big Daddy tells us that she reminds me of some small, cringing animal.

He lays his broad hand on her head and she leans into it like a barn cat.

"Them and us," says Ruth.

Big Daddy nods approvingly. "They try to destroy what they can't understand. What they envy deep in their twisted hearts. What they've forgotten to honor," he says. "It's there in all the old tales." We know the ones he means. The leather-bound books he keeps on a high shelf in the meeting hall, bringing them down to read from on special occasions. There are lessons hidden in the mythology of men, he says. They are histories, not stories. But people have robbed them of their truth and turned them into lies.

"We'll be ready for them," I say stoically. "When they come." Part of me doesn't know why they'd bother with Avalon, but Big Daddy seems so sure and he knows more about the world than I do. I've only seen a sliver of it and don't like it much. If I dare to ask a question in school, they all stare at me, laugh lowdown mean, as if I know nothing.

"Make it back from the mountain first," Big Daddy says.

"Aren't you coming with us this time?"

"Someone's got to keep the women and children safe," he says with a broad grin and a twinkle in his eyes that warms me. "You go on. The mountain will provide," he says, gently pushing Diana away from him, giving her a pat on the head. "Determination. Perseverance. Strength in numbers." And then all my sisters are lining up for a quick caress. I hang back with Aaron, who's sharpening his knife again, although I know he stayed up last night doing it. It's his first time too. He wasn't trusted before. Maybe after he proves himself, Big Daddy will let him sit with the Uncles. Maybe he can formally ask for me then.

We scan the mountain. It protects us, but it can kill us too. I don't think I'll ever get used to how big it is, how it blocks out the sky, how it's been here for time immemorial.

"We're going up there?" Aaron says softly, blinking behind his glasses.

"Not all the way up," I say, trying to sound braver than I feel.

Big Daddy catches my eyes, holds them prisoner with his own, blue and icy. "You go past Old Fire Road, past the foothills and last year's camp, nothing but prey trails then until you're in the shadow of Morganna, the biggest peak. Camp there."

Prey trails are barely rutted paths the deer travel.

He stares at me silently, grey in the dim morning light, carved out of stone. He doesn't need to speak the words for me to hear them anyway. *I'll know if you don't go all the way. I'll know if you fail to complete the test. Honor is everything.*

From the bottom of the first hill, he shouts after us, his voice echoing like a bell. "Which of you will be my Galahad? My Joan of Arc?"

FIVE

— *Min* —

MIN HAD TO ADMIT THAT Spider was pretty adorable when she was asleep. A little less intense with her limbs sprawled out and her long brown braids framing her face with that one little star-shaped chicken pox scar on her cheek, and her lips ruffling with each snore. However, she had also put her seat all the way back and her head was practically in Min's lap. If Min could have, she'd have moved over behind D, but they'd piled their bags and camping gear there, taking up all the available space. She was trapped and squished and she could smell a sourness on Spider's breath, which did nothing for her nauseated stomach.

She should be sitting in the front seat. She should be driving. Those were the best remedies for her car sickness. But Spider had legs twice as long as hers. And She-Ra was D's car and subject to various mechanical eccentricities. Not to mention that driving was mostly theoretical as far as Min was concerned.

She rolled the window farther down and leaned out, closing her eyes against the stiff breeze and trying to ignore the corkscrew turns that rocked her head on her neck.

The odometer had crept forward almost two hundred miles since they'd left the highway. The dashboard clock had flipped ahead a couple more hours. The terrain hadn't changed much though, and it made her feel as if they were stationary next to a screen that was scrolling dull landscapes. Trees. Trees. And hey, trees! Maybe, she amended, slightly fewer birch and maple and more pine as they climbed steadily into the foothills.

Each mile seemed to weigh heavy on D's shoulders, and Min wished she could take some of the burden from her.

"Pines are overrated," she declared into the wind. The trunks grew so close together that they suffocated any seedlings on the forest floor. D threw her a weary smile, shifting in her seat and rolling her neck on her shoulders. Her brown eyes were purple-shadowed. Min wondered if she'd slept much the last week.

"It's this road only now. No more sudden turn-offs or hidden signposts," she said, trying to sound upbeat. *Artery*—that's what the main road to somewhere was called. This artery, Route 12, seemed barely viable. The tarmac was fissured and strewn with loose rock. Each crack against She-Ra's undercarriage made D visibly wince.

Suddenly the sky unzipped and a torrent lashed the car. Min ducked in and hurriedly rolled up her window.

"Can't see a damn thing," D muttered, slowing the car to a crawl. The water came down in a sheet. It was like being at an old-fashioned car wash, the kind where they still let you sit in the car.

"How's old She-Ra doing? She smells a little overheated," Min said.

"She's managing. I might be riding the brakes too hard. The windshield wipers aren't doing a thing though," D said. "I think I have to pull over. Can you make sure I'm completely out of the lane and not on a drop-off or something?"

Min cranked her window open and stuck her head out. She was instantly soaked.

"All clear," she called back, trying fruitlessly to swipe water out of her eyes, "as far as I can tell. No logger trucks, no cliff, a grassy shoulder."

D eased over to the side and cut the engine. The car shuddered and groaned, seeming to settle down in the softer ground like an old weary dog.

Min dug a spare hoodie out of her backpack, wiped her face dry, and toweled her short black-and-blue hair. It didn't make much difference. She was soaked to the skin.

"I feel like my biceps are seizing up. And I've been gritting my teeth so hard my jaw aches," D said. "This road is probably a hoot on the way down. We can just cruise, but I feel like the only things keeping us on the blacktop are my arms and determination."

Spider farted gently in her sleep. D and Min exchanged looks and cracked up. D's smile remained for an instant more but then Min noticed the worry creasing her forehead.

"It can't be much further though, right, Maximin? Got no signal for the GPS," D said. There was a strained note to her voice.

Min unfolded the map across her knees, tucking her long, wet bangs back behind her ears. She had always loved maps, liked checking out the place names and wondering about the historical significance of them. Like this mountain they were heading toward—the Grey Sisters. What was up with that? Nuns? Women in mourning? Or something else entirely? She was reminded of the Greek myth about the three wise sisters who shared an eye and a tooth between them. "We should be seeing the first peak of the mountain any minute now. Or we would if we had any kind of visibility. We probably are close," she said thoughtfully. "Whole bunch of fog mixed with this rain."

D grunted her question. "What exactly does that indicate?"

"The topographical influence of the mountains. Trapped warm air meets cool air. So you get more intense weather patterns."

"Bad news is we're not going anywhere in this downpour. Shit, check that out." D thumped the steering wheel. "Shit!"

"Well, while we're stuck here . . . ," Min said, digging around in her bag. She pulled out a sheaf of papers bound with a bulldog clip. "Let's educate ourselves."

"What's that?"

"I printed it off of the internet. A self-published history of the area by someone called Earl Lumsden, and he's talking about his own ancestors. There's a whole bunch about crop failures and epidemics but also about the people. Listen to this wackness from the late 1800s: 'It was religion that first drove the wedge between the communities. During the hard winters, the single-track road up and down the mountain was almost impassable. Unless you were verifiably on your deathbed, you were expected to attend the lowland churches across the river in Abbotsford. Most of the families in the heights were eventually shunned—the Pembrokes, the Lumsdens, the Moseleys. If you bore one of those names, you were painted with the same brush. The only way to escape the stigma was to leave the area, change your name, and pray you could marry up.'"

They exchanged raised-eyebrow glances in the rearview mirror.

"And listen to this bit. He's talking about the twentieth century here. Like barely thirty years ago: 'Although life on the mountain was hardscrabble, it was the children who truly suffered. The schools were located in the valley, as were doctors and social services and almost all the amenities. Severely undernourished, sickly and weak, the children were ill-equipped to keep up with their better-fed healthy counterparts. For much of the year, they were unable to get to class at all, missing upwards of 140 days per year. They were seen as lazy, shiftless, stupid, and criminal. Most of them dropped out as soon as they turned sixteen. Without diplomas or the ability to read and write, they were relegated to manual labor jobs. Teen pregnancy rates were high—25 percent over the national average. And illnesses easily preventable or rarely seen in more prosperous areas thrived, killing one in five children in infancy.'"

"We're only six hours from a major city," D said. "It's like they were cut off from civilization."

Min nodded. "Even weirder though, there's not too much recent information on the town. It's almost like it's faded away." She stared out the window at the rain-blurred landscape. The fog had settled, transforming the trees into serrated teeth.

"Like a ghost town?" said D.

"Yeah. I mean the last census—the government survey— listed like nineteen people. And that was five years ago."

"How does that even happen? A town can't just disappear!"

Min scratched her nose. "People left. Or people died."

SIX

– Ariel –

I SET A HARD PACE. This is the seventh year that Big Daddy has sent us out, so there's a familiarity for all of us except for Aaron and Faith, although we've never climbed so high before. You might think there's a comfort to be found in that, but the only constant out here is unpredictability. The weather, the mountain, the river, the wild animals—none of them can be counted on to keep us safe. I've been coming out here since I was nine. And, as I look around the small group gathered in a clearing halfway to our destination—Aaron, who's come to stand beside me as he always does lately, Diana, Ruth, Faith, and Hannah—I am aware that every year our ranks dwindle. Three years ago the river ran wild, sending flash floods sweeping down to the compound. People died, mostly young folk who'd been out working in the far fields. Soon after, Big Daddy was able to increase our numbers, but not by much, and sometimes it feels like bad luck dogs our heels. Last year around this time, Eden fell from the cliffs, cracking her head open like an egg. Big Daddy says we don't die. We go to sleep under the mountain until the world has need of us again in the coming apocalypse. But I don't think Eden is sleeping. I think she roams the hills, howling, searching for home. Hannah swears she's seen her in the sky. Soaring like some great grey bird. Our sister.

I hear Big Daddy's disembodied voice echoing from above, telling us that we will be his warriors, that those who survive the trials are natural-born leaders. Natural as in nature. Children of the earth that spit us out, nourished us, and honed us into blades. When he told us this, Big Daddy pinched up a teaspoon of grit from the ground and placed it in his mouth like a chaw of tobacco.

Sometimes Big Daddy has a voice like molasses. His words drip into your skull and warm you from the inside out. He fills you with certainty. He's like a preacher that way. Other times his voice is thunderous and falls like a hammer, or whisper-soft and strikes like a snake. Everything he tells us is anchored here in Avalon.

We've grown up hearing the stories at his knee, the tales of King Arthur and the good life he provided for his people. The sanctuary he built.

Our strength is this dirt, sandy, grey as ash, with threads of reddish brown. And this rock, black and loose underfoot, flaking into shards sharp enough to cut your fingers and the soles of your feet. We have watered the soil with our blood. Home is sour roots and bitter berries and strange herbs and a lot of boiled potatoes. And guns and babies and the wailing of women.

It is in us and always will be. That's what he says. It forms the hard kernels that cramp our bellies and squeeze our lungs and curl our feet with muscle pain. It fills us, the empty space crying out for food, and eventually we become a part of it, like that tree I once saw that had grown around an old iron bar until the wood and metal were one.

Daddy tells us, "There are those who are born to it and those who are brought to it. And those who choose to live on their backs. They serve a different purpose."

We all know who he means: the ones who stay at home and will never be soldiers. They are breeding stock. Cows. My gaze fixes on Faith, still flabby and short of breath after three months, her mouth downturned, eyes hooded. Her baby was a big healthy boy, which was cause for celebration. He brought in enough money to buy ten new handguns. Male children have a different value here at the compound. Big Daddy has to weigh the importance of arming ourselves against growing our family. For as long as I can remember, the boy babies have been sold. Big Daddy praised her at the nightly meeting when she could stand up straight and walk again, invited her to join him, Nana Esme, and the Uncles at the high table for the evening meal. The tables are set up in a big rectangle, four of them end to end, in the communal hall—the youngest children sit along the bottom with a few mommies to make sure they don't throw their food at each other or make too much noise. We have our own place in the corner. On the same night, he gave her the choice to join the rest of us soldiers and she took it, but I don't know if she's got what it takes. After the kid was born, she lay on her mattress with her head turned to the wall for days and days, sobbing and shaking. It was a hard birth and Nana had to use the forceps but the baby came out all right, when he came. No bruises on his face or damage to his neck or eyes. I had to clean up the room after and the sheets had to be burned because there was too much blood and shit on them.

"She's young, she'll heal," was all Nana said. "It's her second one, after all."

Her first was born wrong. I remember the deformed body and the lumpy growths on its back, as if parts of it that should have been inside were not. It was early in the morning, just before sunrise, when Nana placed a cloth over the baby's face. Soaked it with something that smelled sharp and sweet and made my head spin. She sent me from the room when she caught me staring.

Set off a ways from our huts, on the other side of the fence, is a bare field of simple wooden crosses, no dates, no names. Nana wraps the dead ones and the misshapen ones in a scrap of material and sticks them in an empty detergent box, and then in a hole one of the Uncles digs in the rocky soil. They don't live long enough to have names bestowed on them. Names have power, Big Daddy tells us. The Uncle makes it a deep hole and sometimes puts a flat rock on top because the coyotes will dig and worry at anything if they get a scent. The soapy smell helps hide that for a while. I take the long way round if I have to cut past that field. And if I can't avoid it, I run and try to ignore the feeling of all the hairs on my body standing up.

Sometimes I wonder which of us will be the next to die. It could be a snakebite or a fall or drowning in the rapids. It could be in childbirth, though I am careful. There are herbs, black cohosh, goldenseal, pennyroyal. And I am so skinny I barely ever get my period. There are ways, if you are not a coward. You don't have to say yes to the Uncles. You can fight and get a beating instead. And if they hit you hard enough, ugly up your face and bruise your body, then the rest of them won't pay you any attention either. There's this one girl fights so hard I think it's going to get her killed one day. She's in the basement most of the time. We call her Ghost.

Just before this session, we got to pick our warrior names from Nana's old Bible. We are now Diana, Ruth, Faith, Hannah, and Aaron. I chose Ariel. It means Lion of God. It's hard to let the past go, but Big Daddy tells us it is to the future we should be looking. The glorious future.

I'm remembering that first year, the first trial. We ended up in a mossy clearing in the woods about ten miles out from home. It was only us girls then, none of us more than nine years old, and Big Daddy came too. I recall that he had two young dogs with him, and a rifle slung over his back in case of coyotes or a lucky encounter with a deer or moose. We were not allowed to touch the dogs, although one, spotted white and black with swirls of longer fur on its legs, kept pulling on the rope, turning around to sniff and lap at our outstretched fingers. A sharp word from Daddy and we shoved our hands back into our pockets. Once we reached the camping spot, hard up against the foothills, Daddy told us to stop.

He tied each dog to a sturdy branch on either side of the grove. They whined and panted and tried to pull free but he had used a pipe hitch, or, as I called it, a death-grip knot. He sat us around in a half circle facing him.

"You see these pups?" he said, walking back and forth between them. "They're like you. Nameless because they have no knowledge of themselves yet, not long parted from their mothers. Servile." He kicked his heavy hobnailed boot out and got the black-and-white one square in the middle of its pink-splotched stomach. It yelped and curled into its spine. He stood over it and it whined up at him, ears folded flat, eyes rolling white, mouth shaped in a pleading grin. It splayed out its legs like a flower opening to the sun. I ached to stroke its soft head and take it into my lap to comfort it.

He strolled over to the other dog, a black female with fur so short it resembled polished stone. As soon as he got near, she growled, wrinkling grey lips away from her teeth. Her fur bristled in a ridge across her back and she rose stiff-legged to her feet, barking like crazy. He stepped closer. The dog lunged, snapping, at the very end of the rope. He stared at it for a moment. "She'd bite me if she could," he said, smiling. "She'd tear me to pieces and probably eat me. The female of the species." He laughed and then he brought the gun to his shoulder and shot the cowering black-and-white dog in the head.

We were noiseless. He'd taken away our air.

I'm thinking about that day and I'm contemplating Faith. If I have to, I'll leave her out here. For the good of the family.

SEVEN

— *Min* —

AN HOUR PASSED, slow as a slug on long grass, and still it rained. Twenty minutes more. The fog cocooned them, spinning the air into white threads. Spider snored and mumbled in her sleep. D had her eyes shut but Min could tell she wasn't sleeping; her neck was too tight for that, her fingers laced together in her lap. Knowing that her friend was barely keeping her emotions in check, Min kept quiet and played raindrop races on the window—pick a rolling raindrop and see if it reached the edge first—something she'd done at home on wet days when there was nothing else to do. Like seriously, nothing. All her books read and reread; her coloring pencils worn to stubs. Those long days when even the *Oxford English Dictionary* her parents owned that was boxed in two volumes and came with its own nifty rectangular magnifying glass had no power to entertain her.

"We're stopping?" Spider said, yawning widely like a lion. She always woke up suddenly and often fell asleep in the middle of a sentence.

"Yup, here's your chance to pee," D said. "While you're out there, can you adjust the wiper blades?"

Spider propped her feet up on the dashboard and checked

the scenery. "I'm not going out in that." Like a cat, she hated to get wet. "My bladder has sealed itself."

"We're not going anywhere then. I can't see a damn thing."

Min sighed and held her hand out. "Rock-Paper-Scissors."

D put her hand in, and after a moment so did Spider.

"Wait," said Min. "We abide by the results?"

"Yeeesss," said Spider, sounding completely untrustworthy. She opened her eyes wide and grinned. Those eyes were part of the reason Spider was so lucky in love, Min thought. They were a beautiful amber color, the exact shade of sun streaming through honey, set under very thick, straight eyebrows. When they fixed on you, it was almost impossible to tear your gaze away.

"One, two, three," D said, throwing paper.

Min threw paper too, and Spider got rock.

"Ha-ha, karma's a bitch," Min said. "Want a plastic bag for your head?"

"You don't understand. This beautiful hair?"—she stroked her braids—"Cannot be exposed to the elements."

"Actually, I think it's petering off," D said, peering past the windshield.

"Dammit!" Min said, watching the drops slow and stop as quickly as they had begun.

"I'm the golden child. Now you know." Spider threw the words over her shoulder as she exited the car. There was no view—the trees were too thick for that—but Min followed D out of the car anyway, stopping to adjust Spider's seat so that it was more vertical and less likely to crush her kneecaps. Just stepping away from the car settled her stomach, but the sudden quiet was surprising. It wasn't hard to imagine the trees reclaiming the road, breaking through the tarmac in a tangle of serpentine black roots. She gazed up and up into the canopy, the sky like a piece of dull grey fabric slashed open by the web of darker branches. On her parents' Christmas tree farm, the conifers were fat and healthy-looking; these trees were skeletal, wind-burned, sun-starved, hung with beards of greeny-gray moss and scaled with lichen. It smelled like rot, a deep earthy odor like her mom's compost bins. The scent of decay.

She felt a sudden jolt of sadness. When they got back, she'd go visit her parents. After being home-schooled for most of her life, she'd decided on a more social last two years of high school and had transferred to Campbellton High at the beginning of grade eleven. During the school year she lived with D and her mom, Rafaella, the eco-architect who'd helped her family with their carbon footprint. What with the chaos of final exams and making plans for this trip, she realized that it had been a month since she'd seen her mom and dad.

"Might as well pee too," D said to Min, breaking into her sad thoughts.

Spider had found a stubby pine and was crouched behind it, her jeans already pulled down.

"What about ticks?" she asked as they joined her. She was wobbly, and Min braced her with one shoulder. "Do I need to worry about them crawling up my yin-yang?"

"Ticks need undergrowth to perch on, long grasses," Min said. "They don't hang out at ground level. Did you know they can detect carbon dioxide emission fifty feet away?"

"So I should be holding my breath?" Spider said.

Min shook her head. "They sense body heat too."

"How do you know these arcane things, Minty Rosa?" D asked.

"The farm was crawling with the little buggers. I got pretty familiar with them. Arachnids, you know, Spider? Spiders."

Spider grunted.

"She's not called Spider because she *likes* them," D informed Min.

Min raised an eyebrow.

"I'll tell you later. It's not pretty."

"Tissue?" D asked. Min handed her some from the packet she'd brought, along with a compostable garbage baggie.

"You thought of everything!"

Min blushed a little. "Maybe not everything. I hemmed and hawed over the hurricane lantern." She bit her lip. "I probably should have brought it."

"You're the only reason we're not going to get eaten by coyotes," D said. She stood up, stretching and massaging her neck. "At least the sun is breaking through a bit."

It was. A pallid trickle, Min thought, but enough to remind them that it was still daytime.

"God, I'm setting a world record," Spider said. "You should be timing it."

"What's that?" Min said in the middle of pulling up her pants.

She buttoned them quickly and pointed across the road, just above She-Ra's curved orange roof. Something flashed in the midst of the forest. Maybe three or four miles away, where the terrain steepened acutely. Her eyes were sharp. Her dad used to say she could identify a pileated woodpecker on a birch from across the valley.

"What?" D asked.

"There! See?" A bead of light, and then another, flickered from deep within the murky trees.

"Headlights? The road might twist up in that direction."

"It doesn't. I'd have seen it on the map. And it's too small. Reflecting light on a lens is different. I think we should get back in the car. Spider, get a move on!"

"Why? I'm still peeing. Think I might be creeping up on two minutes without a pause."

"Come on," said Min. Spider finally finished and stood up.

"What is it, Min?" asked D.

"I think someone is out there watching us with binoculars."

"Are you sure?" D asked, fumbling for the keys.

"Yes," Min said, snugging her arms around her ribs. The hair on the nape of her neck was standing up. "I felt eyes on me."

EIGHT

– Ariel –

IT IS BITTER COLD ON THE MOUNTAIN and we're wet from a sudden rainstorm. At least it was over after an hour or two and the trees did shield us some, though the ground underfoot immediately turned to mud, rolling and sucking. The sun descends fast this high up, and the temperature drops too, each breath of wind feels like a whip lashing our skin. I'm guessing it's no more than six o'clock, but we're already shivering in nothing but raggedy jeans, our plaid flannels, and those white undershirts the Uncles call wife-beaters. Our feet are clad in hand-me-down sneakers. My big toe pokes out of the front of mine. We chose a large clearing, with the mountain at our back, which helps to cut the wind; a wall of trees curving around most of the other side provides additional cover. First thing, Hannah and Aaron build a firepit, using tinder and Aaron's eyeglasses as a lens to ignite the kindling, racing to get something going before the sun disappears completely. We feed it with pine needles and what wood we can gather, ring it with rocks to keep it contained. Some of the wood is damp and smokes badly, but we hold our hands out to the small heat anyway. We have some bigger pieces of hardwood, but they'll stifle the flames if we put them on too early. Soon I will go into the forest and collect more dry kindling, but for now I rest my feet, which are thrumming and throbbing from a full day of hiking, twenty-five miles of steep bushwhacking. In a day or two we'll climb higher. There are no trails up here. We make our own. The blisters filled with fluid are like translucent mushrooms on my heels. I want to burst them but I know if I do the pain will flare like a bad burn and I'll run the risk of infection, so I leave them be. Tomorrow I can hike down to the river and cool them in the frigid waters or find some mullein leaves to pad my shoes. That's a yellow-flowered plant with leaves that resemble velvet bunny ears. Makes great toilet paper too.

I shiver and Aaron presses closer. He's like a hot stone, giving off more body heat than I do. The firelight reflects off his glasses and makes his soft eyes look even bigger than usual. He's wrapped the broken arm of the spectacles with thread and glue to keep them from falling apart, and the lenses are scuffed and scratched. He frowns, bent over the sapling he chopped down with the folding pocket saw. It's maple, strong and straight, and taller than he is himself, topping him by a head at seven feet.

"Can you feel them?" I whisper. An icy finger brushes my cheek, an unseen hand lifts my ponytail and drops it against my neck. I smell river water and the sharp tang of blood on the wind. Those kids caught by the flash flood drowned, their bones smashed against the mountain until their bodies looked like a tangle of old clothes. No way their spirits are resting easy.

"Who?"

"The ghosts." We're taught not to mourn the ones who are weak, the ones who don't come back, who die, but I do anyway. Eden could climb to the top of the tallest swaying pine in the forest without fear. I remember her scooping honeycomb from a hollow tree, sharing that sweet gooeyness with us all.

He stares at me without comprehension and I decide not to air my thoughts. Idle superstitions, Nana calls them. Aaron only has imagination for practical things—what he can see, hear, or touch. I don't really know what he sees in me. "I like your strangeness," he said once, when I asked him. "It's as if a strong wild thing has decided to walk with me for a while." I didn't quite know how to take that; it sort of sounded like a compliment and an insult at the same time. Maybe he means I make him feel off-balance and just a little scared. Like he does me.

"What are you making?" I ask.

"Spear. Maybe. Haven't figured out all the details yet." His glasses slip down his nose and he pushes them up distractedly.

"I've got string if you need it," I tell him. One of the first things Big Daddy told us was to always make sure we had rope or some kind of cordage with us when we were in the woods. "No end to what you can do with it," he said. Shoelaces would do in a pinch, but my sneakers are already rotting off my feet.

Aaron smiles at me and goes back to his project. I watch his hands, slim and deft, as he transects a deep cross into the sawed-off end. Aaron never hurries. Never moves fast, but every action is precise and premeditated. His focus is crazy: eyes close to whatever it is he's working on, shoulders hunched like he's collapsing into himself. There's a beauty in that and a small joy in watching him. "Hand me some of those little pieces of wood, about the diameter of a pencil." He chooses two peg-like lengths and inserts them into the cuts to keep the four quarters of the spear separated and then uses his fixed-blade knife to sharpen four points. I run my finger over one of them. "You are crazy. Four points. One wasn't enough?"

"Just trying for maximum effect," he says. "Might not work at all." He grins. "But it might." I say it in unison with him. It's one of his catchphrases.

"Remember to harden it in the fire," I say, recalling some experiments that didn't work. Bows that split, arrows that shredded on impact, a new approach to a catapult that nearly blinded me. "You have no fear," he told me that day. "You understand the danger but it doesn't hold you back." He thinks I'm fearless. I think it's because I lack imagination for the worst that could happen.

The others are sitting at the far side of the fire. Except for Diana, they've got their shoes kicked off. "Put them back on," I yell, pointing to their bare feet. I'll sleep in mine. Never know when you'll have to run. They exchange looks but I don't care. After a long moment, they follow my order.

I shoot daggers at Faith with my eyes. Literally, I am imagining a dozen tiny knives pinning her to a tree by the loose skin under her jaw, between her thighs, and under her arms.

Today, Hannah carried Faith's water rations for her and still, Faith slowed the pace way down. Her steady stream of complaints buzzed in my head like the whine of a mosquito cloud. *My feet hurt, my belly hurts, I'm hungry and cold and damp and tired*, and she's acting like she's the only one. I want to slap the shit out of her. This is the first test of our fortitude and she is failing. She turns her back on me as if she can feel the heat of my gaze.

Aaron gets up and hauls a big log onto the fire. It catches, and soon the good warmth beats against my face. He squats there illuminated, firelight dancing along the angles of his body, the length of his bare arms, dipping him in gold. He holds the end of his spear, the four points like teeth, over the flames to harden the wood.

Aaron is the last of the older boys, except for Nicky, and the only one Big Daddy considers worthwhile. Nicky is soft in the head and barely talks, never cries. When he was a baby, some people thought he couldn't hear either, but I saw how he bent his ear toward the dining hall when evening meal was about ready. And how he cowered when one of the adults raised their voice. He spends most of his time in the dog pen, nestled up next to the big black female who snarls her snout at everyone except Nicky. That's the same dog from the first lesson—the one who survived. Nicky named her Biter. Sometimes Big Daddy threatens to shoot her too, but Nicky stays with her, folding his skinny arms and legs over her thick body like he's wrapping her in his flesh, until Big Daddy calms down and forgets his threat, remembering that she is our breeder dog.

"Going to take some time," Aaron says, settling down beside me again. He's propped the spear up against a rock, safely above the flames. Diana and Hannah disappear into the woods, their blonde heads and brown limbs distinguishing them from the shadows until they're swallowed up by the trees.

The air smells dusty, full of must and pollen; the pines are yellow with it. We should be foraging too, but it feels nice sitting here with Aaron, his fingers wrapped around mine. I turn my face up and he kisses me quickly on the mouth. This is a new thing, and we're keeping it secret—although I'm pretty sure Diana suspects—but already I can feel the awareness of him thread itself through my veins.

I drowse, worn out from the long hike, soothed by the smell of sweet smoke and the crackling flames. Faith wanders off into the woods, muttering something about water.

The bushes at the edge of the clearing rustle and Aaron and I are on our feet in an instant, hands on knives sheathed at our hips.

Diana emerges and whoops, Hannah right behind her, carrying an armful of supple branches. Diana holds a limp dead rabbit in either hand. We set snares for the small mammals. I think the most we'd all been hoping for was a squirrel or two.

"Better get those shelters built," I say. We need protection from the wind and rain and a bunch more firewood if we don't want to die from the cold.

"I'll go see about something to pad out that meat," Aaron says. He's the best of us at finding edible wild plants.

I peck-kiss him and join Hannah where she's preparing her pile of slender branches in order to weave them into a rough screen. We've already marked a trio of maple saplings in the shadow of a stand of birch. We'll tie them down like tent rails and roof them with our willow panels, heap the inside with bracken and big flexible branches of spruce, and then all pile in there. I know from past experience that it'll be crowded and stinky but warm. While Aaron is out foraging, I keep an eye on his spear and make sure it doesn't char. Heating the wood draws the moisture out and makes it as hard as iron.

Hannah cusses and sucks on her finger. It's marked with crosshatches of blood. "They're like razor blades," she says. Before we can do the weaving, we have to split the branches. They are young and green and so we use our knives and thumbnails, but the wood gives us stinging cuts all over our hands, and the sap is sticky, making our fingers clumsy.

"Faith could be doing this," I grumble, but she's managed to vanish herself. No one takes longer to complete a simple chore. Finally, we've got something resembling a roof. If it pours again, it won't do a damn bit of good, but maybe the appearance of shelter will help keep us warm.

I check the knots and pull on the support branches a little. They hold. I used a bowline. Big Daddy says there are six knots we all need to know. He made us practice them in the dark. My favorite is two half hitches. You can tie onto almost anything with it. Ruth goes to gather pine needles, ferns, and soft boughs for a mattress and to stuff the holes with.

"Come on, Ariel," Diana calls. She knows Hannah is too softhearted to do what needs to be done. Hannah strokes the closest rabbit as she passes, grimaces, and moves away, eyes on the ground. I pick it up by the hind legs. It's limp, glassy-eyed. The spark of life is completely extinguished. For a moment it reminds me of that dog, the curly-haired white-and-black one, scarcely more than a puppy, with the big splotch on its hindquarters like a black rosebud. After Big Daddy shot him, the other dog went wild. Biting at the air, whining, throwing herself around at the end of her rope. Big Daddy let her tire herself out, and when he went to untie her, the dog never stopped clocking him. That dog knew exactly where Big Daddy was at all times.

I help Diana dress the rabbits. That's a funny expression, because really what we're doing is undressing them, digging our fingers under the fur where the heads used to be until Diana hacked them off with her knife, and pulling the skin free in one long motion. All this work and we end up with two lean carcasses barely bigger than rats. Diana has small hands so I let her deal with the guts. Nothing worse than piercing the bowel and spoiling the meat. She is red up to her elbows by the time she is done. We rinse off with some of our water—I make a note to fill the bottles up tomorrow at the creek that feeds the river—and then I bundle up the heads, feet, and innards and take them out to the woods for the coyotes to fight over. It's quiet among the trees. No birdsong; even the raucous jays have shut up. I smell the peppery stink of a skunk. On the way back, I find some late blackberries and pick as many as I can fit in the pouch I make by pulling my shirt away from my body. I can hear the others, collecting wood and chattering. Aaron comes back with a shirtful of cattail stems and daylily tubers. His short curly hair is gleaming with droplets and he's bare-chested and he smells like marsh water. My world narrows to the pinpoint of him, but I force myself to keep working.

The darkness falls suddenly like a dropped curtain. The woods seem more alive now, filled with sound. Everything screams danger, from the whipcrack of a stick underfoot to the rustle of leaves to the weird cough of a deer. They sound like old smokers emptying their lungs first thing in the morning.

Hannah has an armful of dry wood, which has somehow escaped the last rain. We build the fire up until it flares and roars. I cut and peel a thick stick, sharpening the end, and find two more, forked, to balance it on; we impale the rabbits, head to butt, over the hottest part of the flames. The tubers are wrapped in thick leaves and nestle at the edge of the fire in the ashes. When they're cooked they taste like potatoes, although they don't fill your belly as well. Still, the gnawing teeth of hunger are not unknown to us. I share the blackberries out and we sit around the fire.

I count heads.

"Where the hell is Faith with that water?"

"Haven't seen her for a while," Aaron says. "Wasn't she with you two?" he asks Hannah and Diana.

Diana shakes her head and scowls. "Just thought she was shirking like she always does."

"She was tired out," Hannah says, scrambling to her feet. "I told her she should just go rest."

"Where?"

"Out there." She points into the forest. "Just a little way, I think. She said she was bleeding a little bit. You know. She's been having some pains and such even now from the baby. She looked so sick and pale."

I bottle my anger, bite my tongue hard. Better if she'd kept her lazy ass at home, having babies, getting fat, but instead she's out here, causing problems. Big Daddy had seen the doubt in my eyes. Ranks are thin, he'd said, and I could see the burden of it carved into the deep new lines around his mouth.

"I'll get her," I say. And when I find her, I'm going to drag her back here by her ponytail.

NINE

— D —

D CRANKED THE KEY IN THE IGNITION. The engine turned over but didn't catch. Gritting her teeth, she tried again. She-Ra sounded like a worn-out coffee grinder.

"C'mon, baby," she said. More grumbling, and then sudden silence. *Click, click* went the key, the sound weirdly loud in the confines of the car. Maybe they had all been holding their breath?

Min kept staring out the window, up the hill, as if she were expecting someone to come bursting out of the trees. It was giving D the heebie-jeebies. She twisted the key again.

"Shit." She exchanged glances with the other two.

"Are you kidding me?" Spider said. "Stranded in the woods with a possible cannibal clan lurking and night coming?"

"Let's give it a few minutes. Maybe I flooded the engine."

A few minutes later, spine rigid, she tried again. This time the engine didn't even make a complaint. Just a forlorn clicking.

Spider cursed, got out of the car, and stalked off.

"Stay close," D called, not that Spider was likely to go far. Broken-down car, hidden watcher, the wildness of the woods, and the desolation of the road. It was getting a little too horror movie for D.

"Learn anything about automotive repair in those encyclopedias of yours?" she asked Min.

"Nope. Maybe a wire's just come loose or something?"

"Worth a look."

A stream of curses floated back to them. Spider had her cell phone out, searching for a signal as she marched up and down the road. She drew her arm back as if she was going to launch her phone into the undergrowth, froze in that position for a moment, and then thrust the phone back into her pocket and recommenced with the pacing.

"No reception, I'm guessing?" said Min. Credit to her, she just about kept the smugness out of her voice. Min didn't think much of an overreliance on technology.

"Yeah, well, even without Ms. Sound and Fury over there, it still sucks," D said, popping the hood. She tried to shake the feeling that some superior power was stalling them and then bit back a laugh. Literally and figuratively stalled.

She clenched her hands as she and Min leaned over the hot-smelling engine. "You think that smell is normal?" Min asked. Her face looked pinched and worried, although she erased the expression as soon as she saw D look at her.

"You mean the odor of burning? Not so much."

A wad of dead leaves had gathered under the hood. She brushed them away and then chipped fruitlessly at the scaly white gunk around the battery terminals with her fingernails. Everything seemed normal.

"Hmm," said Min, disappearing around the back of the car and opening the trunk.

"I don't know what I'm doing," D called out, fiddling with the spark plugs. At least she thought they were the spark plugs.

There were more wires going into two boxy things, but everything seemed tight and connected. Dammit, she should have sprung for a complete overhaul, even though the male mechanics at the garage always made her feel as if she'd been taken for a ride.

It was all falling apart before they even reached their destination. They were alone, hemmed in by trees, halfway between nowhere and nowhere. Was someone watching them even now? The faint sun had once again disappeared behind stormy clouds, so there was no way of knowing if a pair of binoculars was trained on them at this very moment. A breeze rattled the tall, dry grass. It sounded like teeth clicking. Her heart rate increased and she forced herself to calm down. Deep breaths, in and out. If this all went wrong, it would be her fault.

Min returned with a container of oil and a rag.

"Let me," she told Min, taking the greasy rag. Her fingers had begun quivering and she wanted to occupy her hands before it turned into a full-force panic attack. She unscrewed the oil cap, being careful not to burn herself. "I checked the levels before we left. Everything was good." She stroked the hood as if the car were an ancient dog. "She-Ra's old but she always gets us where we need to go, right?"

"It'll be fine," Min said with determination. D finished topping up the oil and exhaled. "Ten minutes and I'll try again."

"Not raining," Min commented, patting the bumper beside her as an invitation to sit. "It smells like it though." She scanned the trees. "The maps didn't really show the topography, you know. If you follow the tree line, you really get a sense of how steep these hills are. Solid granite. It must have taken years to blast the roads through here, cut the trees down."

"There could be homes back there, tracks, people—people we can't see." D zipped up her hoodie. It was getting chilly. "Why don't you jump in the car? Try it again," she suggested. "I'll keep an eye out in case anything becomes glaringly obvious. Smoke or something sparking."

Min hopped in, held both hands up with her fingers crossed so that D could see them, and then turned the key in the ignition. D peered into the engine hull as it turned over. Nothing. She leaned back, swearing in frustration. The lights! The headlights were on! And almost as soon as she noticed, they flickered, glowed orange, and went dim. And again, no sound but the clicking.

Min quit trying. "Any idea?"

"Yup," said D, slamming the hood down. "Dead battery. Totally my fault." The morning had been overcast enough that she'd had the headlights on while driving on the highway. "I forgot to turn the lights off. Dammit!" She kicked at a clump of weeds.

"Plan?" Min said.

They resumed their seats on the bumper.

"Can't call a tow. Can't wave anyone down because there isn't anyone," D said, trying unsuccessfully to keep the despair out of her voice. "I'm sorry. I shouldn't have dragged you guys on this wild goose chase."

Min slid an arm around her waist. "Not complaining. Last town we drove through?"

"Miles back. Nothing since we left the highway. Just a few houses along the road. No conveniences or anything, and nothing for the last hour."

Min pulled the map from her hoodie pocket and spread it out. "There's a big highway about sixty miles east of here that passes through Abbotsford on the other side of the river." She pointed to it. "This one we're on must be mostly for locals or people just traveling between Pembroke Cross and Feltzen Corners. No wonder we haven't seen much traffic." Her finger hovered. "Making a guess, I'd put us here. Thirty, forty miles out from the turn-off for Pembroke Cross."

Spider wandered over, scratching her arms furiously. "We good?"

D let Min explain the situation. She didn't think she could deal with the inevitable explosion. Sometimes listening to Spider roar felt a little bit like standing face forward in a windstorm. This time she just closed her eyes and rode it through.

"Why'd we go the stupid way instead of taking the direct main route?" Spider said.

"Because the big road would have taken us totally out of our way. *This* was the fastest since we're not actually going to Abbotsford," Min said. "It's miles from Pembroke Cross, which is close to where the plane crashed."

"Bet there are garages and gas stations and coffee houses all up and down that road," Spider grumbled. "And cell phone reception." She slapped at her back. "And no bugs."

"Let's push her up," D said. They weren't going anywhere, so what was the point of all the what-iffing? Her nerves were jumping again. Small synaptic shocks that raised the hair on her arms.

"Why don't you steer, Spider?" Min said, looking a little exhausted and perplexed. D grimaced. The Spider Effect.

Still grumbling, Spider slid in and released the emergency brake. Min and D shoved until She-Ra was five feet away from the edge of the road.

"Should be safe enough," D said, although anyone blasting down the hill wouldn't have time to stop or swerve.

Spider clambered over into the passenger seat, making room for D, and Min got in the back.

They shared a giant bag of potato chips, passed the bottled water around, huddled under blankets of spare clothes, and used backpacks as makeshift pillows. No one was talking.

It was a relief, if D was honest.

She leaned her forehead against the glass, welcoming the cool of it. All the tension was centered at the nape of her neck. She rolled her head on her shoulders, breathed. Spider's exhalations deepened, punctuated by the occasional snore. D tried to find the rhythm in it, tried to will her body to relax too.

Thunder boomed, and lightning lit up the trees bristling like spears. She squeezed her eyes shut, feeling like a child. Behind the lids, black silhouettes jerked and danced, voices called on the wind.

Another crack, a dazzling flash revealing a bloated sky. It did not rain. She counted Mississippis under her breath, barely getting to five seconds. A mile. No more. Kat used to rub her back during storms, tell her stories, gather the sheets and blankets to make them a safe cave. *Kat*, she thought, *this was supposed to be the easy part.*

"It's close," Min said from her hollow in the backseat. "Right above us." She sounded halfway to sleep but D's muscles were cramping and she had no room to stretch out.

Wind buffeted the car. She-Ra rocked. *Would they flip over?* "Lock your door," she said, fumbling at the button and then leaned over Spider to lock hers too. Spider didn't stir but D could hear her teeth grinding as she dreamed.

She'd thought of the trip as a doorway to some kind of peace but instead she was still trapped on the other side.

"You should try and sleep," Min said drowsily. "Sorry. Dramamine. Knocks me out." She rubbed her eyes and yawned.

"I don't want to," D said. This right here was her fault. The least she could do was to watch over them. Kat would have been reveling in the storm, thinking of this as an adventure.

"Honey, just try." Min's voice was soft, pleading. "There's nothing we can do until morning."

"I can't." Her only thoughts were of the interminable night stretching ahead of her, the crippling frustration that they were stuck.

But she could and she did, sliding into sleep between one breath and the next.

She dreamed of Kat. Her sister running ahead of her through the woods, slipping through the trees like a shadow, always just out of reach.

TEN

– Ariel –

"FAITH!" Hannah calls. "Faith!"

"Faith!" I yell with all my might.

The woods absorb my voice. The air hangs heavy, and echoing down from the peaks we hear the rumble of thunder.

"She's scared of storms," Ruth says. "Hides under the bed."

"So why hasn't she run back here then?"

Thunder growls again, followed by a blinding flash of lightning that leaves pictures on my eyeballs. The sky is swollen with rain but it won't fall.

We've got no flashlights. The moon is a fingernail clipping and the trees are packed so tight it's hard to see more than a few feet ahead.

"Pine sap," Aaron says. I understand what he's saying immediately.

"There's a weeping pine over there by the shelter," I tell him. I leaned against it earlier and the black gunk is puckering my shirt at the back and itching my skin.

We grab a couple of branches and roll the ends in the stickiness oozing from fissures in the tree's bark, and then we poke them into the fire until they catch. They won't burn long and they don't give out much light, but they're better than nothing.

"I'll build it up high," Diana says, gesturing at the firepit. We've added a second row of rocks to keep it contained. Most animals will keep their distance. "Make more of those torches too," she says.

Hannah is at my shoulder. Worry ages her face. She's the one I fret about. She's solid in her body but fragile in her heart. Thin-shelled like a robin's egg, she feels things too much. "You stay," I tell her. "Help Diana and Ruth. Make sure that rabbit doesn't burn." I press her arm. "We'll bring her back." I'm hoping she didn't go near the cliffs. They're shale, so brittle you can snap the rock with your fingers, and cloaked in springy heather that makes the edge impossible to see. I think of Eden's body spread out in a star shape, her head busted open, grey stuff seeping.

"There's coyotes out there. What if something's got a hold of her?" Hannah says, shivering.

Coyotes are normally shy, but if there's an opportunity they'll attack in a pack. Can bring down a moose calf if they're lucky.

"We'd hear the yelling if—" I close my mouth with a snap when I see Diana's eyes dart to Hannah's face. "She's fine."

Aaron grabs his spear out of the fire and shoulders it. "Knew this was going be good for something," he says with a proud grin.

"When we find her, you can stick her with it," I tell him, but low-voiced so softhearted Hannah won't hear me.

We head into the woods, but just out of sight and hearing of the camp I stop, listening and orientating myself. The air crackles with a thousand tiny sounds that are a hair quieter than our breaths. It feels as if every unseen living thing in the earth, under the bark, up in the canopy is waiting to pounce on something smaller and weaker than itself. The beautiful savagery of the wild, Big Daddy calls it.

"She won't have gotten too far. Not really a nature lover," Aaron says, rotating with his pine-pitch torch. Our shadows are thrown up against the trees, the grim bulk of the mountain with its jagged spine. I'm reminded of puppets you can make with your hands. Hannah's really good at entertaining the little ones with those—rabbits and dogs and such. Aaron's spear looks like something the devil would wield. The children would be cowering with fright if they were here.

My ears are sharpening, filtering the noises and separating them. A fox barks, a rabbit or rodent squeals. In the distance, I make out the tumbling roar of the river, swollen from the rains. I visualize the path to the water. Down through a moss-covered glade, as undulating as a bright-green ocean, and then across a meadow of wildflowers and soft grasses, fed by the tiny rivulets of streams.

"I know where we'll find her." Faith lives with half her head in the clouds. She truly believes that some day a prince will come on a white horse and whisk her away to his castle. She probably fell asleep with her hair draped in daisy chains. I gesture to Aaron. "This way."

"You lead," he says, moving to one side with a bow.

My burning torch spits and fizzles. I turn it upside down for a moment and let the flame climb upward, catch again. The flickering light makes Aaron's face appear as if it's carved from golden wood, his liquid-brass eyes gleam.

The moss is spongy underfoot; the trees smell fresh and icy, as if color had a scent. I wouldn't mind lying here with Aaron, tangling my legs with his, lying on top of his chest and kissing his pillow-y lips and feeling his heart leap against my palm like a frantic fish. It's hard for us to find time and space to be alone. At home, there are always kids running around, tasks to be completed, the Uncles making sure no one skips out on chores. Damn Faith and her bullshit!

I walk faster, sliding a little on the slick wet roots that snarl the path like black snakes, wanting to be done with this. The trees thin and open up, and we're at the head of the meadow. In the distance the river pounds against the rocks as it thrashes its way to the sea.

"Faith," I call, pitching my voice to carry. It's hard to hear anything over the water. Our torches throw weak circles of light, and we stumble over tall grasses that twist their way around our ankles and trip on hidden stumps and boulders. I think of Big Daddy talking about seeds that fall on rocky ground. I'm sweating heavily and my hair hangs limp in my face.

Faith, you stupid bitch, I want to say, but I don't. I need Aaron to believe the best of me.

We move slowly toward the river, scanning the ground as carefully as we can, and as we get closer other sounds become clear. Shouting, screaming, high-pitched. We run. Faith is pinned up against a tree, and facing her, reared up on its hind legs, is a bear.

We knew there were bears around. I remember an Uncle telling me how one ripped the roof right off a car parked near the gulley trying to get a bag of jerky some idiot had left in the glove box.

God, I wish we had a dog with us. A dog would draw the bear away, give us a chance to get the hell out of there. Faith hurls a stick at it, which seems to piss it off even more.

"Make yourself look bigger," I scream. Though how she's going to do that when she's an itty-bitty thing, I don't know. I suddenly remember that Hannah said Faith was bleeding from her lady parts. Big Daddy told us that monthly blood is a danger in the wild. I was stupid not to think of it before.

Aaron is yelling too, waving his spear in one hand, torch in the other. First his, then mine gutters and goes out. We hurl them at the bear like javelins but they just thump onto the ground. It doesn't even turn its head. Now we're close enough to see its beady eyes and smell the rank wildness pouring off of it like sweat. Its paws are as big as snowshoes. It's grizzled around the muzzle, missing some patches of fur, and its coat hangs loose on its bones. Old bear, hungry bear.

I could throw my knife but it probably wouldn't do anything and I'd lose the only weapon I have.

Instead, I holler as loud as I can, waving my hands around as though I'm swatting bees. There are a couple of branches on the ground and I scoop them up and hold them out like big arms on a scarecrow. Slowly, even though my stomach is leaping around in my throat, I advance, stamping my feet as hard as I can. I yell, "Here, bear!" Aaron hollers and clicks his tongue like Nana Esme calling the chickens in at night.

But the bear is fixed on Faith. It grunts, slobbering spit from its loose jaws, and takes a swing at her. She barely escapes the claws. They glimmer like black knives.

She is doing the opposite of what I told her: she's hunkered on the ground with her arms up around her ears. Thin-voiced, crying and sniveling and even to my ears she sounds like prey. Once a bear tastes human flesh, it won't fear them anymore. People will just be another food source.

"We've got to get in closer," Aaron yells.

He runs in front of the bear, his spear raised, but the bear just reaches out and swats it down and then it's got Aaron in a tight hug. Faith scuttles away, and Aaron makes a sound I've never heard a human make, a soul's cry. I dart around, grab the spear from out of the tall grass and stab at the bear's back, aiming for its kidneys, but its fur is long and shaggy and snarls the spearhead. I tear it free.

Faith has found a rock or something and is banging on the trunk of a tree, but nothing can distract the bear now. It's pushed Aaron away from its body, although he's still in its embrace. From my vantage point the bear looks like a dancer dipping its partner but then it bats at him with its paws and tosses him aside, and Aaron lies where he falls. I scream—it rips out of my belly—and run at the bear with all my strength, the spear straight out, and the points catch it just under the jaw, in the neck, and they bite into flesh. I plant the end in the ground, brace myself, and push. I'm still screaming, a note like a train whistle that just comes and comes, and the bear is roaring, tossing its head back and forth. The spear rips loose in a torrent of gore. The bear shakes its head wildly from side to side and I feel the hot spatter of blood across my face, and then it drops to all fours and limps into the trees.

I'm on my knees, cradling Aaron in my lap, and tears are dripping down my cheeks like molten wax. "He hit me," Aaron says softly. "I don't feel anything. Am I okay?"

"No, sweet baby, you are not okay," I whisper, too low for him to hear.

"Are you?" he asks. His eyes open so wide they take up half his face.

"It's not my blood," I tell him, my voice cracking.

"That spear though, right?" He makes a sound like a laugh, but it terrifies me, the way it catches like bone on bone.

Faith creeps out from under the tree and kneels next to us. Her mouse-brown hair is braided and a few limp buttercups dangle from it. She's white as milk and trembling so hard her teeth chatter, and I glower at her, commanding her with my eyes not to speak.

Aaron's thick flannel shirt hangs in streamers. Just under his ribs he is torn—a long, deep slash oozing gore into his belly button—and his face is a mess of red from forehead to chin. I know that underneath it, his skin is laid open almost to the bone.

He must read it in my eyes because his breath starts to hitch and his pupils swell and I think I will fall into them and drown.

I try to recall everything Big Daddy has taught us about dressing wounds in the field. If it was Aaron's leg or arm that was injured, I could tourniquet it to stop the bleeding. But his torso? Keep it clean. Let it drain. Lower any fever. There was something about using maggots to get rid of rot, but I can't go there yet.

Taking a deep breath, I turn to Faith. "Run back quick. Get the others and tell them to bring lots of those pine-pitch torches and any spare cloth we have." I can bandage him with it, pack the wound in his side.

"The bear," she says, darting quick glances at the shadows.

"I'll feed you to the freaking coyotes myself if you don't run faster than you ever have in your life."

She takes off and I can hear her labored breathing mixed with sobbing. I hope I've scared the shit out of her. Fear of me is the only thing that'll make her move.

"I'm going to bind you up a little," I tell Aaron, gently dropping his head onto my thigh. I shrug off my raggedy shirt and tear it into long strips, which I wrap around his torso. Even though I try to be gentle it's impossible, and he passes out. It's better that way; I cinch the knots as tight as I can and try not to think about his insides spilling out over the ground, and how grey his face appears, as if his spirit has already flown. Those dead babies looked like they were made of candle wax, eyes like tadpole eggs.

I wait for the others, smoothing my hand over his forehead again and again and dropping little kisses on the top of his head, crooning to him like he's a child, breathing my breath into him and willing the heat of my body to keep him warm.

Should I bring water from the river and try to clean the blood off? It's drying now, the flow sluggish, tacky under my fingers. In the faint light, it shows black. He hasn't regained consciousness but he is breathing. I trace the four crusty ridges the bear's claws left across his face.

The sound of twigs breaking underfoot startles me but then I relax. No animal would make such a racket. Now I can hear Diana's voice, shrill with panic—"Where are you, Ariel? Dammit, Faith, do you have any sense of direction at all?"— and I feel so relieved, I have to choke the tears down.

"Here, by the river, near the oak," I call. An oak's silhouette is distinct and Diana knows that.

I see the flickering flames of their torches coming closer. There are six lights—they must each be carrying two.

Diana runs up, thrusts her torches into Hannah's hands and falls to the ground next to me. Hannah shoves the ends into the soft, marshy soil.

"Faith said bear."

"Yeah." I lower my voice, although Aaron is still unconscious. I don't want Faith freaking out all over the place. She's chewing on the ends of her hair, something she's done since she was a little kid. I have to clench my hands until the nails bite to keep from slapping her. "Ruth," I say, beckoning, "take Faith over there somewhere." Faith is reluctant to go but I telegraph a fraction of my anger and she jumps and walks away. Hannah joins them, slipping her arm around Faith's skinny waist.

"It's bad," I tell Diana.

"How about you?" she asks, looking at my face.

I shake my head. "Not mine. I stabbed the bear, got it near the throat, I think. Didn't kill it though."

She squeezes my shoulder briefly and bends to examine Aaron.

Her face is grim, lips pressed so tightly together they whiten. "We've got to move him or he'll bleed out."

I check his bandage. It's stained red but not dripping.

"Bleeding's slowed." I'm trying to think clearly but it's Aaron and I can't.

She shoots me a look and then answers sharply. "Inside. He's bleeding into his insides. No matter what, he can't stay here. If nothing else, that blood smell might draw the coyotes."

"I know. But how?"

"Take turns carrying him?"

I shake my head. None of us is strong enough. Aaron tops out at six three. And with the additional burden of dead weight? His head already feels like a boulder on my leg.

"Let's get him bandaged better." Diane snaps her fingers at Hannah, who's still wasting time trying to comfort Faith. "Got those shirts?"

Hannah brings over a couple of undershirts and Diana takes them from her. They've all stripped off, wearing nothing but their long-sleeved plaid shirts over their bras.

"Light," I say. Ruth jams the ends of two more pine torches into the ground and holds them steady. The small flames flicker, throwing shadows everywhere, and it's hard to see. In my periphery, Faith is scurrying back and forth, wringing her hands together, and it drives me crazy. "Either get out of my sight or sit down," I snap. "Or better yet, go soak your shirt in the river and bring it back here."

I peel back the strips of cloth I tied on him, carefully cutting the knots with my knife, inhaling sharply when I see how deep the injury goes. The muscle is lacerated, chopped up like hamburger. The blood pools in the cavity like rain in a gorge. I can't tell if any organs were damaged.

Hannah makes a choking sound. I jerk my head, telling her silently to move away. The last thing I need is her puking all over the place.

Diana and I exchange glances.

Her eyes narrow, get stony. She opens her mouth to say something and I shake my head violently, digging my fingers into her forearm. "No, no, no. Don't say it. We can fix this."

Faith comes back, shivering, her wet shirt bundled in her hands. I pray she had the sense to douse it in running and not standing water. Otherwise, I could be infecting Aaron with the same parasites that get into the trout. I swab around the edges of the wound, then tear one of the dry shirts into strips and fold the other one into a pad, which I use to stuff the wound. Aaron groans and his eyelids flutter but he doesn't wake. Sweat beads on his forehead.

"I could run back to the compound? Try to get help?" Ruth says. She's fast, loves to run just for the sheer joy of it, but a vehicle won't be able to get to us. There's a couple more overgrown trails down in the foothills but nothing wider than a deer track up here on the mountain. I'm not even sure Big Daddy would spare one of the trucks anyway.

I don't have to respond because Diana is already shaking her head.

"Shit!" I mutter, trying to work out the best scenario.

If Aaron stays here he'll die; if we move him we risk dropping him and hurting him worse. We could stay put, but Big Daddy won't come to find us for about two weeks. Aaron needs medicine healing. Nana Esme is the only person who can help him. Twenty-five miles down the mountain over rough ground. I'm struggling to think clearly. Perhaps we can follow the river? It won't take us straight home but the land is flatter here along the banks, and if we cut across it could be a shorter distance. We'll end up below Pembroke Cross but maybe we can flag a car down to take us the rest of the way? Or get us to the hospital in Abbotsford? I quickly dismiss that thought. Mountain folk don't use valley services. Even when there was a town doctor who was willing to make the trip up and examine the kids, most people wouldn't unlock their doors. Some of them set the dogs on him or drove him from the property with cursing and rifles.

"We can't carry him," Diana says. "It'll kill him for sure." We lock eyes. I can hear the unspoken words. Big Daddy would say to leave him.

"What if we drag him?" Hannah says. "Take two big branches and tie our plaid shirts between them like a stretcher?"

My heart leaps and I give her a grateful smile. If we use the shirts to make a base, we can cover it with mullein or ferns, make a harness loop with cordage, pull him with the greater strength in our shoulders and legs.

"You and Ruth go find two thick lengths of wood, straight as possible, and cut them down to the same size, about eight foot," Diana says, handing over the pocket saw.

"Take a torch with you," I say.

When they return towing the wood I send them back out again to gather soft grasses and anything that will cushion Aaron's body. Diana and I strip off our flannel shirts. There's a stiff breeze blowing down from the mountain but I'm still not cold, even though I'm in nothing but my bra now. Diana is shivering though, and I decide we'll put one shirt aside and take turns wearing it. Hannah is the biggest of us. Her shirt will cover Faith almost down to her knees.

"Cut them up or not?" Diana says, her knife in her hand.

"Keep them whole," I say, testing the strength of the material between my fingers. They're hand-me-downs and pretty frayed already. "They may last longer that way."

Carefully, I lift Aaron's head from my thigh and lay it on the ground, checking first to make sure there are no stones. He moans and his tongue licks at his lips. "One of you got your water bottle?" I ask.

I've left mine up at the camp, and it looks like I'm not the only one. At least we have our knives. That's something Big Daddy always lectured us on.

Ruth unties hers from across her shoulder and passes it over. I trickle some into Aaron's mouth and he coughs and sputters and raises his head up a little.

His eyes find mine. "It feels like fire," he says. "In my chest." His words are a little garbled, his mouth unable to stretch to form the words. The wounds on his face have gummed up, and I use Faith's wet shirt to try to clean some of the blood away. He flails at my hands so I leave him be. Big Daddy told us that shallow wounds do better left open to the air.

We set the poles about two feet apart on the ground and lash the shirts to them by their sleeves, adding rope crisscrossed and fastened with clove hitches to strengthen the whole area. We roll him onto the sled and he passes out again.

Diana checks out the slope up to the tree line. "It's not going to be easy," she says.

I shake my head. "Not that way. I'm thinking we go back along the river for as long as we can, then cross country. Pick up a ride in Feltzen Corners hopefully."

She drinks from her water bottle and then extends it to me.

"How many miles you guess?" I ask her.

"Easier distance for sure than the way we came. Flatter land. I'm guessing, but maybe twenty miles before we hit the highway?"

I calculate. Normally I can do three miles an hour at a good clip, but Faith is a slow walker and pulling Aaron is going to slow us way down. And we'll need to rest. Plus it'll be full dark in another hour. "So two miles an hour? At least ten, twelve hours of walking, split between the five of us?"

"Faith's a no way and Hannah's not real strong. It'll be mostly you, Ruth, and me."

I shrug. "Soldiers, right?"

"It's going to hurt him like hell," Diana says. "And it'll take all night and a hunk of tomorrow."

"I know, but what choice do we have?" I swipe at my nose with my forearm and get to my feet. I realize I've been tensing all of my muscles this whole time. My shoulder feels tight and sore from hurling the spear. I pick it up. The tips are clotted with bear blood. I hand it to Hannah, who takes it with a grimace. "Share the shirt," I tell her. "Whoever gets coldest. The person pulling won't be needing it. I'll go first."

I loop the rope around my waist, pushing it down to my hipbones. It will chew up the skin but I don't care.

"Where's Faith?" Diana says.

"Faith," Hannah calls.

"Here," Faith says breathlessly. Her face is tear-stained and splotched with dirt, brown eyes reddened. Her jeans are muddy up to the knee. She's holding a plastic milk jug, some plastic bags. "I found them down by the river." She hoists the jug. "Filled this. Thought we could cover Aaron with the bags if it rains again."

For a second, I actually feel like hugging her, same as Hannah and Ruth, but give her a quick nod of approval instead.

"I'll take lead," Diana says. She's a good tracker, has a sixth sense of where north is, and can find home no matter where on the mountain we are. I adjust the rope and focus on the small of her back. That's all I've got to do, put one foot in front of another and follow that dingy white bra strap and knobbly spine of hers, the bobbing flame of the torch. Casting a quick glance over my shoulder at Aaron, I start dragging him, wincing every time I hit a bump, which is every two seconds or so. Hannah and Ruth fall in behind carrying the other torches and the spear, and Faith follows them.

If Big Daddy could see us now would he think "soldiers" or "victims"? I feel the strain in my thighs already but grit my teeth and keep going.

ELEVEN

— Spider —

SPIDER WOKE TO THE SOUND OF D calling her name. The roar of an engine revving. And then Min yelling, "Thanks for the jump." She unpeeled a gummy eyelid just in time to see a baseball cap–wearing woman with a sun-reddened face drive off in a pickup, hand waving out the window.

Was there anything worse than waking up in a car, Spider thought, taking a surreptitious sniff at her underarms. Her breath was rank and she needed a shower stat. But that was an unlikely prospect.

At least they were moving again, although half the morning was gone already.

Min and D both looked tired but energetic. Spider just felt tired. She'd woken up thinking about empty coffins.

Jonathan and Kat's coffins had been empty except for a few family photos and a couple of childhood treasures and books. She remembered how light her brother's was. She'd insisted on being one of the pallbearers. They'd had four: her dad and his brother, a cousin. And two days later, at Kat's graveside service, she remembered D staggering to hold her mother up, and failing, and the sight of the two of them kneeling on the muddy ground. And D's Nonna crying silently, her mouth working as if she was trying to swallow all that pain. Spider hadn't felt anything. Just a cold numbness that started in her chest and spread to her extremities.

They were all buried in the same part of the Catholic graveyard. Nonna too. She'd had a fatal stroke about six months after the crash. Like D and her family needed just a little more anguish.

Spider was on this trip because she couldn't bear not to be. But that didn't mean she understood what was driving D. Her friend had told her it was a way to mark the ending. Go to the crash site, experience it, acknowledge it. Like somehow that would allow them to move forward. But for Spider it had all ended the day she heard the news. The day the cops arrived at the door and broke her parents' hearts. The minute, the second, she had understood what the crash meant and what she had lost. Everything had ceased. And since then she'd been on an endless quest for distraction, hoping she'd feel something different each time.

It didn't matter that Kat and Jonathan's coffins were empty. They weren't there, but they sure as hell weren't here either.

Keep it all inside, Spider, she told herself. *Don't be the one who kills the purpose in D's eyes. The least you can do is not fuck this up like you do everything else. What was that Sinatra song? Regrets, I've had a few.*

Regret most recent? She decided that she probably shouldn't have spent the whole night drinking and making out with someone whose name she didn't even remember. The girl had been sweet and gentle and hadn't pushed her to do anything more than kiss and stroke, and her mouth had tasted of cinnamon, but still, what was her name? She closed her eyes for a second, thinking it might aid her memory. Nope, a total blank. And what did that say about Spider?

Where is your heart? D had asked her once. *Lost*, Spider thought.

Min yipped from the back seat.

"A sign! A sign."

The closest sign to the right indicated accommodations, gas, and snacks. The one further along and to the left pointed up a skinny, muddy road burrowing its way to Pembroke Cross. Both were dinged, as if someone had been taking pot-shots at them.

At the gas station, D swung the car right and bumped them to a halt next to the gas pumps. "Finally," Spider said, unfastening her seatbelt. "I could use some air. It smells like farts in here. I don't know what you two have been eating but it's not good."

For some unknown reason, that made D and Min laugh so hard that Min blew a little snot out onto her upper lip.

D turned off the engine and then faced Spider with a dismayed expression. "Shit. Force of habit."

"Try to start it again," Min said.

D crossed her fingers and cranked the key. *Splutter, splutter . . . roar.*

"Well that's something," Spider remarked, looking out the window at what was pretty much a shithole. The gas station, dingy and off-white, was surrounded by cracked concrete pierced by weeds and tall grasses. Two pumps stood under a rickety metal awning hung with Christmas lights in twisted loops.

"The lady said this was the only gas station around, right?" D asked, adjusting her oversized sunglasses.

"Yeah, according to the map, the next service station is about thirty-five miles down the road," Min said. "In Abbotsford."

Spider pushed her door open, unkinking her neck. The series of cracks it gave off were truly alarming. "Is it even open?" A sign-posted door led to the public restroom, which you could not have paid Spider to use—she could smell the stench from where she stood—and another sign pointed the way along a winding path lined with white-painted rocks to the Mountain Rest Cottages. A couple of junky beige sedans were parked off to the side, next to a collection of rusty oil drums.

D got out, held up her phone. Shook her head. Min did some stretches against She-Ra's trunk.

"Wow," she murmured. "Look at that." Spider followed her gaze. The clouds had lifted, and looming above them, so steep they gave Spider serious vertigo, were the rockiest, most menacing mountains she had ever seen. Spider suddenly felt like a fly crawling across the surface of a glass. She tore her eyes away and yelled, "Hello, anyone here?" No one appeared. She reached through the window and pressed the horn. The sound shattered the air, making both D and Min jump.

Spider sighed. "I'll go poke around." She slipped on her black-rimmed spectacles. They were a spare pair of Jonathan's and she did fine without them, but she couldn't bear to part with them. A memory of her brother blinking as he pushed them up the bridge of his nose flashed across her mind. They were always sliding down; he was always adjusting them. On her, they pinched. *Because I've kept growing and he's eternally fourteen years old.* She forced the thoughts away and eyed the gas station, walked over and tried the door. It was locked but the interior lights were on. The glass was too dirty to press her nose up against, but she made out a bunch of shelves and refrigerated units. Budweiser and Coors neon-lit logos. An OPEN sign winking on the wall. "They sell stuff," she called back over her shoulder. *Snacks. And beer. And aspirin, no doubt.* Aspirin would be the sensible choice, but sometimes you just needed a numbing agent, something that sent you to sleep and didn't wake you up until it was all over and nothing remained but that deep abiding ache. One bottle of something golden or colorless. And then never again. Or at least not for a few months anyway. At the moment though, her head was battling with her stomach.

"Someone just stepped away. Smoke break, maybe," she said.

"Girls." A man wearing grimy coveralls came around from the back, wiping his oil-covered hands with a filthy rag. He was tall and lanky, with stubble and hair the color of margarine, slicked back and oily, his chest pocket embroidered with the name *Guy.* "Sorry, I was busy out back. What can I do you for? A fill-up?"

Spider rejoined the other two by the car. Guy was obvious about watching her walk, and his eyes felt like hot grease running down her neck.

"Yup," she said, chewing the word and then spitting it out. She avoided his gaze but he'd already switched his attention to Min. Spider was reminded of one of those cartoon wolves with the lolling tongues and bulgy eyes.

Spider moved forward so she was standing between him and her friends.

"We can do it ourselves, thanks," she said, picking up the gas nozzle. What would happen if she sprayed him down? Struck a match? Just for fun.

"Suit yourself," he said. "Pump first, pay later." He snickered just in case they didn't catch his drift. His voice was phlegmy. Tongue clacking against the roof of his mouth.

"We need a battery too. Do you sell them?" D said. Spider marveled at how noncommittal D's voice sounded. She, on the other hand, was clenching the handle so tight she thought she might snap it in two.

"I can get you one. Have to call it down to the auto parts store but shouldn't take long. Want me to have a quick peek first? Under your hood."

Min had a startled expression on her face, her fingers worrying the leopard cuff around her wrist, and Spider's blood began to boil.

"Guy!" came a short peremptory bark. Guy instantly stepped back, a red flush creeping across his cheeks. Another man emerged from behind the gas station. He was short, almost as short as Min, but built like a brick shit house, as Spider's grandmother used to say. Shirtsleeves straining over bulging muscles, blond crew cut, intensely bright blue eyes.

"They need a battery," Guy said, a completely different tone in his voice. Gone was the cockiness.

"Get in there and call Lumsden Auto. Leave the price on the notepad for me," Brick House said. Guy scurried away. If he'd had a tail it would have been tucked between his legs. Brick House called after him, "You can go pick it up, along with that alternator I ordered yesterday." He switched his attention to them. "Anything else I can help you girls with?" He stood feet spread, arms crossed over his barrel chest, but a slight smile smoothed his features so he looked less like a white supremacist and more like a kindly gym teacher.

D spoke up. "Actually, we're looking for the site of that plane crash two years ago."

"Up at Pembroke Cross? Nothing but a scar on the land now," he said, frowning slightly. "You won't find any . . . souvenirs, if that's what you're searching for."

D shuddered.

"We lost family," Spider said, hitching the gas nozzle onto its hook and replacing the cap.

"I'm sorry," he said, his tone softening. "A tragedy." He held his hand out to her, shook twice, released. "I'm Art."

"Were you here when it happened?" Min asked.

"Yes. We all turned out. Tried to help."

"Did you see anyone make it out?"

He shook his head. "It was a terrible thing. The fire took hold. In the end all we could do was watch it burn. It was an inferno."

Spider felt desperate for a moment and gulped air, which made her choke. D started toward her, concerned, and Spider waved her away. "I'm okay. I just swallowed my gum."

If D touched her now, she wouldn't be able to bear it.

One of the sedans started up with a roar. Guy peeled out, raising a cloud of dust, and made a right onto the road.

"He'll be about two, three hours," Art said. He seemed to register the frustration on D's face and added, "Won't take but a minute to hook it up."

"That long?" D asked, her eyes on the sky. Art followed her gaze.

"We lose our daylight early here."

Her shoulders slumped.

Min was there beside her before Spider could move. "Tomorrow," she said, hugging D. "Tomorrow we can get an early start." D brightened, and the smile sliding onto her face stayed in place for longer than usual.

Spider stood where she was, feeling an ache in her chest. Her stomach burbled, snapping her out of her thoughts.

"You sell food?" she asked Art.

"Yup. Just plain stuff. Hot dogs and the like."

She followed him into the building. A bell on the door tinkled. She trailed her fingers over shelves of snacks and candy, packaging faded from the sun, and picked up a couple of family-size bags of potato chips. She placed them on the counter and chose a case of beer from the cooler, scooped up a bottle of aspirin as she made her way to the counter. Wieners dripping fat and looking like mummified fingers turned lazily on a spit next to a bubbling vat of fake orange cheese and some flaccid french fries. Working the cap off the bottle, she dry-swallowed three pills.

"Battery comes to forty dollars. All this, another twenty. That it, with the fill-up?" Art asked. Spider rejoiced. He wasn't going to card her. She had a fake ID, but it only worked fifty percent of the time.

Spider debated getting a bottle of Jack Daniel's and decided against it. *Aren't we being mature?* She thought of D. The new creases around her eyes, the way she was holding herself as if she might snap in two. "How much are the cabins for a night?"

"Twenty-nine ninety-five. My wife and daughters wash the sheets weekly whether we have guests or not. They're clean. No bed bugs. Private and quiet."

She tried to imagine how often they had guests.

"Okay, one night."

She pulled a wad of bills out of her wallet. She worked weekends at her parents' antique store and she'd pretty near emptied her savings account for the trip.

Brick House slid her change and the cabin key across the counter. It was attached to a large wooden spoon.

"Number one," he said. "It's okay to leave your car where it is. Keep the hood open and I'll hook your new battery up before I leave for the day."

Spider thanked him, staring at the money in her hand. Why had she withdrawn *all* her savings?

She knew why. The thought that kept dancing in her brain was, *What if I never go back? Just keep moving. Until I make so many new memories that they bury the old ones under their weight.* Could she do that to her parents though? Vanishing would be easy for her. But it would feel like a second death to them.

TWELVE

– Ariel –

WE'VE MADE IT THROUGH the blackest hours of the night and Aaron is still breathing. We snatched a quick hour's sleep but it just made us stiffen up. Diana took a turn after me, then Ruth, and now it's me again. Saddling back up was almost worse. I'm stumbling around, hardly picking up my feet, but I've settled into the numbing pain of it. Big Daddy says there's nothing a body can't endure if one has a mind to. One foot before the other. And my ears aren't twisted back behind me anymore, listening for that bear. Maybe I killed it after all.

Dawn's still an hour or two away but the horizon behind us is lightening and we can see better, and move faster.

Diana calls out treacherous ground, looks out for big rocks and boggy areas, and gradually leads us away from the river. Once we hit the open ground we're traveling blind, guessing which way will be the shortest. None of us know the lowlands below the foothills all that well. My awareness contracts down to Diana's voice and Aaron's grunts, which pierce and elevate my heart at the same time. He's still alive. He's made it this far. Surely that means he won't die?

I'm not going to lie. The rope bites into my skin pretty fast, rubbing a belt of rawness that trickles blood down my waistband. Aaron is thin but he's tall and muscular, and the sled catches against every kind of hump and divot in the ground, sometimes jerking me back so hard I hear my neck crack. At one point, it tilts and almost spills Aaron onto the ground, but Diana catches the edge and rights it, and Ruth and Hannah help to hoist it up and carry it a few yards farther, to where the land flattens again.

None of us has the breath for talking. I think about those rabbits and roots charring in the fire and my mouth waters. Except for that pouch full of blackberries, we haven't eaten anything since the sludgy oatmeal Nana served up the morning we left. I'm glad we dug the firepit deep, cleared the area of brush, and surrounded it with stones. Big Daddy beat that lesson into us when we were young and a bunch of us got hold of a book of matches. Burned down the henhouse, and almost caught fire to the meeting hall. Each one of us got a whipping that kept us standing for a week.

A couple of hours pass. I haul until my feet are blobs of raw flesh, my vision whites out, and I'm slick with sweat. My blisters burst a few miles ago and now my heels throb and sting. I stumble, and pause for a moment, fighting to catch my breath. The chafed area of bare skin above the waistband of my jeans is bright red, almost fluorescent even in this dim morning light, and it sparks with pain.

"My turn again," Diana says. "C'mon."

I duck my head, raise the rope, and hand it over, whatever strength I had that kept me pushing forward draining away suddenly. Hannah catches me against her shoulder and I hold onto her as if I'm suddenly boneless. Faith appears from nowhere. One of the plastic bags hangs from her hand and she upturns it. Orange mushrooms spill out, trumpet-shaped. I know they smell of sweet fruit. We each grab a handful and cram them into our mouths. They might smell like berries but they taste like the rancid stuff you get between your toes. I'd laugh at my thought but I'm too exhausted.

"Let me check on Aaron," I say. His eyes are closed. There's a grey tinge to his skin. The wound in his side has split open and is bleeding again. Faith's bloody, damp shirt hangs from my back pocket. I soak in it some river water from the bottle Faith filled and daub Aaron's face, dribble some more water between his lips, and take a drink myself before passing it around. I've got to believe he'll be all right. He's precious. Not just to me but to the family. Big Daddy always says we're the future.

"Fifteen minutes," Diana says. We sink to the ground.

I feel the cold damp bite into my bones. I look at the girls gathered around Aaron's sled. We're all slump-shouldered, clammy-skinned, too tired to yawn. Pale and sickly, thin as forks in our bras and holey jeans and wet-through sneakers. Hannah's shirt is check-patterned blue and grey, her hair white-blonde like corn silk, and she fades into the misty trees and the mountain always at our right-hand side. My grey sisters, I think. Born of the Grey Sisters.

A cold rain is falling. Not so much from the sky but all around, swirling and seemingly nothing more than a spray, but it soaks our hair, plasters it against our cheeks in rattails. The fog will roll in soon.

"Everyone done eating, drinking?" Diana says through chattering teeth. She does some jumping jacks to get her blood going.

I drink some more in a useless attempt to fill my stomach with something.

Then I haul myself to my feet, teeter a little, and Hannah strips off and wraps the shirt around me. The cuffs reach past my fingertips; the material holds her body warmth. It feels like a hot bath.

I lean down and let my hand barely touch Aaron's face, whisper over the deep slashes in his skin. He feels cool. Too cold? I'm not sure. I tuck the plastic bags in around his body. Check that there's still some padding around his head. My hand drops to his and even though he doesn't open his eyes, his fingers tighten briefly around mine and then release.

"You good?" Diana asks.

I'll be better once I start moving again. I know this. But my foot feels like it's rooted itself into the ground and I have to tear it free to raise it.

I nod at Diana, breathe deeply, take that first step.

"Let's do this," Diana says, looping the rope around her shoulders and setting her heels in.

Diana lasts about four hours and then Hannah takes over. She moves a lot slower—I estimate a rate of less than two miles per hour, but I'm not complaining at this point. My eyelids keep dropping down like rolling steel doors. They're almost too heavy to lift. At first I think I can still hear the river, though our path has led us far from it; then I realize it's the blood slurrying in my ears. The trees have thinned but the ground is covered with tough shrubs and brambles and we have to cut around them often. Ruth trots behind the sled, ready to grab hold if it starts to tip.

"I need to stop," Hannah says with a groan. Her skin is mottled pink and white. Her breath comes hard. I twisted my ankle a mile or two back, turning it on a loose stone. I'm limping.

Somewhere along the way I must have brushed up against some poison ivy. Aaron likes to joke that I have a red thumb and somehow always attract it to me. Even Faith has run out of those nursery rhymes she's always singing under her breath. And Diana has been walking with her head down, straight-lining it, aiming for an end point only she can see.

I tap her on the shoulder. "What do you think?"

She looks around, wonderingly, as if she's been walking in a tunnel.

She sniffs the air. "I smell gasoline. Another five miles, maybe less. It's hard to say since we're off our usual trails. Near as I can tell, we've kept to a straight route to shorten it some." I take a deep breath and smell nothing, but Diana's always been good with that. She can tell what kind of potatoes we're having for dinner even when we're up in the far field. We always hope for fried instead of boiled, but that's happened maybe a handful of times. I remember a dinner once when we had them chipped and cooked up in goose fat—so much flavor and richness it coated the inside of my mouth. We were all ill afterward but it was worth it. My belly rumbles and I feel like I might pass out.

"I think we need to rest again," I say, much as I hate to stop. "Just for an hour or two?" I nod my head to the right. There's an overhang below a big branching tree, a hollow among the thick snarled roots. Hannah unhitches, and Diana, Ruth, and I carry the sled closer to the trees. I settle down next to Aaron, check him. He seems unchanged. No better but no worse. I dribble some more water into his half-opened mouth, prop-ping him up a few inches with my arm so he doesn't choke. Most of it runs out of his mouth but I can feel his heartbeat under my palm. It races like a mouse. I worry it might explode out of his chest.

"He's breathing," Hannah says. "Focus on that."

The ground is sandy and loose. I peel my shoes off, swearing at the state of them. I've got seeping patches on my toes, more on my heels, and a purple blood blister on the sole near my arch on the right foot. The left is a little better. Some soreness and one big flap on my heel that has yet to bubble up. The rash on my forearms is starting to boil too, and I sit on my hands to keep from scratching. Faith brings the water jug to me and I pour a little over my feet, gasping at the sharp pain and sweet comfort of it. Faith might be small and she might be a crybaby, but she's walking more upright than the rest of us. I notice, though, that there's fresh blood spotting her jeans. I can't ask her to haul Aaron, but that doesn't mean I can't still be mad at her either. With an effort I try to let it go. Ruth curls up between two roots. She always reminds me of some bright-eyed woodland creature. Diana is lying on her back with her arm over her eyes, and Hannah is sitting hunched with her head down, her shirt draped loosely over her shoulders. Every few seconds she groans. I give in to exhaustion, just for a moment.

When I wake, the sun is high. Faith squats in front of me with a big smile on her face. She holds out her cupped hands. There are six small brown-and-white speckled eggs in them.

"Six," she says. "Like us."

"What kind?"

"I don't know. Some kind of water bird?"

We could make a quick fire, find and heat a flat rock like a skillet. I have Aaron's eyeglasses in my pocket, though the sun is weak and hidden behind the clouds. Miraculously, they weren't broken in the struggle with the bear, only bent a little when he fell. I put my hands out; they are shaking so badly I don't think I can do it.

"Eat up," I call to the other three, who wipe sleep from their eyes as they come to join us.

We make a hole at either end of the shell and cover one with a finger. And then suck. Raw eggs are . . . not sure how to describe it, but they take the edge off our hunger. Just enough to make me crave fresh-baked bread and potatoes and even the gritty, muddy catfish Big Daddy catches during the springtime floods.

I want to save the last one for Aaron, for when he wakes up, but Diana catches my eye. "You eat it," she says with a wry grin. "He's just lying there." I swallow it down and with a sigh slip my shoes back on. They feel like they've shrunk a couple of sizes, or my toes have swelled.

Getting to my feet again, walking, looping that cord back around my middle is pure pain. Everything in me wants to scream and beg and lie down and never get up. But I go on. And so do they. And after a few miles we've lapsed back into such an automatic dreamlike state that we don't even notice when the ground underfoot switches from grass to packed earth. And then to the concrete of Route 12. I almost want to drop to my knees and kiss it.

A massive pickup truck, the bed stacked high with lumber, rumbles past, horn blaring. And I can see the guy in his trucker hat staring back at us, reflected in his side mirror, because he just passed five girls covered in dirt and sweat and blood, hauling some dude in a sled. In nothing but their filthy bras and ripped jeans. But then he's around the corner and I'm staring at those mud flaps with the big-titty women on them. Wouldn't have accepted a ride from him anyway. I know trouble when I see it. And we lean against each other, in a tight huddle, weary arms draped around each other's shoulders.

"What do you think? Feltzen Corners is that way," Diana says when we break apart. She gestures behind us. We know this road from walking to the school. "The gas station is up that a way. Tad closer." She points up the road. "Over a hill or two. Can probably catch a ride up the mountain road there if we're lucky."

Betting on that is the only thing that keeps me going this last little way, although the sled slides easier now. I check the strips of material and reinforce them with rope where they're wearing thin. "Almost there, baby," I tell Aaron.

Faith stumbles. And then Hannah falls to her knees. Ruth darts in too late to catch her under the arm.

"Hold up a second," I say, trying to catch my breath. The gas station is closed up tight. The signpost to Pembroke Cross is just ahead. *Pray for a ride or keep walking?*

"No one is going to stop," Ruth says, giving voice to my doubts. "I mean, look at us."

"Crap," Diana says, kicking up a cloud of dust.

Hannah gazes at the mountain. "Home's close. Made it this far, we can go a little farther," she says. She's trying to sound all tough, but we can hear the weariness in her voice. Her jeans are torn, knees are all scraped up.

"We've done it before," Diana says with a heavy sigh, echoed by us all.

The rough track road up is familiar. Every twist, every mud-filled pothole, every abandoned shack and backwoods moonshine still and pissed-off fight dog and monster truck with bull bars and plastic testicles dangling from the rear parked in dusty driveways is known to us. We've trudged down it to get to the junior and senior high school in Feltzen Corners, on the rare days when we can make it, and trekked back up it in all kinds of weather, slipping and sliding in ice and snow and rain, and broiling in the hot sun. The overgrown shortcuts through the shrouding woods to the walled compound are sunk so deep into my bones that I could follow them with my eyes closed. Even though the way through is almost invisible if you're not familiar with it. Used to remind me of that story Big Daddy told us about the maze and the monster.

A series of whistles—like birds if you don't know any better —sound from up ahead so we know we're spotted and identified. Diana trills a response back.

When we come out through the thick copse surrounding the compound, see the guard towers manned by a couple of Uncles, and the high fence protecting our home, I just about break down in tears.

I stare at Big Daddy. He stares back, kind of relaxed at first, but then his blue eyes darken and his lips straighten out. His hands, big spoon-shaped thumbs jammed into his belt loops, flex and tighten. We've been back a couple of hours, time enough to grab a chunk of bread—all that's left of the midday meal—and see Aaron settled in.

"She can patch him up, but maybe you should have left him out there," he says. "No telling whether he'll live. Now we got a bear, wounded, probably half-crazed and dangerous, running loose on the mountain." The Uncles had gone out immediately with their rifles and a couple of dogs.

"You could take him to the hospital or call the doctor," I say, trying to keep my voice from shaking.

"No doctors," Big Daddy says. "Esme put some stitches in him. He's young and strong. Not so pretty now." He coughs out a laugh.

I wince. I've just come from the cabin we use for birthing and illness. Four narrow beds in a two-roomed hut set a little apart from the cluster of main homes so that no one is disturbed by groans and screams. The slashes on Aaron's face are swollen and raw and the stitches run crooked, like something hemmed by a five-year-old.

I'm praying it doesn't get infected, that by some miracle he doesn't end up looking pieced together like a rag doll, although it's the wound in his side that's the real worry. Nana Esme used stitches and industrial-strength glue on that and packed it with cotton, but he's also running a fever she's trying to bring down with bark tea.

"Fussing won't make him heal any faster," Big Daddy says. "I won't allow for it taking you away from your duties." He scratches his bristly head. "Henhouse needs mucking out. Esme's doing a heap of laundry today and needs help. Got that fence up on the ridge needs seeing to. And Guy's got a mess of fish to clean. Where are the others?"

I shrug. I know they're hiding out in the woods right now but I'm not about to tell him. Fish guts, chicken shit, beating clothes on a rock until your hands are raw and chapped is no one's idea of a good time. My sisters are in bad shape. Faith is still bleeding from her lady parts. Hannah can't lift her arm above her head, Ruth is limping, and Diana has a pulled muscle that sends shooting pains from her lower back all the way to her ankle. I'm more tired than I've ever been, weaker than a kitten, and my feet feel like ground meat, but I'm jacked up too.

Nana won't use any kind of store-bought medicine. She trusts in herbs and her own magic. Big Daddy trusts in her. I want painkillers for Aaron and ointments that'll kill any kind of bug that's worming its way into his insides. And for that, I need Big Daddy's help.

I want to get in his face and scream, "Ain't we soldiers now?" But I don't. Instead, I paste on a smile and try to make my voice all sweet and high-pitched, like Faith does when she's trying to get candy.

I even dare to place my hand on his iron-hard forearm. "Aaron works really hard. You know that. And he's so smart. A real asset."

Big Daddy grunts.

"He saved Faith. Be bad to lose him if we could avoid it." My voice hitches even though I tried to control it.

His eyes narrow. He brushes my hand off and I know I've lost him. "No doctors," he says. "No hospitals. No outsiders. Once they've got you in their system, assigned you numbers and the like, you are a prisoner. They can do whatever they want to you. The strong survive. The mountain provides."

THIRTEEN

— D —

D SAT DOWN CAUTIOUSLY on the wall-side bed farthest from the door. It bowed under her weight, sinking in the middle. The comforter was a stiff square of polyester that slithered off the mattress.

Min peeled back the covers on the other one. "Not too stained. Seems pretty new, actually."

The rest of the room consisted of brown paneling, an industrial carpet of an indeterminate muddy shade, a simple rod of wire hangers, the kind that always seemed to click together as if by an invisible hand, and a massive dresser made out of that stuff that looks like wood but isn't really. D knocked on it anyway, and silently said, *Tomorrow, Kat.* Her legs were tired and cramped from all the driving but they were also pulsing with a weird twitchy energy. Although the room was small, she walked from one end to the other and back. *I'm here, Kat. I'm so close.* Doctor Octavian had encouraged D to talk to her sister in real time. To keep her memory alive. D had been doing it for so long now that it felt natural. She liked knowing the conversations with her sister were out there somewhere, etched on the ether. A record of them together in the world.

She opened the door to the bathroom.

It was Pepto-Bismol pink—tub, sink, toilet, tiles. Like stepping inside a cupcake. The drains were stained with rust but she was glad to see that the room appeared clean. No curly stray hairs or bad smells. The fluorescent lights buzzed and flickered. In the mirror, her eyes looked sunken, like holes punched in a piece of tan leather, her cheeks far thinner than they used to be.

If Kat were alive would they still look the same? The differences between them were minute, invisible to any but those nearest and dearest. Mamma used to call them Little Spoon and Big Spoon, but not because of any difference in their size. It was because Kat had been curled around her sister in the womb. Protecting her up until they'd been born nine minutes apart. "I'm the oldest," she'd yell at D if they fought. "It's only fifty-four seconds," D would yell back. Counting to fifty-four was one of the ways D calmed herself now.

She splashed water on her face, dried it with the clean yet scratchy hand towel, and smoothed her hair into a ponytail. Took a deep breath, held it, exhaled, and took another one. Tomorrow they would be together again.

"What do we have to eat?" she asked, walking back out.

"Chips, beer, all the food groups." Spider turned from the window. "Looks like the new battery's in. I was half-expecting a knock on the door." She thrust her pelvis out and adopted a drawl. "Can I fill you up, ladies?"

"Oh baby," Min said in a flat voice, and gyrated her hips.

Spider cracked a beer and gestured to the open case on the floor. "Help yourself."

D shook her head. A beer funk. No way. Alcohol would probably calm the nervous energy in her limbs but it would also make her morose. She drank from a bottle of water, downing most of it in one long swallow. She wiped her mouth and bounced a little to loosen up her thigh muscles.

Min stretched out on the bed with the sheaf of papers in her hands.

"More research?" D asked.

"I don't know," Min said with a shrug. "It's interesting, right? I mean two, three communities so close together and yet their lives are so different." She leafed through the pages. "Listen to this. 'In the mid-1970s, after the end of the Vietnam War, new settlers came to the mountain, arriving in repurposed moving trucks, buses, and RVs. These were grim people with set faces and severe clothing, escaping from other places. The mountain folk were blood-bound. A tangled tribe of cousins stretching back two hundred years.

'At first, it was an uneasy relationship. But eventually the lines between them and the first families began to blur and a mixture of past and present ideologies occurred. The old names still dominated the mountain, but these blended kinfolk took on the new ways and started building for the future.'"

"They sound like off-the-grid whack jobs," Spider scoffed.

"Excuse me? I grew up off the grid. Not everyone who wants to heal the Earth is nuts. Some of us are just more aware. Maybe when the seas rise up and drown all the resorts you'll think again."

"I stopped using straws," Spider said gruffly. "Makes it almost impossible to drink a milkshake!"

"Well, that's the Nobel Peace Prize for you then, isn't it?"

"I wonder where they all went?" D said, interrupting the squabble. "The people who used to live here?"

"City, probably. As soon as they're our age they hightail it for the jobs and the donuts," Spider said.

"People usually come home again though," D said, thinking of her extended family in Italy. Her older cousins had gone up north for their educations, jobs, but the ones who wanted to start families had returned to Calabria, married locals, put down roots in familiar soil.

"Not if there's no one to come home to," Min said.

FOURTEEN

– Ariel –

IT'S COMING UP ON LATE AFTERNOON before I'm able to ditch. Uncle Randall thinks I'm fence-patching and Uncle Clive thinks I'm setting snares in the woods. I *am* in the woods but I'm walking in the opposite direction from the way I said I was headed. Not up higher into the mountains but toward the flatlands. It's slow going. I'm tireder than I have ever been in my life and the skin on my feet is raw and weeping. More like limping than walking, although if I can grit my teeth past the pain, it actually feels good to be moving. The farther I go, the looser my muscles feel.

I stay off the blacktop and out of sight of any cars. The only vehicles likely to be on the mountain road at this time of day belong to Big Daddy and the Uncles.

Once I've reached the low country, I cut across to the highway and wait. I keep to the left hand side of the road just in case I have to run and hide in the bushes. I roll my jean shorts up and adjust my bra to make the most of my sparse boobs. I pile my hair up on top of my head. I stink to high hell but maybe they won't notice, or maybe it'll offer some protection. I wasn't able to do much more than change my clothes and get a quick sluice from the bucket.

A big truck heading to Abbotsford would be perfect. Those men are rough, but they're company men and too scared of rape charges to mess with someone as young-looking as me. But it's not a truck that passes by going in the opposite direction, slows, and then does a quick U-turn. It's a carful of young guys, blasting loud music, and with a sinking heart I recognize them from the brief time I've been able to spend at school.

The driver, Jim, is in remedial English with Hannah and me —the class for kids who are behind, stupid, or just delinquent. He stares at us a lot. The other three are his pals: Chuck, who's riding shotgun, and Francis and Blaine in the back. At school they crowd the hallways so you have to pass by them real close to get to your locker. Usually they just say sleazy stuff, low, under their breath, but sometimes they force you to inch past them so that your body rubs up against theirs. They call that a meat tunnel.

Jim has a beer bottle in his hand and he leans out the window, takes a long swallow, and then wipes the foam from his lips. His eyes are really dark, almost black, and they burn into me. He turns the bass-heavy music down.

"Which way you headed?" he asks.

I square my shoulders and walk up to the car, force a smile, and point up the road. If I can just get a ride to Abbotsford, I can convince a doctor to come with me and see to Aaron. Or send an ambulance. Or at the least I can shoplift some pain-killers and antibiotic cream at a drugstore.

"Hey, how's it going?" I say warily.

They exchange glances and snickers. Jim frowns at them, then nods in my direction. "Hey yourself." His grin is easy but it doesn't light up his eyes. I think of Aaron and how his rare, sweet smile spreads like honey, and warms his whole face. And then I take a deep breath; Aaron might not ever look the same again.

"Going into Abbotsford?" I ask. I lean into the window so Jim can get a good gander down my shirt.

"Maybe. We're just driving around. Bored," Jim says. "Want a beer?" He uncaps one for me, hands it over.

I don't but I take it anyway. Pretend to sip. "I would appreciate a ride to town."

"Might be more going on there than there is here," Chuck says. "A party. Some girl action." He and Jim exchange glances and I don't like it. I step away from the car.

"C'mon," says Jim. "Give up your seat, Chuck. Make room for the lady." There's a teasing note in his voice that makes me feel uncomfortable but there's no other cars in sight. I think of Aaron and steel myself. Chuck scrambles into the back and Jim reaches over and opens the door for me on the passenger side.

Once I'm in, he starts driving. Behind me, I can hear the sound of beer bottles being opened, the metal caps skittering on the blacktop as they toss them out the open windows. They've got a couple of cases back there and each of them has probably already had three or four beers. It smells like weed too. As soon as I get in I know I've made a bad mistake, but there's nothing I can do. I press my knees together and hitch the neckline of my tank top up. I pick at my poison ivy.

Jim drives in the direction of Abbotsford and I let myself relax a little. All I've got to do is last another hour and a half. It feels good to be off my feet.

"So what are you up to?" he asks.

"Just some errands."

"I didn't think you ever came down off the mountain except for school."

"Not even for that," Chuck says. "How many absences this year?"

"Might make more sense to ask her how many days she's made it in," Francis says, poking his head between the seats. He's thin, tall, and leggy like a grasshopper. Buggy eyes too. And his acne's so bad it looks like my poison ivy rash. I feel sorry for him until I notice that he doesn't ever make eye contact. His gaze zeroes in on my chest. I fold my arms up tight.

"So, is it like a cult thing up there? You drinking Kool-Aid and worshipping space aliens?" Chuck asks.

"Sister wives," Blaine says. Blaine doesn't talk much. With his bangs in his face, he kind of reminds me of a shaggy dog.

Big Daddy always tells us to brush these questions away. To never give details. It's drummed into our heads. There's them. And us.

I laugh overly loud and overly long. After a while, they laugh with me.

Chuck rolls a joint and the three of them in the back smoke. Jim waves it away and I just shake my head and fake a smile.

We drive through Feltzen Corners. Rows of pretty little houses with fences. There could be a doctor living in one of them but I have no way of knowing. It looks clean. People grow flowers in their front yards, get their vegetables from a store. I bet the kids could go barefoot on the sidewalks all summer long and never step on broken glass, sharp rocks, cigarettes, or twisted pieces of metal, but I bet they never do.

I crank down my window. The skunky smoke tickles my nose. Another twenty minutes and we'll be there. I feel my shoulders relax. They're nicer than I thought they'd be. Maybe they'll take me all the way to the hospital even.

I pull the visor down and check my reflection in the mirror, smooth my hair down, wish I could have had time to wash with a little soap.

Jim taps his fingers on the steering wheel.

"Getting close," he says.

"Yeah. Thanks for the ride."

"Sure. Sure." His voice trails off. "Pretty far out of my way."

The three in the back cut their chatter and goofing around. Francis leans forward. I can feel the air change. It's like a bucket of cold water.

"I really appreciate it," I say, trying to keep my voice strong and confident. We're dropping down the long curved hill and he speeds up. I can see the buildings of Abbotsford in the valley, the quaint covered bridge that crosses the river. The hospital is on the far side of town, I know. I accompanied Hannah there with a teacher once, when she split her chin doing flips on the jungle gym. She's the only one of us who ever got seen by a doctor and Big Daddy almost lost his shit. "Once the government knows about you, they hound you for life. They stick a microchip in your brain and track you. Tell you how to live," he'd shouted.

Jim takes his eyes off the road and glances at me. Those black irises like deep bruises. "Yeah, how much?"

"What?"

"How much do you appreciate it?"

"I don't really have any money. But I can maybe get you some. After," I say.

"Well, isn't that nice. Twenty bucks, you're thinking?"

I've never had more than a couple of dollars in my possession. No one on the mountain does. We don't really buy anything. Except for guns. But I say, "Sure. That sounds fair."

"When?"

"What?"

"When will you pay me?"

He eases the car over onto the weedy strip that runs along the road and stops. His arm is draped over the back of my seat. There's a click and Chuck pushes the lock down on my door. His big meaty hand stays there.

"I don't know. I can get it together next week probably." My palms are sweating.

Jim suddenly pulls out again, back tires sending a spray of gravel up, and whips the car around in the middle of the road to head back in the direction of Pembroke Cross.

"That's not gonna cut it," he says, his voice low and growly.

"You'll have to trade us," Blaine says.

Jim has his foot on the gas. We're going too fast for me to jump out of the car, even if I could get the door open.

"What do you mean?"

"I'm sure you've got something you can give us. Barter? Like the way you do up on that mountain."

They're all laughing again, clinking their bottles, breathing their hot stinky breath on me. I should never have gotten into this car.

Where are they taking me? My mind fills in all kinds of scenarios. This is what Big Daddy warned us about. Outsiders, valley dwellers aren't to be trusted. They will always want from you more than you want to give. And if you don't pony up, they'll take it by force.

My chest feels tight and it's hard to breathe normally. Cold sweat trickles down my spine.

I am a soldier, I tell myself.

I'll wait until they stop and then I'll smash my bottle on Chuck's hand, get out, and run.

"Pull over, pull over," Blaine says, pointing.

My heart jumps and then falls again. I see the gas station and convenience store but it's dark, closed up for the day.

As soon as Jim parks, I put my plan into action. The bottom of my beer bottle crunches Chuck's fingers, I fumble at the door latch, throw it open, and then I'm jerked backward as Jim grabs me by my shirt and pulls me almost into his lap, the bottle hits the dashboard and splinters into wicked thorns. His hand is heavy and hot on my chest and I squirm but he's still got a fistful of my shirt. I drum my heels against the seat, hear the material tear along the neckline.

"Wild one," he says into my ear.

And then I get a hand up. I've got a small piece of glass gripped between my fingers and I rip him across the face. He screams, lets go, and I'm out of the car and they tumble out after me.

Somehow, Chuck gets in front of me and pushes me backward. The rest of them spread out so that they've got me almost surrounded. Their faces are red with rage and I can tell they really want to hurt me now. The road is at my back. I look left and then right, hoping to spot a passing car. I'd run out into the road, force them to stop. Nothing coming in either direction.

"You fucking bitch," Jim says. His cheek drips blood. It reminds me of Aaron's clawed face. I feel a steely knot surrounding the butterflies in my stomach. I will not let them touch me, I swear.

"C'mon girl," says Francis, lunging at me suddenly. "Why

you gotta be so unfriendly?" His voice is slurred, thickened by alcohol. They've got me dancing back and forth, dodging, darting, but I can't break through their ranks. My breath tears itself from my throat, my muscles quiver with exhaustion.

A beer bottle explodes just behind my foot. Shards of glass prick my ankles and calves. I jump forward and Jim snatches at me. Blood from his wound spatters and some of it gets in my mouth. I spit and swipe at my eyes and my hands come away red. I struggle, cursing, and manage to pull free. For a second I think about stealing the car, but what if Jim has the keys in his pocket? I hold up my spike of glass, searching the ground for something bigger.

Big Daddy taught us that everything can be a weapon.

My attention is fixed on the boys advancing.

And then I hear a shout, a man's voice, footsteps pounding, and I run toward the orange car parked in front of the cabins. There must be guests. I squat down near the back, peek out.

The boys aren't paying me no attention. Uncle Guy has a short-bore rifle slung over his shoulder and as soon as he gets close, they break and run, pile into their car and peel off, burning rubber into the road.

"C'mon out, girl," he says. His shadow is long and stretches halfway across the parking lot; the gun hangs by his side. His tone is mild, though, so I come out, trying to pull my ripped shirt together to cover my chest.

He waits for me to come to him. I can't read him. His hair is loose, hangs in his face, one blue eye glitters.

And once I'm in grabbing range, his hand closes around my upper arm and he squeezes it so hard my fingers start to tingle. His jaw clicks; he's grinding his teeth.

"What in hell's name are you doing down here, girl? Sneaking around? Whoring? Who were those boys you were messing with?"

"I just . . ." My mind is scrambled, the pain shooting through my arm like liquid fire driving thoughts away. I'm a soldier, I remind myself, not just some girl. "Big Daddy sent me down to—"

"You're telling me you're on some errand for him. Dressed like that? He said nothing to me about it."

His hand moves from my arm to my jaw, pinching along the bone, forcing my head up. There's a heat coming off of him. And a stink that speaks of a long run of drugs or booze, most probably both.

"You hold yourself apart," he says in a low, growly voice. "But I got your number now, girl." His eyes drill holes into my body. "You're all grown up."

I aim a vicious kick at his junk but he pushes me away so hard I hit the ground on my butt. He's stowed the gun now, and his hand is working at his belt buckle. I start yelling at the top of my lungs.

FIFTEEN

— D —

D SAT UP, DISORIENTED. Shouting had woken her. She rubbed the sleep from her eyes.

"Someone's out there," said Spider. "I heard shouting, a car revving, but it's stopped now. I can't see anyone."

D joined her at the window and pulled the curtain back a little. She must have crashed for only a couple of hours but her body was stiff and sore. She massaged her neck. "What time is it?"

"Just gone six."

"Should we check it out?"

"Survey says no," said Spider. "What can we do about it? Plus, it sounds like it's resolved itself."

Min came out of the steamy bathroom, a towel over her wet hair. "Why are you guys sitting here in the dark?" She clicked on the light, took in their expressions. "What's going on?"

"You missed all kinds of excitement," Spider said.

"Shh," D said, holding up a hand. "Listen."

"That's a girl yelling," Min said.

"Shit!" said Spider. She pulled on her boots and started lacing them up.

Before they could get to the door, someone was banging on it. "Let me in!" It was a female voice. "Open up, please!"

Spider, D, and Min exchanged a look and then Spider, motioning the other two to get ready, flung it open.

A girl bolted in. Spider slammed the door shut and locked it.

"Who you running from?" she asked. "Do we need to be worried?" She'd grabbed a desk lamp and was brandishing it like she wasn't exactly sure what to do with it.

The girl flattened herself against the far wall, her breath hitching, eyes sliding from face to face. She had blood smudged across her cheeks, all over her hands, her threadbare shirt gaped from a torn collar, but D couldn't see any wounds on her. "No. He's gone." Her voice was low and scratchy, a burr harshening the vowels.

"Hey," said Min, drawing closer. "You're safe." The girl tensed, bunching her fists, then relaxed. Min was the smallest of them, and also wearing bunny pajamas. "Have a seat." Min pointed to the armchair in the corner. "Did he hurt you?"

The girl ignored the chair, pressing closer to the wall. She was painfully thin, sinewy, and her tight clothes were too small, barely covering her stomach, which was round in that way that spoke of too little to eat, not too much. Her curly red hair had escaped from the ponytail and snarled around her shoulders. Angry-looking scabs dotted her arms.

"You okay?" D asked. The girl was also older than she'd first thought. Pretty near their own ages.

"I handled it," she mumbled.

Spider passed her a bottle of water. She had to stretch her arm way out like she was feeding steak to a wild animal, and once the girl had hold of it, she ducked back into her corner again. Opening it, she drank it down in one long swallow, wiping her mouth and smearing more of the blood when she was done. Her eyes, wide and grey like one of Margaret Keane's waif munchkins, were fixed on Spider's face.

"You live nearby? Got somewhere to go?" D asked. "We can take you there if you like."

The girl's eyes flicked to the door and back again.

"No," she said, her voice quavering. D couldn't decipher the emotion. It was fear, but desperation and anger too.

"I've got to go," she said. Her gaze fixed again on Spider.

"What's up?" she said. "Don't you know it's impolite to stare?"

Min put her hand out, stepping closer. "Why don't you have some food first? We have chips, granola bars, chocolate." Her fingers brushed the girl's arm. "I'm Min. We can get you cleaned up?"

For a second, the girl relaxed, staring at Min's hand.

"Don't touch me," she yelled, and hurled the empty bottle at Min's face.

Dodging past Spider on her way to the door, she fumbled at the lock and she was out, running into the woods at the back of the cabin.

SIXTEEN

– Ariel –

I'M THINKING ABOUT THE SHORT GIRL, blue and black hair, concerned expression, the one who held her hand out toward me. "I'm Min," she said. For a moment I let myself believe she'll help me, get medicine for Aaron. Her voice is soft and kind and I am so worn out and worried that I relax, but then all my training kicks in—these are outsiders, strangers, these are Them. They'll ask questions about us and Avalon; they won't understand, and that ignorance will lead to our downfall.

I get free and I run into the woods back behind the cabins and I watch for a couple of minutes until the lights dim behind the curtains and I can sneak around the front and get to the road. I find a suede bracelet in the dust, spotted black and yellow all over. It's soft as puppy fur and finer than anything I own. I slip it onto my wrist.

By the time I get near the compound I can barely keep my eyes open. I'm covered in dirt and sweat and blood. My breath razors in my throat. I took the roughest, fastest route, away from the track road just in case Uncle Guy was still searching for me. If he goes to Big Daddy will his lies be believed? As a soldier, one of Daddy's own, am I protected? I'm not sure. I go as quick as I dare, falling more than a few times, my legs collapsing beneath me. My knees scab up, encrusted with grit. I just want to give in to exhaustion but I have to get home first. The gates are closed up, so I sneak around the back to a shallow trench under the fence where the boards are loose.

Even though I shouldn't spare the time, I run to the hut where Aaron is, my heart in my mouth until I see the quick rise and fall of his chest. He's still asleep. Is that good? Bad? I can't tell. I lean in and sniff him. He smells sweaty but there's no sweet stink like I've noticed with injured animals. The ones that are going to die.

A big bandage covers half his face. The eye I can see is swollen, a mass of bruising. Beside him, there's a half-empty coffee cup of some muddy-looking greenish liquid. I lift it to my nose. It smells like dirt and plants and something sweet, probably honey. We keep hives. Nana's own magic, she says, goes into her tinctures. She activates them by rolling the tiny bottles in her palms, praying all the while under her breath. That's some old-woman magic there.

He's thrown his blanket off. I tuck it in around him, lean my head against his chest. I listen to his heartbeat flutter, kiss his dry, flaking lips. "Back soon."

The meeting hall windows are all lit up with candlelight, so I know that everyone is in there, gathered for the evening assembly. I linger for a moment but hear just the usual babble. Near as I can tell, it's just past eight—Big Daddy has probably given his sermon already; read from one of his books. The mommies are likely cutting thick slices of bread, ladling up a soup or stew, serving the littlest ones first. Maybe Guy isn't back yet? Or he hasn't had a chance to speak his piece. What was he doing down there anyway? I need to wash up before the meal. I can smell Jim's blood on my face, and it's gummed up under my fingernails. If I'm going to play the innocent, I can't go in looking like I've been fighting. I go around behind the henhouse, slip past the dog pen. The pups jump up against the fence, yipping and shoving their noses into my hands. There are three, all black like their mom, but one of them has a white splotch covering his eye. I named him Patch. The other two are Tooth and Claw. Nicky, curled up beside Biter, raises his head. He makes a questioning sound. I ruffle his hair, ignoring the growls coming from the big dog. She won't attack me unless Nicky reacts in fear or cries, but it's unsettling. Her whole ribcage vibrates like there's a motor in there.

I notice the water bowl and feed trough are empty. This could be the excuse for my lateness. I grab a bucket and go over to the shed where we hang our hunting kills. We keep the guts and such for the dogs. First, I pocket my new bracelet so it doesn't get dirty, and then I fork up a soggy handful of something white and bloody-red and mix it with some grain and vegetable peelings until it makes a stinky porridge. I empty it into the trough, keeping clear of the dogs' teeth. The puppies bury their noses, all in a row, butts up, tails wagging. I take another bucket to the well and fill it. Wash my hands, gasping at the cold, rinse myself off, pouring most of it over my head, and then fill it again and take it to the dogs. Nicky is eating alongside the pups. He shouldn't be eating raw meat and offal, but he's been doing it since he was a little kid and it hasn't harmed him yet. "More dog than boy," Nana Esme always says. I wipe my face with my shirt, twist my hair until most of the water runs out, then put it back in a ponytail. Slip the bracelet back on like it's a good luck charm. Even now I can feel Guy's hands on me.

I'm hoping Nana Esme doesn't notice my torn shirt and how filthy I am. She's very particular about cleanliness. Makes us line up and show her our fingernails on the weekly.

I enter the hall from the back door, sticking close to the walls and away from the candles, where it's darker, and inch my way along until I'm down at the end by the littlest kids. My sisters are here too. In our corner. I squeeze in among them. No sign of Guy but there's a big knot of Uncles over by the high table. Hannah is coaxing some of the reluctant eaters and Diana sits next to her, then Ruth. Hannah is quite motherly, happy to play games with them and wipe their snotty noses, but Diana would sooner kick them away than soothe. I know she's only sitting here because the kids get served first and all our meals taste better warm.

Diana raises her eyebrows at me. "I'll tell you later," I say, shaking my head. "It's not good."

"Did you get some medicine at least? You were taking a big risk, girl."

I hunch my shoulders, blinded suddenly by hot, angry tears.

Hannah presses my hand.

"Where's Faith?" I ask.

Diana stops gnawing at a piece of tough meat and gestures with her head. Faith is sitting with the Uncles.

"Did she choose to sit with them?" I ask, my stomach turning over. One of them got Faith pregnant this last time. She can't risk it again.

"She asked him." Diana's face is like stone. We exchange disbelieving looks. "Clive."

"But why?" Clive is the nicest of the Uncles, not that that's saying much. A big soft mattress of a man with a lumpy, mushy kind of a face, sort of like a cold bowl of oatmeal.

I can't stop the shiver of disgust that worms up my spine. She chose to give what Guy wanted to take from me. It makes me want to puke.

"Can't she just—" I break off, not sure how to finish the sentence. Faith isn't really a fighter. Me, I fight with everything I have. And now that I have Aaron, I'll fight even harder.

"Why are they even messing with her? What about the cows? Any of them not paired up?"

I know it's mean to refer to them that way but that's the purpose they serve. They have the babies and they feed them until they're old enough to be sold. It's mostly rich white people who have no problem operating under the law. For the male babies, that is. The females stay and are reared up until they can become cows or soldiers.

"Once our ranks are filled and we have arms enough, the trade will cease," Big Daddy says. I think we girls are tougher anyway, built to endure pain.

"Three of them are knocked up and Ghost took a beating. She's been down in the cellar all week," Ruth says.

I wince. Big Daddy made us dig the basement out of the earth with a few shovels and our bare hands—one of his teaching lessons. I know how dark and dank it is. There are three rooms down there: two cells, A and B, for malcontents like her, and one, way bigger, taking up an area almost the same size as the meeting hall, filled to the ceiling with sacks of grain, root vegetables, canned fruit, and jarred pickles. There's even a well. It has a heavy steel door, concrete walls and ceiling, and reinforced metal beams. Big Daddy says it could withstand a nuclear attack. We store the guns and ammo behind dry-wall panels.

"What did she do this time?" Diana asks.

"Run? Resist?" I don't think I've ever exchanged a word with her, but I feel sorry anyway.

"They say she's bad luck," Ruth says.

She's as pale and wispy as a wraith, although I do sense some quiet stubbornness in her. Not that that'll help her any.

"Faith's one of us though. Not a cow anymore," I say to the other two. A soldier. That's all we have. It can't be that easy to let it go.

Hannah shrugs. "Maybe this is easier for her?" It's true that if you're mating the Uncles or pregnant you get better food, and more of it. The choice bits, not like this tough-as-leather strip of something I just pilfered off of Hannah's plate. I'm hoping it's an old deer but worry it's roadkill. Once you've eaten opossum you don't ever get that greasy taste out of your mouth.

Diana slides her plate over. I fork up some boiled potatoes and wish for salt. I'm always wishing for salt but it's something we don't have up here. There's that tale about the king's daughter who was banished when she told her father she loved him as much as salt. He thought that was an insult until he had to do without.

Diana shifts uneasily on the hard wooden bench. "Your leg still bugging you?" I ask.

"Yeah, plus we were hauling rocks out of the far field most of the day until well past sundown." She punches me on the shoulder. Hard. "You missed all the fun."

"Did Big Daddy tell you it was preparing you?"

According to Big Daddy, everything is preparing us. All the crappy chores we do, the shit jobs like moving big rocks from one place to another, is prep for the war that is coming. Even canning carrots and beets until our fingers are stained and we puke a little from the smell of vinegar is some kind of testing. War is a glorious thing, to hear him preach it.

Hannah snorts and then her face gets serious.

"We had to cover for you though," she says. "He was gone after breakfast, but he did come round late afternoon. He asked where you were."

"What'd you tell him?" I scratch at my poison ivy. It's scabbed over and my nails make the rash bleed but I can't stop myself.

"Bathroom break in the woods," says Diana. "So what happened?"

I fill them in on Jim and the others. I tell them about Guy.

"He crossed the line," Hannah says. Her voice is shaky. "How could he?"

Part of me is glad it was me and not her. I can take care of myself but Hannah takes things to heart.

"Not the first time." I'm not sure what to do about it. Kill him in his sleep? "He was jacked up on meth for sure." She slips her warm fingers into mine. "Maybe together we can make it right," I tell her.

"You going out again?" Hannah asks me.

"If I can sneak away. Aaron's not getting better. He needs real meds." It feels weird to say that out loud. Like I'm turning traitor.

Diana's face hardens but all she says is, "It's a big risk."

"I think if Big Daddy found out, he'd kill you," Hannah says.

Diana nods. "Yup. You broke the first rule: don't fraternize with the outsiders. And that's the only one that matters."

"Please be careful," Hannah says.

I squeeze her hand. "Ready for anything. Like always."

SEVENTEEN

— *Min* —

THEY'D VACATED THE CABIN the next morning in a coffee-deprived woozy state, none of them sleeping much after the incident with the girl. And the gas station wasn't open yet, so Min had just slipped the key through a mail slot in the door. Then they piled in the car and headed off, taking the turn up to Pembroke Cross. "Only twelve miles," said D happily, although Min noticed her smile slipping before they'd gone much more than a mile. It wasn't a road so much as a deeply fissured track.

She-Ra's transmission was clearly not happy. Some of the potholes seemed deep enough to tilt the car all the way over. It was like being in a small boat in a choppy ocean. Min was not overjoyed either, and her torment was escalating by the second. She'd swallowed some more Dramamine but it hadn't kicked in yet. She opened her window all the way and tried to focus on something immovable on the horizon. Of course there was nothing she could fixate on, just the gnarled pines as they lurched past, and the cloying stink of the exhaust. In the end her mantras became "please don't vomit please don't vomit" and "we're almost there we're almost there" as she wiped the sweat from her forehead, swallowed the saliva collecting in her mouth, and tried not to think about the very real possibility that she would lose this battle.

Min didn't want to risk speaking, but D must have read her mind or her body language—stiff as a board, leaning as far out the window as she could without being beheaded by a branch. She pulled over.

"Did we miss a turn-off?" Spider said, scowling at the trees.

"It's up here somewhere. Probably just around the next bend," D said, switching the ignition off. She winked at Min. "Just want to check the radiator, and let her cool down for a minute or two."

"Thank you," Min said, and got out hurriedly. She felt as if she was going to puke at any moment. What was worse: vomiting on an empty stomach or a full one?

"Min?" called D. "Can I help at all?"

Min waved her hands, signaling "no," but she didn't unglue her lips, just in case, and kept walking down the road.

She just had to wait out the waves of nausea. She sank down on the ground, dug her fingers into the carpet of pine needles, and tried to root herself in stillness. After about ten minutes, she opened her eyes. Directly ahead of her was the mountain. The uppermost peaks gleamed with caps of snow. Three steep, craggy spires rose into the clouds, tufted here and there with greenery. Her parents farmed. She knew how hard it was, how long the days, how much could go wrong. Why would anyone choose to live here? Where were those nineteen people who had filled out the census?

She stood up carefully. No wobbliness. No cramp below her waistband. She'd stopped sweating so profusely.

"Better?" D asked, when Min got back to the car.

Min nodded. "For now."

"She-Ra's ready to go."

Spider handed her a bottle of water and a box of crackers, which Min accepted with gratitude.

"Thought for sure you were going to spew," Spider said with one of her sly grins. And just like that the gratitude dissipated.

"Maybe later," Min said, giving her a hard thump on the shoulder.

"I'll drive extra slow," D promised.

The road snaked around a bog—inky waters smelling of iron, a stand of rotting birches—and climbed a ridge. The trees tilted in, obscuring the way ahead.

It was a guess when they hit the town. The woods opened up a little and a crop of hand-painted NO TRESPASSING signs sprouted at numerous muddy trailheads that seemed too narrow to fit a car. A barking dog came out of nowhere, snapping at their tires and leaping at the windows. D gunned the engine but the dog chased them for a few hundred yards before halting in the middle of the road, sides heaving, black lips curled.

"There's people," Spider remarked. "Somewhere back there."

Min, hanging out the back window, watched the animal retreat into the distance behind them. Once she'd trained her eyes to see through the tangled undergrowth, she caught glimpses of RVs tucked under the trees, a cluster of dilapidated houses no bigger than her parents' goat shed and so derelict they seemed uninhabited, a few tiny shacks covered with tar paper, which she guessed were outhouses, many abandoned sites strewn with bags of garbage, old refrigerators and wrecked cars, but no people. No one sitting on porches or working on their cars. She wondered if they were standing behind the dingy curtains watching the VW go by.

"How are we even going to find this site?" Spider said. "What if it's deep in the woods? Are we going to ask somebody? Some nice man with a pit bull and a hatchet?"

D shot her a look, which Min caught from the backseat. "There's a roadside memorial. I saw it online," D said. Her voice was clipped, and her hands on the wheel were whitened with tension.

Min checked her map hurriedly. Tracing the squiggling line of the road and the topographical circles made her feel dizzy, so she cut her eyes away as soon as she'd located one of the black stars she'd drawn. "Two more miles, I think."

They almost missed it. At first glance, it looked like another abandoned site, a dump of moldy papers and assorted garbage, but Min spied a thicket of handmade wooden crosses marking the head of a dirt road leading back through the trees. "Stop. Right here," she called. D pulled over and they got out.

It was a mess.

People had come here with their white candles and prayers and their tears but now all that remained was what they'd left behind. Brightly colored plastic flowers trodden into the dirt, photographs too rain-soaked to identify, pinwheels and lots of toys.

Min leaned against a tree trunk and closed her eyes. The ground seemed to sway and melt underfoot and the odor of hot engine clung to her nostrils.

When she opened them a minute later, D had moved past the memorial, pausing halfway down the wide track as if to prepare herself before disappearing from sight.

Spider made to follow her but Min held her back.

"Give her a minute," she said, her voice cracking. "This is all —it's too much, isn't it?"

"What were you expecting?" Spider said, nudging a ragged pink teddy bear with her boot; the heart embroidered in the middle of its chest like a splash of blood, Min thought. Spider slid her gaze away from Min and jammed her hands into her pockets as she followed D.

Min walked after them more slowly. The road terminated in an open area dotted with tree stumps. Min guessed they'd cut the forest back to make room for the emergency vehicles and later, the trucks and machinery necessary to haul the wreckage away. Other trees close by still showed signs of fire and impact damage. She stopped in shock. She supposed she'd expected something more tranquil. But instead, what had happened here was etched into the bones of the land.

She had always believed that anger and grief had no foothold in nature. "Go for a walk," her parents said when she was wrestling with something. She didn't believe in God but she did believe in something bigger. A goodness that made things right. Sitting at the base of an oak, smelling the earth and the growing things, listening to the whirrs and thrums of bugs and birds was like being in a cathedral of trees. All peace and busyness at the same time.

But this place. It was a wound that had still not healed. Somehow, the wilderness had been held back and the rough circle of the crash site was clear, even two years later. The path the plane had taken as it fell from the sky was delineated in the trees shattered by the impact, and the shallow canyon where the plane had bellied up. She felt a different kind of nausea.

Slowly, she walked the perimeter. It was about the length of a football field, roughly oval. The ground rose in gentle ridges on either side; beyond, clustered groves of deciduous trees softened the harsh, rigid rows of pines. Outside the crash site, it felt different. Untouched.

At the far end, Spider bent, picked something up and brushed it off against her shirt.

D was sitting in the middle, in the trough left by the plane. The ground was wet but she'd made a cushion out of her raincoat.

Min held back. It felt like a private moment. She waited until her friend met her eyes before approaching. D moved over on her cushion, patted it, and Min settled in beside her, wanting so much to gather her friend up in a big hug.

"I bet they held hands when the plane was going down. I can see it," D said. "They grew up together. Jonathan was like our kid brother." Tears slid softly down her cheeks but she didn't brush them away.

Min gave her a squeeze, wishing she could carry some of the grief.

"There's that, at least. We were apart but there was someone there who cared for her."

For the first time Min wondered if D felt guilty. That she had lived. How much would that add to the pain?

Min stared at her hands, listening to the sound of her friend crying, hoping that her presence was giving D some kind of support.

At long last, she heard D take a long shaking inhalation and release it. When Min darted a glance at her, the weeping had eased. Her expression was still somber but relaxed.

"Is this helping?" Min asked.

D drew her eyebrows together, uttered a small laugh. "Not sure yet. Weird. I've got a whole lot of different emotions going on. Doctor Octavian said it would take time to process. Sitting here with you feels good. Like a reminder of all the good things."

She leaned back, tilted her head up. "I do feel like I can breathe. And I feel closer to her. Isn't it strange how something can hurt and make you smile at the same time?"

"Maybe the hurt you feel is a way of telling yourself that she's still in your life," Min said, and wished immediately that she could take the words back. D looked so haunted, but then the expression smoothed and she nodded.

"Yeah. My fear is that maybe there will come a time when I don't think about her every day, when she starts to slip in my memory. Being here feels like I'm saying to her, I miss you. I love you. I remember you."

"Can we go now?" Spider said, striding up to them. Her long-fingered hands fussed at the zippers on her jacket, dug into her pockets, pulled out some lint and stared at it for a moment, perplexed. "Shit," she said, slipping her glasses on. Behind the lenses, her eyes glistened, brows like angry, jagged pencil lines. "This is a waste of time. Why did we come?"

"I had to see it," D said quietly.

"See what? A ghost? An angel? Some kind of a sign?" She flipped her braids back. Her lips thinned. "What did you expect to find? They're dead. And we're here in this . . ." She choked and then spat the word out: "Graveyard."

"I thought it would help to make sense of it all," D said, jumping to her feet. Her voice wavered for a second, and then she straightened her back. Her voice stronger now, she continued. "The question I'm asking myself is why you're here. Clearly you think this is bullshit."

Spider said nothing, just blinked convulsively. "I thought . . . hoped . . . dammit!" Her hand went up to her throat. Her voice got thin and reedy.

"Spider!" Min said, reaching out for her. Spider danced backward, fists up as if she were going to throw a punch.

"You could be home, getting drunk, getting laid," D said. "Isn't that all you care about?"

Spider's mouth fell open. Her face crumpled and then reformed itself into something harder.

"Is that what you truly think?"

"Well, it's not like you're giving me anything else to go on."

They glared at each other.

Min studied each set face. It was as if her friends were wearing masks, stripped of emotion except for the shimmering heat of anger that smoldered in their eyes.

She got between them.

"Stop, please! No more. You're not mad at each other, so stop acting like jerks," she said pleadingly. "It's the pain of being here. I feel it too. I never even knew them and I can feel it! There's just so much sorrow here," she said, her voice dropping to a whisper.

D deflated all of a sudden. "Jesus, Spider," she said. "Why are you like this?"

Spider turned her back on them.

"Kindred spirits, remember!" Min said desperately. One of their first bonding moments had been over their shared childhood love of *Anne of Green Gables*.

"Seraphine," D whispered. Min didn't think she'd ever heard D call Spider by anything other than her nickname.

Spider grunted and turned around, her shoulders loosening.

Min stared at her, injecting a mute appeal into her expression, until at last Spider's eyes softened. She shook herself as if dislodging a cloud of flying insects and took off toward She-Ra.

With a mumbled curse, D ran to catch up with her while Min watched, helpless. D's hand went to Spider's forearm, forcing her to stop; her head bent in close, speaking rapid-fire words that Min couldn't hear. A flurry of gesticulations from both of them and then they hugged. Min released her breath. She knew each of them so well, but their history together was unknowable. She would always be on the outside of it.

Once she got back to the car, she paused. Her stomach was in knots again, and thick saliva flooded her mouth.

"Let's get some coffee and food. My blood sugar is nonexistent. Maybe find a B&B with an old lady and some cats," Spider was saying, her arm hugging D close.

Min was happy that the fight was over but the thought of eating made her head spin.

"What's up, Minsk?" D asked, opening the driver's-side door.

Min tried to paste on a smile. She didn't think she could bear to get back in that cramped car again. The memory of She-Ra pitching and bumping up the road was enough to make her abdomen churn.

"Why don't we stay here? I noticed a small grove, just over the low rise there." She pointed to it. "I was thinking we could camp. That was the original plan. We came all this way."

Spider nodded. "I'm in. There must be a grocery store in one of those real towns. We could grab some stuff, come back."

"I am a little tired of potato chips and bananas for dinner," D said.

"Let's go," Spider said, her mood obviously better. "There's probably a Starbucks."

At the mention of coffee, Min's throat convulsed. She hurried to get the words out.

"You go. I can set everything up." She looked around. "There's a perfect spot over there by the aspens." She eyeballed it quickly. "Why don't you drive the car down with all the stuff? See? There on the left." She pointed. "I'll walk."

She got there first and watched as She-Ra lurched over the rough ground, arriving at the western edge of the clearing.

"Are you positive, Cinnamint?" D asked, getting out of the car. She stared at the rocky, muddy ground.

"Yeah, you guys are useless with the tent. It'll be faster without you." She breathed deeply. The air smelled sweet and she felt her energy flood back.

"Yeah . . . ," said D, still sounding uncertain. "I was talking more about this particular location. Seems a little . . ."

"Cesspool," Spider interjected. "It's a pig wallow. A mud spa. A . . ."

"It'll be great," Min said, amused and slightly perplexed that they couldn't see it. "The ground is flat here. We've got a windbreak right there"—she pointed at the trees—"and this little ridge for cover." She started hauling the camping gear and sleeping bags out, piling them into Spider's arms, who pretend-staggered under the weight. "We can build a fire."

"Kumbaya," said Spider. "I'll dig out my tambourine."

"We'll only be a few hours," D said, once they'd finished unloading. "Less if we find what we're looking for in Feltzen Corners."

"We can leave you the beer," said Spider. "And be back in time for dinner."

"Dinner, eh?" Min peeked at the sky, the sun directly above. It was late morning as far as she could tell.

Spider slung an arm around Min's shoulder, almost buckling her.

"Country dinner. Four p.m. You can rustle up a five-star meal out of some acorns and a squirrel."

EIGHTEEN

– Ariel –

WE GET UP WITH THE DAWN and flee to the farthest field. Me, Ruth, and Diana hauling rocks and tilling rows so that we can plant cabbages and more potatoes there in the spring. Hannah lucked out and got chicken duty in the compound. The roughly rectangular fields are laid out in a half circle. It's mostly shale, loose underfoot, pitched steep, with a thin covering of ashy soil. From the very top field, we're high enough to just see the huts, sheds, and big circular hall surrounded by the timbered wall, the two guard towers, and the big gates, the muddy road snaking away through the thick trees. There are glints of metal roofing that flash in the sun, wisps of wood smoke, but if you're approaching from the other side, from the road, it's damn near invisible. Especially if, as happens most days near dusk, the fog descends.

I've been able to keep low, out of sight of Big Daddy's piercing eyes. And, better than that, away from Guy. Hannah told me he went out to the east side of the mountain last night hunting that bear. I hope it hunts him. We got word it killed a goat and destroyed a shanty hut up near where we were camping. Big Daddy gave us all a speech about our sworn duty to protect the weak and slay monsters, and I think a few of the Uncles aim to bring back its head.

Diana leans on her shovel. Her blonde hair hangs in wet strands. She pulls it back into a knot.

There seems no end to these rocks. It's like they grow here. Even after they're all cleared, we still have thistles and brambles to deal with. Ruth's already whacking at them with her scythe. We'd all rather be napping, and we could do it safely, unseen, but old habits die hard. Idle hands and all that.

Ruth keeps watch in between swings. From here we can see anyone approaching from below when they're still a mile off. Mostly, though, she's got her eyes sweeping above us, to the rise where the trees grow dense and shaggy. She's watching for Uncles; she's watching for that bear or anything else dangerous that might run at us.

The air is still and close. Feels like a thunderstorm is brewing. Truth be told, I'm only working this hard because moving stops my poison ivy rash from itching so bad and it kills time.

I'm dying to get back to the compound. When I checked him last, Aaron was running a high fever, and I'm worried. Nana Esme is trying to bring it down with cold compresses and more bark tea but so far nothing is shifting it. He's looking yellowy around his eyes too, and I know that means something terrible.

The cow who's knocked up and close to her time is in the sick hut as well. The baby is lying against her spine or something, the wrong way round. Whatever it is makes it hard for her to stand up. I wonder if she's going to die. The baby too. There's only a thin curtain between her bed and Aaron's, so

I dare not linger long enough for the cow to notice and rat me out. You get perks for telling secrets here.

"You hear that racket last night?" Ruth asks, pushing her damp brown hair behind her ears.

My arms are sore and feel all stretched out. My shirt sticks to my back.

"Yup. A couple of the heavy trucks came in," I say, heaving a rock onto the pile we've made.

I heard them in the small hours when I was lying next to Aaron, and I peeked out the window and watched as the Uncles unloaded a bunch of big metal boxes covered in tarps. They must have taken them down to the basement.

"Guns this time, pretty sure," Diana says.

She's probably right. Drugs or the stuff to make them comes in wooden crates, not metal boxes. And Big Daddy doesn't store the chemicals anywhere near our living space. He's got a trailer in the middle of the woods, with its own well, so there's access to water if something catches fire or explodes. That's one of Guy's special duties. It's his job to move it out, sell it, or trade up for something else we need. He's not supposed to get high off it, but everyone knows he does.

Ruth shields her eyes from the sun. Points.

"Faith is coming with the water."

I toss another rock, exhale in relief, wiping sweat out of my eyes.

We watch her limp her way up, her back bowed by the big jug she has in her hands. Hannah runs over and grabs it from her. Faith presses her hand against her belly. Her cheeks are bright red but she's all white around her mouth, like a ring of paler skin.

"I'm okay," she says. "I came fast as I could. Had to go over to North field too." She grimaces and bends over double. Her breath is coming rough and fast.

Diana makes her sit down where she stands.

"Big Daddy wants you back in time for day meal," Faith says when she can. Her head lolls as if it's too heavy for her neck. Ruth rubs her back, brushes her hair out of her eyes.

"Serious?" says Ruth. She can't keep the happiness out of her voice. Usually we work from sun up to sundown, and sometimes well into the night depending on what needs to be done. Lunch is the hard hunk of bread or cold baked potato we shove in our pockets. We've labored maybe five hours today, but that's nothing.

Diana passes me the water jug, and I swallow half of it and wipe my mouth on my shirttail.

"What's going on? Is it the bear? Do we get to go hunt it?" I ask.

Faith's more in the loop than we are. She sits quiet as a mouse next to Uncle Clive and he forgets she's there and doesn't mind his mouth.

Since we got back she hasn't slept a night in our hut. I scan her arms for bruises or fingerprints, signs she's being forced, but she seems fine. Pasty as a toenail clipping, but fine. She swears he treats her well though I have my doubts. He might not lay hard hands on her but he still treats her like something he owns.

She shakes her head. "Clive and Randall were out all night. They took the dogs but couldn't run it to ground. They heard it though. Roaring and bellowing up on the heights."

The heights are half scree, half sheer cliffs. Hard enough by day; impossible in the dark.

"Hope it's not crazed enough to come down to the compound for easy pickings," Diana grumbles.

I glare at her. I know she thinks I should have killed it, doesn't understand why I didn't. Dammit, she was there. She saw how it was. I turn my shoulder to her. "So what is it then?" I ask Faith, trying to keep the snap out of my voice.

"It's definitely something to do with Guy. Maybe some of those outsiders he messes with? Something he's got up to."

Could Big Daddy have discovered what that pig tried to do to me? But no, if he knows that he'd know I snuck into town and he'd have called me to account. I exhale, feeling the knot in my chest loosen. Something else must be going on. Most probably Guy was up to something shady when I ran into him and he's got his own secrets to keep.

Uncle Guy is not quite right. I mean, all of them are mean as brown recluse spiders but there's something different about him. He's never been someone you want to spend time with, but lately it's gotten a whole lot worse.

"They're doing something to the fence too. By the main gate. Reinforcing it," Faith says.

"Wonder what Uncle Guy did?" Diana says. She's lying back, chewing on a stalk of grass.

We all shrug. I'm not alone in knowing what he's capable of.

"Something stupid, I bet," Ruth says.

NINETEEN

— D —

D SIGHED.

For the ten arduous miles back down the mountain, and even after they made the left turn onto Route 12, Spider had stared resolutely out the window, her fingers restlessly playing with the small object she held. That was fine initially, since all of D's attention had been focused on avoiding potholes and taking the sharp curves in the narrow road at the slowest speed, but now it was starting to irk her a little. Were they cool or not? After some deliberation and a throat clearing that Spider ignored, D let her be. She could rekindle the argument, but why? That sort of thing made Spider dig her heels in and D was not in the mood for another fight. Plus, Spider had agreed to camp *and* said she was sorry. Words that came hard for her.

Besides, she knew it wasn't her Spider had a problem with. It was a classic internal struggle. She would talk when she'd figured out what she really wanted to say.

They drove past woodland and mailboxes at the end of long drives and small cottages with sloping porches. The mountain reared over them to the left. It felt like they could drive for miles and never escape its shadow.

"How can you be so okay?" Spider said finally, turning to face her. The object in her fingers was a muddy button, D saw, shaped like a flower. A rose maybe. The kind of thing you'd find on a kid's shirt.

D shrugged. "I can't explain." Her feelings were confusing, half-formed, but there was an underlying calmness she hadn't felt before. Like all the frozen parts of herself were starting to thaw.

"Didn't seeing that just make it harder?"

"Actually, no. Visiting them in the graveyard? That was hard. Because I know they're not there. They're here," she said. She tried to describe what she was feeling. "This filled a hole. Just a little bit. Can't you just . . ." What? Get open? Try? She didn't know what word to use but Spider seemed to hear her anyway.

Spider shook her head. "But you," her voice softened. "You can show me how." Her face was filled with yearning. It lit up her golden eyes. She heaved a deep shuddering sigh, as if something inside had loosened too.

D smiled at her. "I will."

Her phone pinged and she hauled it out one-handed, gave it to Spider to check. "It's a text from your mamma," Spider said.

"Oh shit, I was supposed to message her last night. Can you? Tell her we found a campsite and we're fine. And kiss kiss kiss."

Spider tapped in the message and then fluttered her fingers over the screen. "Hey, we can google," she said with a wide grin. "Civilization at last!"

"Okay, so tell me where we're going," D said.

"Keep heading straight ahead. Looks like Feltzen Corners has nothing but fast-food burger and corporate taco joints."

D shook her head. Min was pretty much a vegetarian. And D had been too spoiled by her mamma's cooking to enjoy the whole fat-fryer experience.

Spider whooped. "There's a family-style pizza place in Abbotsford. Four-plus stars on Yelp and an exemplary salad bar." She smiled. "That's a quote. Let's hit it and get back to Min. She will love me so hard!"

TWENTY

— *Min* —

SETTING UP CAMP TOOK MIN TO HER HAPPY PLACE. She remembered the summer she'd turned eleven. Her parents had decided to drive cross-country, camping all the way.

The first night it had taken them hours to get the four-person tent up. By the end of the first week, Min could do it herself, in the dark.

She surveyed the campsite. The land rose in a gentle washboard ridge here, then dipped, making a snug hollow bordered on one side by aspens. Sitting down on one of the logs she'd dragged over, she couldn't see the crash site at all, which comforted her.

The tent was up, ground tarps and sleeping bags laid out ready. She'd treed what was left of the snack food and water, built a firepit, and swept the whole area clear of brush and rocks. But now that she was finished, sweaty and a little proud of herself, she noticed the heavy quiet. The dry-skin-scratching noises of leaves whispering together in the breeze. The absence of car or human sounds—radios, TVs. Even the birds seemed hushed. Just one unseen warbler trilling, and that cut off abruptly, leaving Min to wonder if something had just swooped down and killed the bird.

She knew how far sound carried. It made her feel as if the clearing, the campsite were somehow outside the world, in some place where she was caught and time stood still. Could a place be cursed? Before they'd built their straw-bale house, her mom had scattered rock salt in a wide circle and burned sage around the site. "Just in case," she'd said.

A trickle of watery light caught the silvery underside of the aspen leaves, glimmered there. Min was reminded of the flash glimpsed from the trees while they were peeing. She snugged her arms around her torso and raised her hood, suddenly cold.

Where were Spider and D? Checking her watch, she saw with surprise that two hours had passed. She hoped they hadn't had to drive all the way to Abbotsford.

Her wrist seemed bare and she realized her leopard bracelet was gone. She tried to remember when she'd last seen it. At the gas station, maybe? In the cabin? That reminded her of the girl from last night and suddenly the silence took on a greater weight, an oppression she could feel in her chest. The mountain loomed, scattering shadows like a tattered net. The peaks stabbed the grey clouds. If she leaned back, it almost seemed as if the mountain was tilted toward her. As if just a push would cause it to topple and crush her.

"Get a grip," she muttered to herself.

She pulled one of the larger sticks from the campfire pile she'd accumulated, laid it close by. She'd be able to hear anyone who approached. Her mind was racing and she wished she'd braved the car and gone with her friends.

A sharp crack came from behind. Min whirled around, reaching for the stick. An unseen force pushed through the undergrowth, trees bending as it moved. She imagined she could hear labored breathing. Straining her ears, she wheeled in a circle. Saw nothing but trees swallowing the sky.

TWENTY-ONE

- Ariel -

AS SOON AS WE GET BACK DOWN THE HILL, we hear the big bell sounding. Usually that means someone got injured.

"There's men manning the towers," Diana says as we enter through the west door.

All our vehicles are parked inside the wall, and the heavy timber that bars the wide gates has been lowered in place.

I check out the guards as we pass the cooking fires. "Armed." Who are they keeping watch for, I wonder? It's not like that old bear is just going to wander up to the gates, is it?

Hannah runs up to us, her blue eyes round with alarm. She clutches her ribs and tries to regain her breath. She's got chicken shit plastered on the knees of her jeans, a feather caught in her white-blonde hair. "Big Daddy called an emergency meeting. Now."

Diana frowns. "What about?"

"Don't know but he's mad as a hornet. The kids are all gathered up in the meeting hall."

"Maybe it's time," I say. "For the war." I say it mostly as a joke but they all look at me and there's fear mixed with excitement in their eyes.

"They've turned the generator on," Hannah notes. Strange, that. We don't use it except maybe once or twice a year if we get a cold freeze and we all end up bunking down in the hall. Then it's head to toe, squished in tight, and if you have to pee in the middle of the night, you can't help but step on people. The only other building on the circuit is the supply shed, with the bunker and basement cells below it. Otherwise, it's wood-stoves and candlelight. A mommy stands outside the hall striking the giant brass bell. When she sees us, she silences the clapper with her hand and jerks her head. "Hurry up now," she says. "You're the last. Don't keep him waiting any longer." We push inside with her, past Uncle Bob and Uncle Norbert, who close the door behind us. Both of them hold rifles. We hardly ever see those two. They're our primary hunters and spend most of their time up high on the mountain. They look like mountain men too, all hairy, bush-bearded, and smelly, like moose walking around on their hind legs. "Find that bear?" I ask one of them. Don't ask me which is which. He just grunts at me, spits something brown and wet onto the earthen floor, and jerks his thumb toward the benches. I glower at him but his eyes have already passed over me.

Inside, it's like someone kicked a wasp nest. People are bustling around, chattering, excited or scared, maybe. I can't tell. Kids running all over. Nicky is hiding under the table. He hates being away from the dogs and this harsh light must be doing a number on his eyes. They are the palest grey I have ever seen. As if he's been touched by the moon.

Uncle Clive summons Faith to his side, and with a sideways glance at us she goes over to sit by him. I notice her posture, head down, hands clasped in front of her. She may not admit it but I think she's made her choice.

The adults are looking to the front of the room where Big Daddy is in a huddle with three more of the Uncles and Nana Esme. Even though we can't hear what they're saying, we catch the rhythm of it, the words bitten off, sharp and angry. An argument. We sit down on our usual bench near the far wall and wait, but I keep my eyes on the elders. My mind is whirling and fear twists my guts. *Is this about me?* Uncle Guy is throwing his hands around and yelling and his voice carries all the way over to us. "I didn't do nothing wrong! She wanted me. No one saw me take her."

Not me, then.

"Fool!" Big Daddy says in a voice like thunder.

Guy throws his chest out like a skinny-legged pigeon and Big Daddy steps toward him, arm raised, hand fisted, and the three of us are half out of our seats because we're sure he's about to hit him, until Esme steps between them. And it seems like things have calmed down a little but then, suddenly, Guy lunges, catching Daddy off guard, and they wrestle, their momentum carrying them closer to where we're sitting. It's a violent fight, but oddly silent. Guy is pop-eyed and red in the face, spittle spraying from his clenched lips, and I'm wondering if he's high on something that's making him extra fearless or incapable of feeling pain because in normal circumstances I'd have bet on Big Daddy to clobber him in no time. His head rocks back from a blow but he's holding on. Finally, Uncle Randall, who's bald, big, and muscular, breaks it up and pushes Guy hard onto the bench, keeping his hand on his shoulder.

"We've got rules for a reason," Big Daddy says, breathing hard. He speaks quietly but you can hear the threat in his voice. "You've brought a world of trouble to our doors." There's a muscle bunching in Guy's jaw and he's trembling with the strain of staying put. But after a few seconds with his head down, Guy surges up, knocking Randall's hand away, and stalks out of the hall, slamming the door against the wall. Norbert is halfway out the door behind him, his big gun ready, but Big Daddy barks a couple of words at Clive, who nods and goes after Guy. Norbert closes the door again and takes up position, gun tilted up toward the ceiling. I'm betting he's clicked the safety off.

A hush falls over the hall.

Faith scurries over. She's practically shaking with excitement. "I could hear Uncle Bob and Norbert talking. They're saying this is all over some girl Uncle Guy fixed his eye on. Little bit of a thing from away."

"His eyes are always roaming where they aren't supposed to," Diana says, trimming her fingernails with her knife. "It's just the way he is."

"He did more than look this time."

We all struggle to process this.

"What's that mean?" I ask, but Faith just shakes her head. People drift in here. Big Daddy or the Uncles'll meet them at the gas station or in town or on the road and get to talking. They can be real charming when they want to be. Sell a girl a whole story of a Garden of Eden and a fresh start, a close and loving family, a safe community, the magic that is Avalon. You'd be surprised how many people jump at the chance. But this, this doesn't sound like that. Normally, new blood is something we celebrate with a big welcoming dinner and a bunch of speeches. Could Guy have kidnapped this girl?

The kids swarm and surge. They've got up a game of tag or something. One of them runs up to the adults and hides behind Nana Esme's voluminous skirts.

I'm wearing the bracelet I picked up outside the cabins. It's pretty and new and I've never had anything like it before. I'm probably fiddling with it too much but it's so smooth and the clasp is shiny. "What's that you got there?" Hannah asks.

"Just something I found."

Diana tries to snatch a peek and I shove it up higher on my arm, pull my shirtsleeves down.

"Enough!" says Big Daddy. We hear him but the kids are clamoring and shrieking and they don't.

Uncle Ronald slams the hilt of his buck knife against the wooden table. It's a big hunk of moose thigh bone and it makes a hollow sound.

"Enough!" Big Daddy says again. He doesn't raise his voice like someone else might, but it still carries like a wave, crashes against the walls.

The kids stop their fooling, and they're quickly wrangled by a squad of mommies, who assemble them at the far end of the room. The babies are put on the nipple to keep them from fretting.

Big Daddy raises his arms, palms up, as if he's about to recite a thanksgiving. His face is stormy, shaggy eyebrows drawn low over his eyes. I can tell that a big rage is bubbling just under the surface, but he's holding it in.

His voice is thunderous. "This is our community. We are strong in one another." He pauses as his eyes travel around the room, pinning random people under his gaze. It finds me and I am transfixed, scared even to breathe. There's something about that piercing blue gaze that makes me have to pee. When his attention passes down the line to someone else, I feel a surge of relief. He's not talking about what happened with me and Guy. It's something else.

"We *trust* in one another." The word weighs heavy in the stillness. "We do not betray one another. When a tooth is rotten, we pluck it out."

Ruth mutters an assent, eyes glittering. I notice she's gripping her knife with the blade angled, like she's ready to go to battle.

Diana exchanges looks with me. *What the heck?* she mouths. Hannah is sitting on her hands, rocking slightly back and forth on the bench. I grab her arm and fold her hand in mine. She is trembling like a baby bunny. What happens if you betray trust?

"We're on lockdown," he says. "No one comes in and no one leaves without my say-so. Everyone must remain in the compound."

My insides freeze. We're restricted as far as town and the valley go but we've never been forced to stay inside before. The whole mountain is ours. I never realized how much I need that air, the icy wind that blows over the peaks. And what about Aaron? How will I get out again?

"The fence will be guarded at all times."

My heart plummets.

Chatter breaks out and he frowns and raises his hands up again.

"What's happened?" someone dares to say. Uncle Ronald scans the crowd searching for the speaker.

Big Daddy gestures that it's okay.

"We're under threat. From the outside. But we have prepared for this and all will be well." Done speaking, he sits down at the big table with Randall, Ronald, and Nana Esme. The mommies start a clapping game with the young ones. After a while, Nana Esme leaves with a clutch of people to see about dinner. Meal prep is done outside during the summer months. I'm amazed at how fast everyone settles down.

"What do you think the danger is?" asks Diana. "Must be something big."

"I don't know. It doesn't make sense," I say. People from the valley have stayed away from us for years. Cops don't come up here unless they can't avoid it. There was some kerfuffle about stolen cars a few years ago. An Uncle. He'd been ousted already though. Ousted is when a family member is forcibly banished from Avalon. There's also shunned, which is when no one is allowed to speak to you or even acknowledge your presence. You stare right through the person like they're a ghost. It can go on for weeks and weeks and it really messes with people's heads.

"At least we won't have to work up in the fields," Hannah says. "We'll be stuck here until the trouble dies down."

We all nod, contemplating this. I brighten. If Guy is on the outs and they're having to deal with him, then there's only maybe a dozen Uncles to guard the fence. They won't be able to cover all of it, nor will they be able to trade off shifts. My escape hatch is round the back, away from the road, and it's likely their attention won't be on it. I'm wondering if I should go out tonight, while people are all worked up, when a hand falls heavily on my arm, sending my stomach into my mouth.

I look up into Uncle Bob's beady blue eyes. All of Big Daddy's six blood brothers share that same brilliant eye color.

"Big Daddy wants to speak to you," he says to us. Ruth jumps to her feet, all eager, but he stops her in her path. "Take some food down to the basement. B cell," he tells her. She opens her mouth as if she's going to argue but thinks better of it. With a jerk of his head, he sends Faith scuttling off to where the young kids are sitting. "Just you three." His eyes bounce from Diana to Hannah, then back to my face, skewering me like a fish on a spear.

Hannah makes a little whimpering sound.

I square my shoulders.

Big Daddy is still in deep conversation with Uncle Ronald and he finishes what he's saying before he looks up at us. It's excruciating, standing there waiting. All my muscles are jumping but I know how much he hates fidgeting so I will my feet to stay planted on the floor. He's frowning but gradually his face clears. We stand with our hands clasped behind our backs, chins up, spines rigid, the way he likes us. I'm breathing low and slow, trying to ignore my hammering heart.

"There's some people in the woods," he says. "Over in the area where that airplane crashed a couple years back. I need you to run them off. Secure the perimeter."

"Run them off?" Diana asks.

"Get rid of them."

TWENTY-TWO

— Spider —

"HONEY, WE'RE HOME," Spider called out, looking around the clearing. "And we brought salads and pizza! And it's still freaking hot." She'd managed to talk the guy behind the counter at the restaurant into one of those thermal padded carriers and she was feeling pretty pleased with herself.

"Min!" D called, climbing out the driver's side. "I wonder where she is?"

"Digging a latrine in the woods?" Spider said, resting the food on the hood of the car. She swept her gaze around the campsite. It was positively homey. The tent was up and Min had built a firepit complete with log seating. "Wow."

"She is truly amazing," D said.

"Check that," Spider said, eyeing the complex rope system Min had devised to get their food up a tree. She wasn't even sure she'd be able to figure out how to work it. She just bet there was some trick to the knot. One tug and it all came down. Or more likely, one tug from her and it would turn into something impossible to ever untangle. "She set it all up. Where the hell is she? Min!"

She reached in through the car window and honked the horn. The sound shattered the stillness.

"I bet they heard that all the way in Abbotsford," D said. She raised her voice, "Min! Min!" and looked worriedly at Spider. "We weren't too long, were we? We shouldn't have left her alone."

"She's probably gathering more wood or something." Spider didn't like how drawn D seemed suddenly, the dark smudges under her eyes. "Nothing to worry about." She held D's gaze until the stricken look left her, and followed it up with the broadest smile she could muster.

"I'm sure you're right," D said, relaxing her shoulders. She poked her head into the tent. "Aw, she arranged our sleeping bags already."

"God, I hope I'm in the middle," Spider said, sitting and patting the space next to her on the log. "I hate being on the edge. Last time I woke up half outside and it was raining. Plus, I like to cuddle."

D settled in. "I recall. It's like being in bed with an octopus."

"You love it. Who else is giving you any action?" She pulled D closer. How long had it been since they had sat with no space between them? Just the two of them together? Her own doing, she admitted to herself, not D's.

"Min," Spider yelled again. Her voice echoed. The mountain soared above them, seeming to lean in crazily against the darkening sky. Spider averted her eyes. Tucked into her shoulder, D swallowed audibly.

"This is weird, right? That she's not here," she said, sounding childlike.

Spider tightened her hold on D's arm. "Weird as in the rapture? She hasn't been summoned. Her clothes and shoes aren't sitting here empty. She's getting something. Filling a bottle at a clear mountain spring or some shit. She's our little survivor queen. She knows the woods."

"But not these woods," came D's stilted voice. Spider racked her brain for distractions. They could eat.

She retrieved the pizza, the case of beer from the previous night, and a coffee tray from the car, and walked back over to the firepit, balancing everything precariously.

D was on her feet, peering into the trees.

"Sit down," she told D. "Drink your chai tea." This was a common joke of theirs. Since *chai* essentially meant tea. Tea tea. She pressed it into D's hand, hoping for the glimmer of a smile, but D's face was set. Although she did sit down.

"Relax. It's been a crazy time."

She massaged D's neck and shoulders, happy when D slumped against her and made small noises of pleasure.

"When Min gets back we can gorge ourselves on pizza and drink beer and build the fire up until it's roaring," she said. If she closed her eyes, she could imagine it. The flames driving the darkness back, the good heat that would soak into their bones. "We can dance around it naked!"

"It's too cold for nudity," D said, with only a tiny hint of amusement. Spider hated the strain on her face.

She stood and held her hand out in invitation. "Let's go look for her."

D gazed up at her, an eyebrow raised.

"Come on!" Spider gulped down her coffee, tossing the empty into the case of beer, and picked up a big stick. "We can whack through the bush with this. Do I sound like a Girl Guide?"

D couldn't help but laugh. "Bushwhack. Are you sure you don't want to eat first?"

"Let's eat together *à la famille*. Do you know how to get a good fire going?"

"Flick a match and pray?"

"There you go, then. We'll have to wait for our feast. Let's find the Minimizer."

"Okay, but we should put the pizza somewhere safe. Probably Min's drink too. Do bears like coffee?"

"We can stow it all in the car," Spider said, handing her the pizza box and grabbing the beer. They piled it onto the front seats.

"If she comes back before us, at least she'll know we're around," D said, scanning the tree line. "Which way?" She sounded more like herself again.

"Pretty much only two directions, toward the mountain or away from the mountain," said Spider, thrusting her stick like a pointer. "Or how about that way? It's as enticing as either of the other two possibilities. I can already hear the soothing whine of stinging insects."

"Alongside the mountain? Okay."

There was no path of any kind. They had to move branches aside and hold down thorny bushes and scuttle through small overgrown spaces, calling Min's name periodically. It was tough going. Plus, it was hard not to feel like they were traveling blind. The trees and shrubs were so thick that Spider had no idea if she was about to lead them off a cliff. She couldn't hear any other noise besides their breathing and grunts. And how normal was that? Shouldn't there be birdsong at least?

"Jeez, why do people choose to put themselves through this agony?" Spider griped as she waited for D to free her braids from a persistent bramble. Once she was loose, she stomped on it, grinding the stems into the earth.

"It's therapeutic, I guess, being around nature."

"I'm more of a garden center girl myself. All those neat rows," Spider said, forcing D to backtrack because there was no way in hell they were going to be able to push themselves through the impassable wall before them. "And what's the point of all these thorny things if they don't have berries on them?"

"I don't know, but I think nature is winning." D leaned against a tree trunk. She had a livid welt across one cheek where a branch had sprung back. Spider was covered in scratches and had leaves caught in her hair. D reached out and pulled them loose.

"Stop awhile?" Spider said, hunching down against the tree. "I feel like I went ten rounds with Ali." She sniffed her armpits. "Man, I stink, and what the hell is up with this?" she said, pointing to her battered arms.

"That is what happens when you whack bushes," D said. "They whack you back."

"This is dumb. We have no idea where we're going, but Min knows where the camp is. We should just go back and wait for her."

Finding their way back to camp was marginally easier, since they were walking in their own footsteps, but they were still sweaty and tired by the time they broke out into the clearing. Clouds had gathered overhead and a light rain fell, making strange shapes out of the bushes and trees. A hard knot formed in Spider's throat. Everything was just as they had left it. She realized she'd been praying the whole way back that Min would be there, ready with a huge grin and some joke about their wilderness survival skills. She'd so convinced herself of the scenario that she had to stand stock-still and blink a few times when Min was nowhere to be seen.

"Damn."

D swayed a little. "It's getting dark. Where is she?"

"She's on her way. We just went looking in the wrong direction," Spider said, avoiding D's eyes. "We'll make a fire. She'll see the smoke and the welcoming glow and that'll make it easier for her to find us." She paused. D was rooted in place. Spider snapped her fingers. "D! D!"

D's eyes cleared.

"Throw me the lighter," Spider said, hating the harsh sound of her voice but rejoicing when D started moving. "And get me a bunch of twigs and some dry stuff."

— *Min* —

MIN WOKE, HER THROAT SWOLLEN, her body bound, and her cheek pressed against a hard surface. She was in a dark, cramped space. She coughed and spluttered. It hurt to swallow. The thirst blazed through her.

Drifting in and out of wakefulness, she struggled to figure out where she was exactly. Her ankles and wrists were tied with a coarse rope, which looped around her neck. When she struggled, it got tighter, cutting off her breathing. She forced herself to relax her muscles, trying to breathe past the pain of her pounding head. Her stomach twisted with nausea.

She screamed until her throat was shredded. No one came. She couldn't even tell if there was anyone near. Perhaps she was somewhere completely isolated.

It smelled like dirt and standing water. She peed herself. Hours passed.

She jolted awake. She could hear someone singing. A child's song, words garbled. *Twinkle twinkle little star* . . . "Who is that? Who's there?" she said.

The singing stopped. Scrape of something against a wall, a body shifting nearby. "You awake? Don't move around too much. It makes the knots tighter," said a low female voice. It was muffled, as if she were behind thin sheetrock or plywood. "We're in the basement."

TWENTY-FOUR

– Ariel –

WE'D ALL DRESSED IN DARK COLORS, and I daubed wood ash on our faces and hands. The three of us look like creatures born of smoke or river mud. By the time we get down the mountain into the foothills, the sun is hovering at the horizon and the air is filled with a misty drizzle. Diana and Hannah still as statues squat beside me in the dark of the forest. Grey Sisters, I think again. Formed from the granite rock of our home. Sisters to it and to one another. Only our eyes glimmer in the shadows.

The clearing is several hundred feet below us, but for now, we wait and listen. I'd say we are still an hour out from dusk falling, so the birds have quieted down. Just the soft flutter of owls on their heavy downy wings and the occasional swoop of early bats. My ears are sharp enough to hear their squeaks. A couple of vultures ride the air currents high above. Those scavengers are ugly as sin but nothing to worry about unless you're dead already, and then they're just cleaning up.

There's no movement coming from the campsite but I can pick out their car, bright orange, a cleared firepit ringed by stones and an army-green tent. *Where are they?* I'm thinking about whether this is an opportunity for me and Aaron. That car spells freedom if I can just figure out how to work it. We have one tractor up at the compound and it's Uncle Clive's baby. He's always tinkering with the engine and yells at any kid who tries to climb on it. Question is: Is the key in it? Or do I need to threaten someone to get a hold of it?

"What's that up the tree?" Hannah asks.

It's a shapeless, lumpy silhouette but I follow the rope tied to it and then hitched around the trunk. "Food. Cached," I say. "Someone knows something about sleeping rough after all."

I lean my rifle carefully against the tree. It's the first time Big Daddy has trusted us with guns. "As long as that bear is still wandering around, you need to be watchful," Big Daddy told me. "You warn those people off," Big Daddy continued. "Don't go doing anything foolhardy."

It's just a small-bore shotgun but I feel warm with pride. I've never shot any living thing bigger than a squirrel, but we've been training with target practice since we were nine. I think of that bear. How much easier it would have been if I had been armed? When it went after Aaron I'd have fired as many times as it took to bring that animal down.

There's no fire or light coming from down there, which seems odd. Most people feel safer with a fire, and these are likely city dwellers jumping at every hoot and hiss. Still, if they're scared already that's half the battle, and I'm hoping we can carry out Big Daddy's orders and get back home quick so I can check on Aaron again. He was awake when I stopped by before we headed out here, but his eyes were confused and the skin around his lips was chapped and raw. Nana Esme said he'd stopped taking broth, just a little water, which she had to dribble between his lips.

"It's just a matter of time now," she'd said. I almost punched her when she said that.

Maybe I'll see what these people have stashed in their car before I scare them away. Painkillers, first aid kit, something that might help him.

"Think we should go down there? Poke around?" I ask Diana.

"Too risky."

"I'll go."

"Shh." She frowns, nudges me, and tosses her head to the west. I can hear them well before I see them, stomping fit to scare every deer for miles and cussing up a storm. Females from the sound of it. I lean forward and now I can just make them out. I have a passing thought about those girls down at the cabins but these are only two, dressed in jeans with hoodies shadowing their faces. One of them carries a big stick, swatting it back and forth as if the mosquitos are giving her an extra-hard time. They're bad this time of year. Breeding in every pool of standing water, and I know that clearing is marshy and wet. The drizzle isn't enough to keep 'em down, but we'd all smeared Nana's lemon verbena paste over our exposed skin before we left.

"Wait for full dark," I murmur to Hannah and Diana. "We probably won't have to do more than holler and wave the guns around to get them running."

We settle in more comfortably, pushing leaves into the hollow of a tree's gnarled roots, and huddle together.

TWENTY-FIVE

— Spider —

THE FIRE WAS PITIFUL and barely enough to keep the mosquitos at bay. The persistent rain wasn't helping matters either. They had to keep rotating around the fire to avoid getting a face full of smoke. Hunger had finally won out too, and they were eating congealed pizza and washing it down with bottled water. Well, D was drinking water and Spider was trying a warm beer.

Beyond their camp, fog settled above the trees like a cotton ball wall, and the temperature was dropping. They had both pulled their logs as close as possible to the tiny flames. Spider shredded a piece of wood with her fingers and tried to focus on something other than the nagging worry: the hardness of the log against her butt, or the sound of a small animal snapping twigs in the undergrowth, or maybe the dank swampy thickness of the air. But her brain kept returning to Min—*where was she?*—and her eyes kept returning to D, who was pretty much the only thing clearly visible. Everything outside their little circle of fire was being rapidly gobbled up by the shifting shadows. With her shoulders hunched, D looked smaller and younger. As young as Kat was when Spider first realized that her nose wrinkled up when she smiled, and how when she didn't use product in her hair, it was this big wild soft curly mass that you could tangle your fingers in. And it smelled so delicious, like rainwater and flowers and spice. It was in July when she'd noticed, a year before the crash and a really hot day, and they'd flopped around the house, bored and complaining until Spider's *maman* had made lemonade from scratch, the perfect combination of sweet and tart, and inflated their old wading pool. They were all much too big to be playing in it. She remembered that Kat had tried to sit on the edge and it had collapsed and spilled all the water out, flooding the rose beds. And she'd been all tanned knobbly legs and freckles and crazed hair, lying on the grass, helpless with laughter. And it was in that moment that Spider knew. She loved D like a sister, but she loved Kat with all her heart.

She shivered suddenly. It was an all-over shudder, as if something electric had sparked through her veins, and at the same time she felt an unbearable tightness in her chest. She downed her beer, focusing on the way it made everything tremble and shimmer, and slowly the pressure eased. She looked up to see D watching her and was glad for the cover of darkness. Dusk had fallen without her really noticing. Darker even than the shadows was the silhouette of the mountain above them.

"She's fine. We'll laugh about this," Spider said. Her own voice sounded fake to her. Inside her head all she was thinking was *Please don't let anything bad happen.* D must have heard her, in that psychic way they all used to share, because she climbed into the tent and came out with their sleeping bags. She draped one over Spider's shoulders, wrapped the other around her own body, and stood poking at the dying fire with her stick.

"I found this too," she said, showing Spider a flashlight. Spider held her hand out and D gave it over.

"Should we go to the cops?" D asked. "Before it gets too dark and scary on that road?"

Spider clicked the flashlight on, moved it in an arc. Its beam was pitiful. She'd hoped for something more like Batman's sky signal.

"What if she comes back and we're not here?"

"Wait until morning then? But what if she's . . . hurt . . . lost?"

"She could have had an accident." They stared at each other, the words hanging in the air.

Stay? Go?

It seemed like an impossible decision. If Min had been there, she'd have suggested Rock-Paper-Scissors.

But they couldn't leave, because then Min would come back to pitch-blackness and that thought was unbearable. Wherever she'd gone, she hadn't planned on being out for this long; she'd left the flashlight. Round and round went Spider's thoughts, leap-frogging from one to the next. She picked one.

"I think we should find a signal and call 911."

D's face fell, and Spider realized how much she'd been holding onto some hope that Min was going to come skipping out of the woods any second now.

She took a shaking breath. "Yes, of course we should. They've got search crews and rescue teams"—her breath caught on a sob—"and helicopters. If . . . if . . ." She dug around in the ash and embers with her stick, her shoulders quivering. The fire wakened. Flames licked the underside of the log and cast leaping shadows on D's face. Tears tracked across her cheeks.

"No. Nothing like that," Spider said. "Just a backup plan." She hunted for the words that would soothe. She was shitty at this. It was Min who always knew exactly the right thing to say. Finally she said, "The sensible thing to do. What would Min do if it were one of us?"

Ten feet beyond the fire they were in full darkness again, the wavering flashlight D held in one hand distracting as they tripped over each other and their drooping sleeping bags searching for bars.

"One, shit no, it's gone."

"Nothing, nothing."

Spider whooped. "Don't move! I've got two, no three. Damn, my battery is on low though."

"Mine too. Should have charged them in the car."

"It's cool. I've got enough juice to make a call."

Spider tapped in 911 and pressed the speaker icon. The line crackled to life.

"911, what's your emergency?" a woman said.

"Hi, we're camping up on the mountain and our friend is missing."

"Where are you now?"

Spider tried to contain her impatience. "I don't know. Near the big mountain."

D interrupted. "We're camping at the site of the plane crash." They could hear the sound of tapping on a keyboard, machines humming, other people talking in the background.

"What's your name?"

"Seraphine Legault. Can we hurry this along?"

The woman ignored her and asked her to spell her name, give her age, home address, and phone number. She took down all of Min's information as well, including what she was wearing.

"Okay, Seraphine, how long has she been missing?"

Spider exchanged glances with D. "She was here alone from about noon. We got back from Abbotsford around four."

"Any sign of a disturbance?"

"No, nothing. Can't we tell the officer all this when they get here?"

"This information will be relayed to the unit en route, and it helps speed the process up." She sounded like an automaton reading from a script.

"Do you have reason to suspect foul play?"

"No."

"Does she have any outdoor experience?"

"Yeah, she does."

"Okay, I need you to remain calm. We'll send a squad car up but it'll be a few hours, maybe even longer."

D made an outraged sound. "Why so long?" Spider asked. "She could be injured."

The woman's tone changed slightly, sounding less mechanical and more engaged. "Try not to worry. People get lost on that mountain all the time and turn up fine. A unit will be there as soon as they can. Not much searching going to be happening at night, but they'll be there by morning." She hung up.

D slouched against her. Spider looked back at the dim glow of the fire, the indistinct shapes of She-Ra and their tent, the menacing bulk of the mountain. Daylight seemed like an eternity away.

TWENTY-SIX

– Ariel –

"VERBENA'S WEARING OFF," Hannah says, raking her arms with her nails.

The mosquitos are biting me too, a thick haze of them just above our heads. I know scratching just makes the itches worse but I can't help it either. Uncle Guy burns his bites with a smoldering match head, swears it stops the itching immediately. The skin on his arms is pitted with tiny holes like a piece of chicken skin. I half wish he'd come looking for me now. I could blame the dark for putting a bullet in him.

"We should just do this," Hannah says. "Big Daddy didn't want it to take all night."

"He didn't say nothing about time or strategy or any of that," I say. Truth be told, I wasn't thinking too much about what Big Daddy wanted.

"So how much longer we gonna wait?" Diana grumbles.

"Not full dark yet."

"It's pretty damn dark."

"We wait." Diana and I often fight over who takes lead, but she knows and I know that Big Daddy was looking straight at me when he gave us his orders.

My mind wanders back to the whole scene with him and

Guy. It looked like a challenge, Guy getting in Daddy's face like that. It seems out of character. He bullies the children and the women but he's careful around other men. Kisses Big Daddy's ass so much you'd swear you can see his lip prints. I can only remember one time when someone tried to take power from Big Daddy. A guitar-playing drifter who was hitchhiking around the country with two young women in tow. He had big ideas and a real persuasive way of talking and the kind of attractiveness that gets people listening, and it split us down the middle for a while. In the end though, Big Daddy gathered the Uncles and their guns around him and had the guy booted out. The women remained, absorbed into the Avalon community.

The two girls are still down by the fire, although they'd both gone off briefly. "Peeing," Hannah guessed. Probably so. Now one is kicking at the fire.

"Not a clue," Diana mutters. "She'll end up burning her toes." A log catches, flames leaping, and for a second she is silhouetted—tall, her hair hanging in long braids around her shoulders. Her companion, on her feet too but still in shadow, says something sharp-sounding and the tall girl steps back from the fire. In that brief moment, I recognize her from the gas station, remember her amazing eyes. What are the odds that they turn up here? And where is the third girl? The small one who'd taken my arm and spoken with a kind voice? A terrible suspicion grabs me.

"I know them. They're the ones who helped me at the garage."

"What the hell are they doing down there?" Diana breathes into my ear. It tickles and I swat her away. "Are they drunk?" she continues. "Stumbling all over the place like fools."

I'm thinking lucky for them that all the mountain lions were hunted out years ago. Guess this proves that wounded bear isn't around anymore. He'd have thought they were prime pickings.

"No, they're upset about something. Listen to them yelling," Hannah says.

We listen. "What's that they're saying?" Hannah asks.

"It sounds like men? Or min? What's a min?" Diana wonders.

An image of a sympathetic face flashes in my mind. "I think it's 'Who's a Min,'" I say. "They've lost their friend."

TWENTY-SEVEN

— *Min* —

MIN SHIFTED ON THE HARD BED, blinking until she realized it was not going to get any lighter. The grogginess she'd felt when she first regained consciousness had risen up again and sucked her under. She couldn't call it sleep—it felt more like suffocating or passing out, but she was surprised that the pain and discomfort of the restraints hadn't been enough to keep her awake. As far as she could tell, she hadn't moved for hours. Face down, muscles as cold and as immobile as stone, throat parched. She tried to change position. Her stomach muscles protested. She had never realized how necessary her arms were, how much she took for granted. Her balance was totally off. It was almost as if she had to force her limbs to obey her. It took a few attempts to build up enough momentum but eventually she managed to roll over.

Afterward she shook for a while—a combination of cold and fear and an all-over weakness that reminded her of a really bad flu. Her bones felt as if they'd been grinding together. And *bed* was not the right word either. It felt more like a thin mat on top of a low wooden platform. She inched to the side carefully and her face hit a rough wall, shuffled the other way and found a drop-off. So, wall on the left, edge on the right. She didn't think she'd hurt herself if she rolled off, but it probably wouldn't be good.

The space smelled like earth and rotten food and the sharp tang of her urine. It shamed her to think she'd urinated in her clothes, and the wet material chafed her thighs, but she couldn't do anything about it. Even the smallest movement made her feet and hands buzz as the blood flowed back into them. Otherwise, they just felt like lumps of meat at the end of her limbs. She worried that if she was kept bound for much longer, she might end up losing them. That could happen, couldn't it? If her blood supply remained restricted? Like a tourniquet gone wrong.

The voice had come from this side. It sounded like a girl in another room next to her. Whoever she was had been right. The knots *were* tighter—Min must have tensed somehow, involuntarily, maybe when she was passed out. The tension pulled her head back and there was a constrictive feeling around her neck.

She felt the panic rise and willed herself to lie still. If they, whoever they were, wanted her dead, she'd be dead, right? Surely, someone would come soon. If rape was on their mind, maybe the stink of pee would ward them off. She'd heard that was a way to deter a rapist.

It felt like a bad dream. A cataclysm in the path of her life that was never meant to happen.

"Are you there?" she said into the dark. "Please, are you there?"

"Yes."

Her heart leapt and her muscles immediately tensed. Breathing deeply, she forced herself to relax.

"Can you get to me?"

"No, my door is latched from the outside."

Her voice sounded like she was only a few feet away. The headache lingered but Min's thoughts were clearer than the first time she'd woken.

"Are you tied up?"

The girl shifted and Min heard her footsteps advancing, a slithering sound as if someone was dragging a bag of potatoes against the earthen floor. "No."

Now she was so close it was almost as if she were whispering in Min's ear.

"They don't tie me up anymore. They know I won't . . . can't run. I spend a lot of time in B cell."

"If I yell, will someone come?"

"Eventually they'll bring you food and water, but not because you yell. Yelling doesn't do anything. No one can hear. We're under the supply barn."

"So they're keeping me a prisoner? Why? Ransom?" Her pulse raced. All those horror stories in the pulpy grocery store magazines she and D and Spider had mocked. The organ thieves and the sex traffickers. A world so far removed from their own that they'd found it impossible to comprehend.

"You must have caught someone's eye," the girl said, her voice weary.

"I don't know how I got here. I was at the campsite, waiting for my friends to come back." Her voice croaked, and she tried to work up some saliva. She was so thirsty. "I set everything up." And then . . . the memory came crashing back. "It was that letch from the gas station. The one giving off the creepy vibes. He grabbed me, shoved a cloth over my nose and mouth.

It smelled sweet." That explained the sick feeling in her belly and the swirling confusion in her head.

"Ether. They use it on the babies too. The sick ones." She sighed. "You met Guy, I bet."

Min's heart was pounding like a jackhammer. Questions were piling up behind her closed lips but the girl was still talking.

"While you were sleeping, Big Daddy came down to see if I've learned my lesson. You must have met him too. At the gas station. He owns it. Arthur Pembroke is his name."

Min remembered the muscular, short, blond man with the buzz cut. Art. He'd been friendly, sympathetic about the plane crash. She recalled how Guy had obeyed him without question.

"You call him Daddy?" She felt sick to her stomach. What the hell was going on here?

"He's the father of us all." She uttered a harsh laugh. "That's what they drum into our heads, every minute of every day here in Avalon. He believes that this is a sacred place."

"And people follow him like he's a leader?"

"He is very persuasive."

"How did you manage to avoid being—?"

"Brainwashed? I knew all the stories already. They kind of lose their punch if you remember they're not original."

"So do you know why I'm here?"

"I could hear him out in the hallway talking to one of the other Uncles," the girl continued. "He was so angry. He said Uncle Guy took you without asking."

"Took me? Why?"

"He must have wanted you."

"Wanted me?"

"Like a man wants a woman. There aren't enough to go around."

"What does that mean? He wants to rape me? Why didn't he do it when he grabbed me? Why bring me here?" She thought she might be sick but she swallowed the sourness down. Every instinct was screaming at her to get loose, to run, but, trussed like a turkey, she could barely move. She forced herself to listen.

"He wants a wife. The last one died having a baby."

The bile rose again. She could feel the sharp prickle inside her nose.

"How long have you been here? Who are you?"

"It feels like forever."

She was silent for so long Min was afraid she'd vanished. Like a voice in her head.

"They call me Ghost but that's not my name. I'm Kat. Katerina Amandola. At first I couldn't remember, but then it came back to me."

TWENTY-EIGHT

— D —

EVEN WITH THE FIRE ROARING NOW, there was a bitter wind blowing down from the mountain that cut through the sleeping bag and her clothes and knifed straight into her bones. D huddled by the flames. It didn't feel like she'd ever be warm again. Next to her, Spider rocked and moaned. "I'm going crazy. I always hated that *Survivor* show, you know. They'd have eaten me for sure."

"You got the fire going," D pointed out.

"That was pure luck and you know it."

D went to the tent again and brought out spare clothing. They put plaid shirts and jackets on over their hoodies, pajama bottoms over their jeans.

Beneath the groaning of the pines buffeted by the wind, D could almost hear Min's pealing laugh, her giggles that all too often ended in a snort. It was contagious. It was necessary. That kind of helpless laughter cleared out all the bad stuff. Afterward, D always felt empty, but in a good way, and her stomach muscles hurt as if she'd done a hundred crunches.

There was some good reason that Min had gone off. Something she and Spider hadn't thought of yet. And when she came back—soon, soon—they'd laugh about it. Like they laughed about so many things. "Min," she yelled. And Spider, who was adding more wood to the fire, shouted out Min's name again until the vast silence of the trees took their voices from them.

Unexpectedly, she felt her eyelids droop. The darkness was so absolute there was a mass to it, like they were enveloped in a thick blanket. A weight to the thick soupy sky as well, with its underlay of fog. An owl wafted by, hooting softly.

She stared off into nothingness, fuzzy headed, half-asleep, Spider a warm, comforting presence beside her. It was a few seconds before her brain caught up with what her eyes were staring at. People. There were people. At the edge of the clearing.

"Spider!"

"Wha—Holy crap!" Her fingers bit into D's shoulder hard enough to make her cry out.

"You see them too? Is it Min?"

No. There were three of them. Hooded, dressed in dark clothing, they looked as if they were pieced together from the shadows. Even their faces were fuzzed out except for their eyes, which caught the firelight like the shiny discs of animal eyes and threw it back.

"They've got guns," Spider breathed into her ear as the figures moved apart, coming closer, still silent.

D felt a dizzying surge of adrenaline, a quickening of her heart. Yes, all of them had rifles slung across their backs, and as she watched they smoothly slid them forward, held them close against their chests with the muzzles pointed toward the sky. There was something military about the way they moved. No wasted effort.

She lurched to her feet, dragging Spider up with her, wanting to run.

"Sit back down," one of the figures barked, gesturing with the gun. D could feel her leg muscles spasming. She was petrified, too scared to move. There was something so inherently evil in the gleaming metal barrel, the black hole at the end of it like a hungry mouth, now pointing straight at her. The hands that held it shook ever so slightly, and that was enough to ramp her fear up another notch.

Clutching one another as if they were drowning, Spider and D slumped to the ground.

"What are you doing here?" the same figure said.

"Camping. We're just camping," D said, trying to control the quiver in her voice. "Our friend went missing earlier today. Maybe you've seen her hiking?"

The speaker leaned forward and scanned their faces, took a step back and pulled one of the others close, speaking rapidly into their ear. They appeared to be arguing about something, their voices rising. D caught some of it.

"No. That's not what we were told to do."

"I don't care. This might be our only chance."

"You're acting stupid, stubborn . . ."

Finally, they broke apart. The tension between them was palpable.

"Oh my god," whispered Spider. "Are we about to die?" She slid her hand into D's. D wondered if she could get her phone out. Dial 911 without anyone seeing her. She had no signal though, and if she were observed it would make things worse.

The figures stepped closer, revealing more of themselves. They were slight, two of average height, one a bit taller. They'd camouflaged their faces with mud or special makeup, but their clothing was regular—hoodies, jeans. Nothing military about them, D revised in her head.

So who were they? Hunters? Crazy people?

"Is it money you want? You can have everything we have," D said, tensing as two of them split off and took up position on either side of her and Spider. "Take it. Take the car too." She rummaged for her keys with shaking fingers.

The one who'd spoken shouldered their rifle, moved into the firelight. One of the others uttered an explosive noise of irritation, darted forward, and grabbed the speaker by the arm. After a brief tussle and a barrage of angry whispers, the speaker shook free and slowly pushed the hood of their sweatshirt back. Spider gasped beside her and D recognized the girl from the gas station by her sharp features and bright red hair.

Were they all just kids?

"What the fuck? Is this some kind of sick joke?" Spider shouted. "The cops are on their way here. Right now!"

Waves of hot and cold washed over D's body. Fear. Anger.

"What do you want from us?" she asked. The words fell like stones in the sudden quiet.

"You need to get off this mountain," one of the other two said, pushing her hood away from her face as well. She was a corn-silk blonde, strongly built.

The third paced back and forth, muttering "shit" under her breath.

"Calm down, Diana," the redhead said, over her shoulder. "Just let me talk to them."

"Don't say my name," she yelled. "And why the hell are you showing yourselves? They said the cops are coming. We need to get the hell out of here."

Spider and D exchanged looks. "Maybe we can overpower them?" said Spider under her breath.

As if she'd heard, Diana whirled on them, her gun poised, her finger hovering above the trigger. "Just give me a reason."

The redhead stepped in front of the gun, placing her hand on the barrel, and slowly Diana lowered it. "Just let me, please?"

Diana grunted and backed away a few feet. "This is all kinds of messed up, Ariel."

"You remember me?" Ariel said, switching her attention to D and Spider.

She crouched down, staring at them. Her eyes widened and a puzzled expression traveled across her face. D struggled to identify the emotions she saw there. Hope, desperation, resolve? But Ariel wasn't looking at her, she realized. Why was she so interested in Spider? After some kind of internal debate during which her eyes never wavered from Spider's face, the girl seemed to come to a decision.

"These two are Diana and Hannah." She ignored Diana's new storm of curses. "We're from Avalon, the mountain. There's a boy, he's one of us, hurt bad. Bear attack, two days ago." A shudder ran through her. "We need to get him to the hospital in Abbotsford. I need you to help me get him there."

"Why should we help you?" D asked.

"Yeah, you going to kill us if we don't?" Spider hissed, her face twisted with rage, thick eyebrows bunching across her forehead. Again, Ariel seemed almost transfixed by her. The redhead shook her head violently, as if trying to dispel a troubling thought.

"Your friend? The one who's gone missing? Min? I'm pretty positive we've got her. You help me and I'll help you."

"What do you mean 'got her'?" D said, sitting forward. The guns stayed down and she felt some energy flood back into her limbs.

"I mean she's being held prisoner. Tied up, locked in a room up at the compound."

"And what do you mean 'pretty positive'?" Spider snapped.

"I saw her," said Hannah suddenly. "Thought she was a newbie. Small girl, black hair with a blue streak." Her face sobered. "She was sick or something."

"Min," said Spider.

D moaned. "What have they done to her?"

"Nothing yet . . . ," Ariel said.

"Jesus, Ariel, I don't know what the hell you're doing!" Diana said. "Who cares about their friend? We have a mission."

"Dammit, Diana. Uncle Guy took her. He stole her. You know how he is, what he tried to do to Ruth and to me. If Guy put his filthy hands on either of you, I'd kill him for it."

Guy, D thought, picturing the lank ponytail and lecherous gaze.

"That sleazy man from the garage?" Spider shouted. "He's your uncle?"

"He's kin," Ariel said, raising her hands. "But—"

As she gestured her shirtsleeve fell back. Spider gasped and D followed her eyes. The redhead was wearing a leopard cuff. They both recognized it.

"What have you done?" Spider was on her feet, her entire body shaking. "That's her bracelet, you bitch."

"I found it. Outside the cabins."

"I don't believe you."

175

"Spider," D yelled, but Spider didn't seem to hear her.

"Sit down," Diana yelled. "Now." The gun swung around again. Spider bared her teeth and then slowly sat.

"*We* haven't done anything to her," said Ariel. "But I can't guarantee her safety if she's up there for long."

"So what do we do?" D said, putting a hand on Spider's arm to calm her. "Where is she? And how do we get in there?"

"We'll figure a way. You've got a car, we've got guns. No one knows these woods better than we do," Ariel said.

"Doesn't sound too safe," D said.

"How about we just wait for the cops? Tell them what you just said," Spider snapped.

"If the cops come, they'll kill her, bury her deep where no one will find her. You don't understand how it works up here. We've been preparing for war. We're on lockdown right now. If they bring it, we'll fight back. And people will die."

TWENTY-NINE

— *Min* —

"YOU'RE KAT," MIN SAID. Her voice echoed in her ears and she could feel her heart speeding up. Now she understood why the girl's voice had sounded vaguely familiar. The way she pronounced her *r*'s with the same rolling emphasis D did. "D's sister."

Silence. A void that stretched for seconds, minutes, hours, measured out by Kat's quick, labored inhalations and Min's pounding heartbeat. She closed her eyes, imagined this girl with D's face, in shock. She was sure her own face must look similar. It was hard to believe.

Kat exhaled, a long wavering sigh. "I haven't heard anyone say my name for so long. Who are you?"

"I'm Min. A friend of D's." Her breath caught in her throat. She felt a laugh building—and close behind it, hysteria. "We thought you were dead."

"I'm not."

"No, you're not." She gulped, suddenly afraid she couldn't get enough air. The ropes tightened around her wrists, sending shooting pains up her arms, an answering pressure against her throat. She forced herself to relax.

"Why can't I feel her?" Kat murmured. "After I started remembering, I could. Especially at night when it was quiet. Where is she?"

"We were camping at the crash site. Where the plane went down. She and Spider went into town but they'll be back now . . ." *They'd be back. They must be freaking out!*

"Spider is here too?" Her breathing was coming so fast it sounded as if she were hyperventilating, and Min felt her own respiration pick up pace. Suddenly Kat wailed. An animal sound, sharp and wild, and then the tears came, a flood of them.

Min drew as close to the wall as she could, trying to transmit her concern somehow. She couldn't place her hand against the wood, so she rested her cheek there, whispered, "It's okay," even though the words seemed meaningless. It wasn't okay at all. She had to get out of here. She had to free Kat. She wriggled, trying to ease the constricting bonds across her chest, and felt something shift. The cord that ran from her wrists and looped around her neck seemed a tiny bit looser. She clenched and unclenched her hands over and over, feeling the ropes around her wrists pull apart a little. It was excruciating. Her fingertips tingled as the sluggish blood flow was awoken. Her shoulders felt as if they were ripping apart; her thigh muscles screamed under the pressure of not straightening out her legs.

Something dug into her hip. Was it a part of the wooden platform? She rocked, inching her body into a new position. No, it was still there. Her mind replayed the moments before Guy had grabbed her. She'd just trimmed the frayed end of her rope after tying the barrel hitch to suspend their food supply. She'd slipped her clasp knife into her hip pocket. It was a good titanium knife, a present from her dad.

A new sense of purpose flooded into her veins. She twisted her torso as much as she could, the fingers of her right hand scrabbling to extend to their fullest length, beyond it even. She could just feel the edge of the pocket but she couldn't slip her fingers inside. Why were her jeans so tight? If they'd been baggy she could have done it, but these were molded to her hips. She swore in frustration.

"What are you doing?" Kat asked, her voice clogged with all the tears she'd shed.

"I've got a knife. If I can just reach it, I can cut this rope and get us the hell out of here," Min said breathlessly. She curved her spine, reaching, reaching, her fingers tantalizingly close. *An inch, Min, that's all. You can do it.* She couldn't do it. She slumped against the hard board, shaking from her tears of anger and frustration.

It was as if her arms were being pulled out of their sockets, and all this squirming had tightened the rope around her neck even more. Houdini had been able to dislocate his shoulders. That's how he'd escaped from straitjackets and padlocked chains. A home-schooled friend of hers who lived in a neighboring straw-bale house had been double-jointed, able to bend her fingers all the way back so they lay flat against her wrists, but Min could do neither of those things. She was going to strangle herself if she wasn't careful.

Every fiber of her being longed to explode in a flurry of action, fight like a cat in a bag, but she had to bottle the frustration, tamp it down.

Think. Her hands were tied at the wrist, crossed like you did when you made a shadow puppet of a bird; the ropes, as far as she could tell, looped over and under in a butterfly shape. Could she move a hand so they were palm to palm? That could give her more strength in guiding the hand nearest to her pocket; she could brace her wrist. She tried, gritting her teeth as the fibrous rope shaved away a few layers of skin. There, now it was as if she were praying. She extended them as far as she could, hooking her fingers. She still couldn't reach the knife.

Think better, she told herself furiously. She was bleeding from a wide strip of raw skin like a bracelet. She could feel the warm, wet blood and she felt the rope slip a little. Blood was a lubricant. Could she make herself bleed more, then wiggle her hand until she could slide it out of the loops? She sawed her wrist back and forth across the rope, opening the wound wider, gripping her lower lip with her teeth, moaning in pain.

"Min? Min?" Kat's voice, so similar to D's. She sounded calmer now, all cried out, which was probably a good thing. Her sobs had pierced Min's heart.

"Almost . . . there . . . I can do this," Min gasped. Her wrist was on fire, the blood dripping, the noose around her throat inexorably tightening from all the movement, black spots dancing in front of her eyes. Oh god, she was going to pass out, she was going to die of asphyxiation before she got this hand out, and then it was sliding free, slick with blood, and her other hand shook free of the coils too. She tore at the bonds around her neck, taking huge gasping breaths, then huddled, sobbing, clutching her poor torn hand to her chest.

"I'm loose," she cried, reaching for her knife with shaking fingers and opening it. She cut the cords around her ankles, her muscles trembling with the need to be free, but trying to slow down so she didn't jab herself. A good knife is a sharp knife, she heard her dad say. She sawed through the last knot and hurled the rope from her. Slowly she sat up, stretched her limbs. *Oww.* Jeez, it was like pins and needles times one hundred. She knew the only way to get through it was to force herself to move, so she got to her feet and hopped around, screaming with the agony of it, until the feeling returned and the tingling dissipated.

"What's going on?" Kat whispered.

"I'm up."

A thin wedge of light was coming from under the door and she could see how small the room was. Maybe eight feet by four, bare other than the bed. No light switch that she could see. The walls were rough board, the door something that had been salvaged from somewhere. It was shored up around the edge with scrap pieces of wood. She hooked her fingers in at the bottom where there was a two-inch gap between it and the concrete floor and pulled on it until it rattled. But whatever lock was engaged held. There *was* some give though, a looseness that made Min think that her captors relied on their ropes more than any kind of complex security system.

"I got the ropes off. Trying to figure out this door now."

"They might be coming to check on us anytime."

"I can't worry about that! Just be ready to get out of here. Anything you can use as a weapon? Grab it."

"There's nothing. They're always afraid I'll hurt myself."

"Give me a couple of minutes," Min said, with more confidence than she felt. She used her knife to pry away the two narrow pieces of wood nearest the knob, exposing a gap between the wall and door. Min bent down and inspected the bolt, squeezing her fingers in to feel the mechanism. She could tell by touch that it was beveled, sliding into a simple notch in the frame. Not a dead-bolt scenario, and the notch was not too deep either. Offering up a silent prayer to luck, she guided the blade to where her fingers had been and jimmied it back and forth, applying a steady pressure. The lock clicked open.

"I did it!"

"Min, hurry."

She peeked out into the corridor. It was narrow and filled with shadows. To the right was a dead end. Next to her, illuminated by a bare bulb hanging from the ceiling, was another door. Kat's cell. And further along, another bare bulb, a double-width door, and a dark alcove she hoped was a stairwell. So just the one way up and out.

She unbolted Kat's door and swung it open. The girl was standing just inside it, thin arms wrapped around her torso, her face mostly covered by her long, matted dark hair. She was wearing a short shift, torn and dirty, and a pair of battered boots, clearly too big for her. For a moment, they just stared at each other. Min knew her expression mirrored her thoughts and couldn't keep from making a small noise of surprise. She shut her mouth with a snap. The height and coloring were all the same, but Kat was an anemic, broken copy of her sister, as if she'd been kept out of the light for years. Min thought of those cave fish, sightless, like blobs of unflavored gelatin. And she looked starved, not just for food but also for affection and love. Her face a portrait of grief. Min was overcome by a wave of pity. She stowed her knife in her back pocket and pulled Kat into a hug, tightening her arms around her even as she felt the sharp bones under the girl's loose clothing.

"Come on," Min said, releasing her from the hug but clasping her hand. She resisted the urge to pat it as if Kat were a child or an old person. "You can show me the way out."

Kat stared at her feet. "You should leave me here." Her eyes rose, fell. She seemed mesmerized by her clunky boots. "They won't hurt me. They barely pay me any mind," she whispered. "I'm not the same person I was."

Min said, "Hey, what's going on? You're not saying you want to stay in this shithole?" She gently nudged Kat's chin until she'd raised her eyes. Staring into them, she said, "There's no way in hell I'm leaving you here. I'm taking you to your sister. You have a family."

"I can't run. I can't even walk very well. I'll slow you down." And now Min could see how her left foot was curled inward, the calf above it thinner than the right one, muscles wasted.

"I'm injured. You go. Send help after."

"Not going to happen," Min said, pulling her forward. "How would I explain that to D? Hell, Spider would kill me with her bare hands." Reluctantly, Kat followed her. Min closed and latched the door to Kat's cell, thinking it might buy them a little time if anyone came down. She did the same at her door. They crept toward the exit.

"Hold on," said Kat, shoving her against the wall. "Someone's coming. I can hear them on the stairs." There was nowhere to hide. "Quick, my cell," she said. Min hurriedly unbolted it and they ducked in. "Will they come in here?" Min whispered. Kat shook her head. "Might be my dinner, might be an Uncle getting something out of the bunker." They stood side by side just inside the door, listening. Min took her knife out and flipped it open. "Go lie on the bed," she told Kat, "like you're sleeping." She had some experience with self-defense—a course their high school had offered last year to all female and LGBTQ students—but none in offensive tactics. Only a fool takes a knife to a fight, she remembered her father saying when he gave it to her. "It's a tool, Marianne. A useful thing." But she figured she could threaten someone with it if she needed to.

Footsteps came closer, paused, and then paused again just outside the door. A weak semicircle of light was now visible under the crack. Flashlight? Candle? Min kept quiet, pressing her body against the wall. She heard the clink as something was placed on the concrete floor, then a soft exclamation as the person realized the door was unlocked. The door swung open and then closed behind a girl holding a steaming bowl and a cup on a tray, lantern held high. "Kat," the girl said, with a hint of menace, "you better be in here." Min held her breath as the girl directed the beam, squinting toward the bed. She was about Min's height, brown-haired, wiry. "Can't see nothing," the girl muttered. "Oh, there you are." Min let her pass, so close she felt the air move, and then stepped in close behind her.

"You awake?" the girl called, stowing the lantern by the wall. "I've got food and water for you. And a fresh shift."

"Stay where you are. Don't move," Min said, grabbing her arm and applying steady pressure. "I've got a knife." The tray went flying overhead. Min ducked, keeping her hold on the girl's wrist, and felt the spatter of some hot mush on her leg. She shoved the girl forward and adjusted her grip so the girl's arm was pressed against her spine.

"It's Ruth," Kat said, grabbing the girl by the other arm. "She's one of Big Daddy's soldiers."

"Hey, Ruth," Min said, trying to sound as vicious as she could. "You're going to help us get out of here."

THIRTY

— Spider —

SPIDER THOUGHT SHE'D PROBABLY worn a groove in the dirt with all the pacing back and forth that she'd done. She felt as if she were about to explode with nervous energy. She checked the sky, trying to find the moon, but it was obscured by clouds.

"You sure you can get us in?" D asked Ariel. "Without anyone seeing us?"

"Sure," said Ariel thickly. "When it's dark enough."

Spider bit back a curse. It seemed dark enough to her already. What was it? Ten? Eleven p.m.?

They were sitting around the fire eating cold pizza. D and Spider had no appetite, but Ariel and Hannah were digging in, licking their fingers, rapturous.

"Haven't you ever had pizza before?" Spider asked, amused despite herself.

Ariel stared at her, all big grey eyes and freckles. She looked much younger than the fierce gun-toting warrior she'd been just an hour before. She had sauce at the corner of her mouth and Spider watched as she licked it off, like a cat. "Our goats all died," she said. "We haven't had any kind of cheese since then. Although we did eat a ton of goat," she said as an afterthought.

"Mostly we just get potatoes and porridge," Hannah said around a huge, greasy mouthful.

Of the three of them, only Diana was still on her guard, sitting on the periphery farthest from the fire, her gun laid across her knees, refusing to eat although she stared at the pizza for a moment as if she could absorb it with her eyes. Afterward, she didn't take her gaze off of them, not once, somehow able to keep both D and Spider in her sights. And Spider was hyper-aware of her hands on her gun, inches from the trigger.

"So what are we waiting for?" D said impatiently, leaping to her feet. They'd stripped off their extra clothes; the adrenaline had raised their body temperature. Spider felt like frogs were leaping under her skin, pushing her to move.

"Midnight. No one except the patrols to worry about then," Hannah said.

"And the patrols are these Uncles you mentioned? And they're armed too?"

"Yup," Ariel said, sucking on each of her fingers. Her hands were filthy, fingernails black—God knew what kind of bacteria was scurrying around on them. Spider glanced away.

"Bigger guns than we have," Diana pointed out. "Plus, there's more of them."

"How many more?"

"A dozen, maybe fifteen. Depends on if some of the families up mountain have come down to help out."

"Way to sell it, girl," Spider said. Still, she felt a rush of excitement that they were going to do something.

"We can sneak in. Sneak out. They won't even see us," Ariel said.

"Like the Greeks and the wooden horse?" Hannah said.

"Exactly." She rounded on Diana. "I'm not talking about going head to head with them. What's Daddy always telling us? *Brains over brawn. Use stealth.* That's what we're gonna do."

"Be stealthy," Spider said with a sigh. "Okay, so how close can we get the car?"

Ariel and Hannah exchanged glances. "Old Fire Road?" Hannah said, using a stick to draw some lines in the earth. "It hooks into Fish Peddler a few miles in, before the river, pretty much hugs the mountain."

Ariel nodded. "Turn the headlights off for the last six or seven miles, push it for the last little bit."

"By little bit, you mean . . . ," Spider said.

"Just a few miles," Ariel said with a nonchalance that made Spider want to hit her with something big and hard. *Are they all crazy like you?* is what she wanted to ask her. But of course they were.

"The trees are thick back there. Should give us enough cover," Hannah said, nodding.

"The guard platforms are at the front of the fence. Facing the mountain road. They'll be walking the perimeter but only every half hour or something." Ariel blew air out her nose. "We can do this," she said.

Spider had to admit that they sounded like they knew what they were talking about. It was hard to reconcile the commando speak with these half-starved teens though.

"You want me to drive on some itty-bitty road with no lights?" D said.

"We'll guide you. Take it slow."

Diana kicked at a stump. Spider just bet she rolled her eyes.

"What do you think?" D asked her. "Think this is crazy?"

Their eyes met. Spider shrugged helplessly. What choice was there?

Diana snorted. "You love your friend? You're this close to finding her." She pulled her hood back over her head, slung her gun across her back. "No one left behind, right? Let's do this."

THIRTY-ONE

— *Min* —

MIN SCOOPED UP A HUNK OF BREAD from the floor, dusted it off, and gave half to Kat. It was hard and stale and tasteless but Min nibbled on it, wishing the cup of water hadn't spilled all over the concrete. Even the splattered stew—brown and chunky, looking a little like vomit—made her stomach rumble.

They'd released Ruth for now, told her to sit on the bed. Although she was reluctant, she did what they asked. Min kept the knife in her field of vision and tried her best to keep up the appearance of strength and unpredictability.

"Who are you?" Ruth asked.

"Me? I'm the girl your Uncle Guy kidnapped. What do you think about that?"

Ruth's eyes flicked up to hers, flicked away again.

She stared at her hands, chewing on her lips. "He's not my uncle," she said finally.

"Do I need to gag you?" Min asked fiercely.

Ruby held her eyes for a second. "I won't make a peep."

Min drew Kat away, closer to the door. "She doesn't look like a soldier," she remarked, watching the girl pick at her nails.

"She is. He starts training them when they're young. Puts them through all kinds of endurance exercises. Sends them out on the mountain with nothing but knives and the clothes on their backs."

It was hard to believe.

"They're tough. Like old leather."

"What should we do with her?" Min asked in a low voice.

"They'll come looking for her soon, I'm guessing. The soldiers are a team. They stick together, watch out for each other. It's not like how it is for the rest of us. I've been down here for as long as a week before and it's like they forget I exist."

"Why did they do that to you?" Min felt tears prick her eyelids. She took Kat's hand in hers.

"Because I ran. Some of us, a month after the crash, tried to get away. Me, Henry Chen, and John Brewster. We were in pretty bad shape. Head injuries, broken ribs, a piece of shrapnel went through my thigh. Severed some muscle or tendons, I think." She pulled her shift up quickly and showed Min the raised scar on her leg. "John was basically okay though. Had some burns on his arms but he was lucky. If it hadn't been for me slowing us down, he'd have escaped."

"What happened to him?"

"They shot him in the back. Henry died too. There was bleeding in his brain but no one knew it. He went to sleep and he never woke up. I kept running though, every chance I got." She raised her head and looked into Min's eyes. "Until I just couldn't anymore. I couldn't remember where I was trying to go."

"This will be the last time you have to, I promise," Min said, squeezing her hand. She jerked her head in Ruth's direction. "So you're saying we should bring her with us? How about if I tie her arms?"

"You don't have to do that," Ruth said. "I won't make a fuss. Swear." She half-stood, sat down again when Min raised the knife. "But I can't go against *him*." There was a sort of reverence in her voice.

"Big Daddy?" Kat asked.

"Yeah . . . I just can't. We're his."

"It's bad, Ruth. This girl's got family out in the world. When her people start looking for her, they're going to come here. This could bring it all down," Kat said, her voice pleading. "We just need to get out. We won't tell if we're caught."

Ruth stared at her hands for a while longer, then met Min's eyes. "Okay, but once you're past the gates you're on your own."

Min nodded, sheathing her knife. Ruth rose and searched the room.

"What are you doing?" Min asked.

Ruth picked up a piece of dingy white clothing from the floor under the bed. It seemed to be a voluminous nightgown. "Brought it for you," she said, nodding at Kat, "but I think you need it more," she said, looking at Min.

"Why?"

"You stink like pee."

Min felt her face flush. Somehow, she'd managed to wipe that event from her mind.

Kat snatched the clothing from her and gave Min a quick, reassuring smile. "Let me borrow your knife." Min handed it over and Kat used it to cut a good three inches off the bottom. "You'd be swallowed up in this," she said. She tore the remnants into strips and proceeded to bandage Min's wrists, and then turned her back while Min shrugged off her hoodie and kicked her stiff underwear and jeans into the corner of the room. Min slipped the shift on, thankful that it came down to her knees, and then covered up with her hoodie and pocketed her knife. Throughout the whole procedure Ruth stared at her with unconcealed curiosity. She appeared to be particularly interested in Min's bra.

"Never seen that color before," she muttered.

"It's turquoise."

"Turquoise," Ruth repeated. "Pretty."

After checking to make sure it was all clear, Min and Kat followed Ruth down the corridor. The walls were hard-packed earth, reinforced by metal girders. The floor changed from dirt to concrete as they got close to the exit. Min paused as they passed the doublewide metal door, padlocked and chained.

"Stored food. Guns," said Kat.

"Last resort," said Ruth.

"Like a bunker?"

Kat nodded. "For when the war comes."

Ruth raised a finger to her lips. "Once we're outside, keep your head down, don't speak. Stick with Kat and they'll just think you're one of the cows."

Min stopped in her tracks. "Cows?"

Kat grabbed her by the elbow. "It's what they call the women who aren't soldiers."

"And that's supposed to make me feel better?" Her anger must have gotten through to Ruth, because she coughed nervously and put her hands up. "No offense meant," she muttered.

"Oh, offense taken," Min said grimly. "*So* taken."

Ruth grinned at her like a dog that was afraid of being reprimanded. She had a big gap between her top front teeth and a spray of freckles across her nose. Min felt her anger dissipate and shrugged it off. She was just a kid repeating what she'd been told all her life.

"This way," Ruth said, climbing the rough wooden stairs. She moved like a shadow creeping on cat feet. Min tried to imitate her as best she could while helping Kat, who was hampered by her old injury.

Upstairs was a barn with high rafters, straw littering the planked floor, and farming tools hanging from hooks on the walls. Ruth eased the door open, slunk out, and scanned the area before beckoning them to join her under the eaves. They hunkered down. "Fog's lifted," she said. "Was hoping for some cover."

Min glanced around. Solar torches cast puddles of light onto the graveled paths weaving around the buildings. Closest to them were two small wooden sheds, wire enclosing a yard set between them. She could hear dogs whining, and smell chicken shit. Just beyond, a large round building. Farther off were rows of corrugated metal–roofed huts set out in a grid, and she glimpsed another dark huddle of structures. Encircling it all was a periphery fence, probably twenty feet high and topped with coils of razor wire. A massive gate was set into it, flanked by two tall towers. "Was this some kind of army base?" she asked Ruth. Actually, it looked more like a prison than anything.

"There was an old community here before, logging camp at first. A lot of the outbuildings existed already but we built the fence. Took us years."

"How many of you are there?"

"Including the children? Over one hundred now that live here. More up in the hills." She sounded proud about it. "Come on. Keep close." The ground underfoot was sandy, deadening their steps. "Stay in the shadows," Ruth whispered, peeking around the corner. "Everyone must still be at dinner." She indicated the squat round building to the left. Flat-roofed with porthole-style windows set high up on the timbered walls. A stronger, harsher light blazed from it; the difference between the diffused light and electric bulbs was obvious. Generator? Her parents had had one too, but only used it for emergencies. Otherwise, it was candles and hurricane lamps. One of the hardest things to get used to at the high school had been the harsh fluorescent lighting, which often gave her cluster headaches.

Beyond the hall, she spied more huts, more fence, and the flat silhouette of the encroaching trees.

"Can we just walk out the gates?" Min asked, her voice stuttering with nervousness. The desire to get out of here was a mounting urgency. At any minute, she felt as if a large hand was going to grab her from behind.

Ruth shook her head and pointed to the gates—two huge doors, wide enough for a Mack truck to drive through. They were closed and barricaded with a big piece of lumber that spanned their width, supported by metal brackets. "Takes two men to lift that piece of wood." The tall fence stretched in both directions as far as Min could see. "Lockdown," Ruth muttered. "And," she pointed again, "guards in the towers." With horror, Min saw that the men were armed with long guns.

"How can we get past them?"

"They'll switch over in an hour or two. It'll take about ten minutes for the next watch to show up. Can you climb?"

"What do you mean?"

"If we can get up on top of the platform, you can climb down the other side of the fence." She patted her hip. Min saw she had a coil of rope attached to her belt.

"There's razor wire."

"I can get some bolt cutters."

"I can manage but—" She looked at Kat, who shook her head.

"You could leave her?" Ruth suggested.

Min ignored her and gripped Kat's hand. "There's got to be some other way." She squinted. "There's a door in the fence there."

"Padlocked. Not likely to be open any time soon. And the hasp is as big around as my thumb. No cutting through that. Up and over is the only way."

Min swore. Ruth turned her head suddenly and threw a cautioning arm out. They flattened up against the wall. Small groups of people were leaving the meeting hall, talking feverishly amongst themselves. They seemed fearful, full of anxious energy, mostly women and small children, although Min also caught sight of more men with guns. One of them, tall and imposing, with hands so big his weapon resembled a toy, yelled over the crowd, "People, to your quarters. No dawdling. Stay there until daylight."

The crowd grumbled, drew back but didn't disperse. Instead, the nervousness seemed to escalate.

Another man stepped out from the meeting house and with sickening dread, Min recognized the short, burly man from the gas station. Arthur Pembroke. Big Daddy. Ruth drew in her breath. Min could feel her quivering beside her. She searched the crowd for Guy's yellow ponytail but didn't see it.

"Randall," Arthur said, clapping the tall man on his shoulder. Randall immediately stepped back and all eyes turned to Arthur. Although he was a small man—especially in comparison with Randall's massive girth—and soft-spoken, he commanded the crowd. Even the children ceased their babble.

"Your safety is our main concern," Arthur said, a wide smile on his face. The warmth that Min recalled emanated from him like something tangible. "We will prevail." He spread out his arms to those standing nearby and they massed around him, reaching out to touch his hands, drawing closer for a hug. "We have made many preparations for this." He picked up one of the children, a girl with riotous brown curls, and held her against his chest, dropped a kiss on the top of her head. "All will be well," he said. "Go along now."

The hum of conversation calmed and the crowd thinned, people vanishing into their homes. Arthur's warm smile vanished; his expression hardened. More men joined him and Randall. Some of them were wearing green army fatigues, all carried rifles, and some had handguns holstered at the hip. Arthur barked a few commands and then walked toward the gates, Randall at his side. The others peeled off in every direction.

"I shouldn't be doing this," Ruth said, voice shaking. "I'm betraying him. He'll find out and then he'll punish me and it will be awful."

"Please," Min begged. "I don't belong here. If I can get away, I won't tell anyone, I promise." The lie came easily.

"Guy is the enemy, Ruth," Kat said. "Keeping her here is helping him and threatening everyone else."

Ruth swallowed hard, eyes downcast. Min waited, panicky, until Ruth finally came to a decision.

The girl glanced around, scanning the buildings. "They're patrolling now. We can't stay here. It's too dangerous. We need to wait it out."

"Where can we go?"

"There'll be Uncles everywhere. Plus, the rest of my team. Big Daddy will have us all working tonight."

She bit her lip and then her face cleared. "Okay, I've got it. Follow me."

She led them around the corner behind the supply building. For half a second, Min thought she was returning them to the basement cells. She hung back, and Ruth noticed. "Come on," she commanded in a harsh whisper.

They skirted the building safely and Min took a deep breath. "Careful near the dogs," Ruth said, motioning to the right. The pen was shrouded by shadows, but Min could hear an ominous growl building steadily the closer they got to the fence, and then caught a glimpse of a pair of furious black eyes, a flash of white teeth. She turned away, unwilling to lock gaze with the animal, but not before she saw something—no, some*one* —crouched in the middle of the pile of furry bodies. A young boy, tousle-haired, barely clothed. He wrinkled his nose at her and uttered a series of short yaps.

"Shh, Nicky, everything's fine," said Kat, and the kid sank into the sea of fur.

Ruth had halted a few yards ahead before a muddy yard enclosed in chicken wire with a rickety structure in the middle of it. The smell of chicken shit was eye-wateringly strong.

"No one will look for you in here," she said. Min searched her face for deceit and saw no evidence of any, but still— seriously? "Just for a few hours. Until it's quiet and we're sure all the civilians are asleep. Then I'll come get you and we'll figure out how to get you over that fence without cutting you to ribbons."

THIRTY-TWO

— Spider —

SPIDER WAS REMINDED OF some science program she'd seen that talked about the blackest black of a black hole and how the human eye couldn't discern it because it was the almost total absence of color. That's what it felt like to her right now, riding through a dense forest in She-Ra with all the lights off, following three figures who were only slightly less black than the surroundings. On the plus side, the car had started right up. For the first little while, they'd had the high beams on, all of them crammed together in the Bug, but steadily the track had curved around, leading them on switchbacks up into the foothills, and Ariel had told D to cut the lights. "We're above Avalon right now," she'd said. "We'd be easy enough to spot if they happened to look this way."

Spider couldn't see anything when she peered in the direction Ariel pointed. The compound must be at the bottom of a dip of ground, a valley of some sort. Turned out Min had brought multiple flashlights, bundled away in her pack—of course she had—and the three mountain girls held them under their hoodies so the lights were dimmed by the material. It probably helped them traverse the potholes without breaking their necks but it didn't do much for the occupants of the car. D was hunched over the dashboard, her nose practically pressed up against the windshield, trying desperately to see.

"I didn't know that She-Ra could go so slow. What are you doing, Speed Racer?" Spider said.

D glanced down for a millisecond and uttered a brief laugh. "It's not even registering. I don't know—less than five miles an hour?"

"So we'll get there tomorrow then," Spider said, pounding her fist on the dash.

D swore in frustration. "These are some crazy people, correct? Why are we even trusting them? This could be a trap."

"Hey, preaching to the choir, honey."

D gave a little screech of frustration mixed with terror. "I hate this. It's so hard to know if we're doing the right thing. Maybe we should have waited for the cops?"

Spider straightened up. "No, seriously, D. I do trust them. Well, that girl Ariel anyway. She's pretty transparent. She needs our help for this kid who's injured. Not sure about the other two but she'll keep them in line. Did you notice that they defer to her? Even though she's a scrap of a thing?"

D braked suddenly and She-Ra coughed and spluttered. The rumble of her engine sounded unbelievably loud to Spider's ears. "What are they doing?"

Spider rolled down her window and leaned out. The three girls had stopped. Far ahead, like a ghost light, Spider could see a hazy glow illuminating the trees.

Ariel came to the window. "The compound's about four miles that a way." She gestured to their left. "Kill the engine."

"Is this where the stealth begins?" Spider asked. She couldn't help it. Something about these girls made her snark come out.

"We've gotta get the car closer. Sneak up from behind," Ariel said, nodding. Spider decided that sarcasm was wasted on the oblivious.

"We're pushing it?" asked Diana. The sour look she'd been wearing this whole time was still in place. It must be her regular expression, Spider thought. She had a brief urge to smile at Diana, to see if she could break through the sullenness, but decided not to press her luck. The girl was armed and tightly wound.

Ariel nodded. "Track's not so bad up here. Plus, we start going downhill just up past the hunting hide."

"What's that?" Spider asked.

"A little hut up a tree. Covered in camo. You squat up there and you shoot the deer when they come and eat the carrots you threw around," Diana replied.

"Seems a little unsportsmanlike."

"Not if you want to eat, it ain't."

"She-Ra is old but she's solid steel," D pointed out. "She weighs a ton. We could get stuck."

"Only option," Ariel said, her eyes shuttering.

Diana shook her head. "You're not talking sense. What good's the car going to be if we hit a mud hole?"

"Yeah, maybe we should walk it from here?" Hannah said. "It's the safest way to get in unseen."

Ariel swore, kicked at She-Ra's bumper. "We need the car close by so we can transfer Aaron into it as soon as possible." Her gaze traveled between their faces, maybe picked up on the doubt she saw there. "Your friend Min might not be able to walk either."

Spider felt a surge of rage bubble up inside her chest at the thought of someone hurting Min.

"Once we get to the compound, we can grab a couple of ATVs," Diana said. "Ride them back here."

Ariel's stormy face cleared. "Okay," she said finally. "Cover the car with some branches."

"Where you going?" asked Hannah.

"I'm going to go scout ahead. Heard some noises I don't like."

Spider sharpened her ears but she heard nothing.

"The trailer is pretty close. Think that's it?" Diana said. "Men up there?"

Ariel nodded grimly.

"Shit!"

"Trailer?" Spider asked.

"Drug lab," Ariel said.

"You mean like meth or something?"

But Ariel was gone into the shadows.

"Will she be okay by herself?" Spider asked Diana.

"Yup."

"Will we?"

"Yup." She jerked her head at Hannah, who slung her gun over her shoulder and started piling branches on top of She-Ra. Her flashlight lay on the ground beaming a small pool of light.

"You don't talk much, do you?" Spider said.

"Nope." Spider said it at the same time, but it didn't even raise a smile. Sighing, she went and joined D, who was also scrabbling on the ground for sticks and brush.

"Did you hear anything?" Spider asked her, watching Diana. She was standing like a sentinel, a slightly less tree-like shape among the close-knit trees all around her. These girls all had some ability to dissolve into the landscape.

D shook her head. Her face was a pale disc.

"How are you holding up?" Spider asked. "Feels like a Tarantino movie all of a sudden."

D swallowed a laugh that sounded more like a sob. A thin wail escaped her lips.

Spider ignored the furious shushing coming from Diana. She dropped her stick and ran over to her friend.

"I'm freaking out about Min," D said, hanging her head. "I can't bear to lose her." Spider pressed her hand. Her fingers were quivering. It was like trying to keep hold of a terrified bird.

"I'm here. Hold onto me," Spider said. D's fingers tightened and Spider felt her own hands go numb from the pressure. "Breathe with me."

Slowly D stopped panting. Her eyes lost their frantic look.

"It's my fault. She's in danger because of me—"

"No," said Spider cutting her off.

"This is just so awful."

"I know. But we'll get her out. Promise."

A twig snapped somewhere off to the left. Ariel rushed up, making them both jump. She was dripping with sweat and a wild light danced in her eyes. Hannah and Diana drew closer.

"There's something going on. A whole bunch of men down there. I don't recognize them."

"Are they cooking?" Hannah asked.

"I don't think so. Couldn't smell anything fresh. Sounds more like a meeting, but they're heated."

"Got a bad feeling," Diana said. "Planning meeting?"

Ariel nodded. "Guy's definitely up to something."

"Called on some of his tweaker friends for reinforcements?"

Ariel grunted.

"What's going on?" Spider asked.

"Uncle Guy, the man who stole your friend. He's had a falling out with Big Daddy and the rest of them. Guess he's not feeling welcome up at the compound, so he's down here with some business acquaintances. Sometimes we get money from stuff that's outside the law."

"Why are you candy-coating it?" interrupted Diana. "Since you're spilling all our secrets."

Ariel shot her a look. "We sell drugs or trade them for other stuff. Guns, building materials, that kind of thing. Not us soldiers, but Guy uses these guys to distribute for us. He rendezvous with them at the gas station and now they're here."

"He must have promised them something," Diana said. "To bring them on board."

"Can we cut around?" Hannah said. "Sneak past?"

"It'll take too long. We need to get back as soon as possible."

"Checks?" Ariel said, unslinging her gun and cracking it open. The other two crouched down and followed suit, carefully loading the cartridges they pulled from their pockets, and then clicking the safeties on.

"I'm good to go," Diana said, sounding amped up. She cradled her gun in front of her using both hands.

"Make sure you stay behind us," she told D and Spider. "Don't want to shoot you accidentally."

They exchanged troubled glances.

"She's mostly kidding," Hannah said. "But still, don't get in front, okay?" She reached her hand up toward Spider's face. It was filthy, and Spider recoiled. "Just a little mud," she said. "For camouflage." Spider closed her eyes as Hannah daubed the swampy-smelling goo onto her cheeks and forehead and then onto D's face.

Ariel glanced at the car under its heap of branches.

"Leave the keys," she said to D. "Right there, on the front seat."

D froze, staring at her.

Ariel fidgeted. "Sorry. Just in case."

"Just in case I don't make it back?" D said.

Ariel dropped her gaze. "Got to be prepared for all outcomes." D reluctantly dropped the keys in through the window.

Diana took the lead. "We're going to be passing real close to the trailer. You see anything, anyone, you hit the ground."

"No flashlights," Ariel said over her shoulder, "so go slow and stick close together."

Hannah mumbled what sounded like a prayer. For a moment, she was next to Spider, her breath hot against Spider's cheek. "These are bad men," she said. "The last thing you want is for them to get ahold of you."

THIRTY-THREE

— *Min* —

MIN'S MOTHER HAD KEPT CHICKENS for a while until a fox had gotten them. Min had been amazed at how mean they were to each other, terrible bullying and pecking that resulted in half the brood strutting around with no feathers on their heads or rumps. The rooster had crowed from morning to night—and sometimes in the middle of the night—and Min, who at the time had still been flirting with vegetarianism, had not been entirely sorry when he ended up in a delicious soup.

Couple of things she did like about them, though, was their soft expansive fluffiness and the warbling, cooing noises they made when they were settled in for the night. So, despite the smell, it was cozy in the henhouse on the hay with a tier of drowsing birds dreaming above her head.

"Used to hide in here sometimes," Kat said. Her hair had drifted in front of her face and Min wanted to push it back, rest her eyes on those dear familiar-yet-unfamiliar features.

"Can we trust Ruth?"

"I think so. She's loyal, but she's also . . . righteous and honorable. Like, Guy's gone rogue and should be punished for what he did. He's not deserving of help. They've got this code here in Avalon. It's kind of tied up in that whole Knights of the

Round Table mythology. All the soldiers hold themselves to a standard, even though they just look like ragged kids."

"You know her a little?"

"She talks to me sometimes when they let me help with food prep. You saw how she brought a clean shift for me. She's not unkind. She's bought into it—this whole brave new world thing that Big Daddy is pushing—but she truly believes in doing the right thing."

She inhaled sharply. Min could feel the tremors traveling through her body even though they were sitting apart. She struggled to think of something calming.

"Tell me why Spider is called Spider?" she said finally.

Kat made a curious noise, like an exclamation mixed with a cough. "I remember," she said, sounding a little surprised. "We'd heard that people swallow as many as eight spiders a year while they sleep. This was in third grade or something. And Spider got so freaked out that she slept with a dust mask on for six months. Even then, she was convinced they were finding a way to get inside her."

Min laughed and Kat joined in, a thin sound that ended abruptly, as if she were out of practice. Her breathing quickened again, the fear in her almost a tangible thing to Min.

"I won't leave you, you know. No matter what. Tell me what's wrong?" she asked Kat, who was twisting pieces of hay into ropes and then shredding them between her fingers.

"Stuff is coming back to me. Terrible things. The crash, afterward." She swallowed hard. Her voice was shaking so much that her speech sounded choppy. Min thought about soothing her, telling her not to talk if she didn't want to, but there was a note of steel in Kat's voice. Min knew she had to get it all out. Although she wanted to hug her more than anything, she kept still, giving her the space she needed.

"I told you about Henry and John."

Min nodded. "The plane survivors."

"There were two others who were alive, hurt but alive, when the men came." She took a long, quavering gulp of air. "One was Sally. Sally Beaumont. I never liked her much when we were in school. She was mean to D especially. Cornered her in the bathroom once with a bunch of other girls, hurt her."

"Did they kill her too?" Min asked.

"No, she's still here. She's a mommy now."

"How's that different from . . ."—Min could barely bring herself to say it—"a cow?"

"She's got status. She's Uncle Randall's wife. She's about to have his baby."

"Why would she do that?" Min asked.

"You have to understand. They made us weak. Starved us. Kept us separated and in the dark. For weeks. Months. The only kindness we got was from Big Daddy. He'd come down to the cells and talk to us in that soothing deep voice he has, and at first it didn't mean anything, but eventually, some of us started listening. Started forgetting that we had families and lives from before. He convinced us that this was a calling. That we were special and that all of us had our roles to play in the great future that awaits us. He said we came through fire for a reason."

"But not you. You didn't believe."

Kat raised her eyes to Min's; her face was streaked with tears. How long had she been silently crying, Min wondered.

"Just stubborn like that, I guess. At first, you know, with the head injury, I didn't remember anything about my past." She parted her long hair above her ear and Min saw a thin scar snaking across her skull to the back of her neck. "But then one day, it started coming back."

She slipped her hand into Min's. Her fingers were cold, her palms calloused.

"I have to tell you. Jonathan, Spider's brother, is here too. I don't see him much but I heard he was injured a few days ago."

"How bad is it?" Min felt her breath catch in her throat.

"I think he might be dead."

THIRTY-FOUR

— D —

D SMELLED IT FIRST. A chemical stench like a mix of cat urine and rotten eggs. Ahead, Diana held her fist up, and Ariel pulled on D's sleeve until she crouched down in the leaves. The trailer was parked in a clearing just below them, faint lamplight picking out the contours of the metal roof and the trim and throwing a wan puddle of illumination on the ground. All of its windows were blacked out and the shredded grass around it appeared burnt in places. KEEP OUT signs were posted on many of the trees, and piles of garbage bags were heaped all over, interspersed with dilapidated lawn chairs scattered around a rusted barbecue. A black van with big tires and a reinforced grille was parked alongside a bunch of souped-up ATVs.

There were people inside. They could hear them hollering. As they watched, the door swung open and two men, beers in their hands, nearly fell down the wooden steps. They were young, dressed in jeans and muscle shirts. One had multiple piercings along his brow bone and ears. A third, thickset and older with a bushy greying moustache, stood in the doorway. His leather vest was stenciled and adorned with numerous patches and pins, most of them skulls. D felt Spider's hand tighten on hers as the two guys moved in their direction. One lit a cigarette and the other leaned up against a tree. D could hear the sound of a zipper, and then the flow of urine.

They were going to be spotted. She cradled her head in her arms, tensing and releasing her muscles in turn, striving for invisibility.

"Move further on down," the man in the doorway yelled. "You gonna light that and not even think about what we're doing here?"

"Sorry, Luke, my bad."

The smoker stalked into the trees, passing not ten feet from where they all crouched. Bald-headed with heavy black tattoos that covered most of his arms and neck. "Old fucker," he muttered, blowing plumes of smoke into the air. D put her face down, feeling the tickle of coarse grasses against her cheeks. Her throat tightened. To her own ears her heartbeat sounded like a drum. It was hard to believe he couldn't hear it.

"Stupid ass," the old man said, hawking phlegm over the railing. He banged his fist against the side of the van before taking a seat on one of the chairs. "Let's go," he yelled, and five men exited the vehicle, pulling on leather jackets, rubbing their eyes.

"Could use a pick-me-up," one of them said. The old man just stared at him steadily and then spit again.

More men spilled out of the trailer. The smell of cat pee grew stronger carried on the breeze. Even though the night was cool, they were wearing tees and undershirts. D didn't like to stereotype but they all looked like white gangbangers. Face and neck tattoos, bulky muscles covered in a sheen of sweat. One of them hauled a suitcase. D sucked in her breath as she recognized Guy by his greasy yellow ponytail.

Ariel made eye contact with D and placed her finger across her lips.

"Where you want it?" Guy asked the old man. His voice sounded thick with mucus.

"Let me check it over first. Not that I don't trust you." He chuckled, but it wasn't a pleasant laugh. Guy opened the case. It was filled with large plastic bags of glistening powder. The bald man, Luke, sliced open a bag and used his knife to lift a measure to his nostril.

"My best cook ever," Guy said. "Primo shit."

Luke sniffed loudly and then pinched his nose.

"We good?" Guy said.

"We are." Luke beckoned to one of the other men, a swarthy, muscular fellow who swung open the back of the van revealing metal cases and semiautomatic guns.

Beside D, Ariel gasped.

"You can use my men. Think that'll be enough for you to get it done?"

Guy grunted. "If we've got the firepower, sure. Easy in and out, that's the plan," he said, swiping at his nose with his forearm. "Maybe wait till sunrise. Take out the old man and start changing things." A man with an eagle tattoo on his neck high-fived him.

Guy picked up one of the guns and racked the slide. D didn't know anything about guns but she recognized that noise from the movies. It meant he could fire it. He sighted down the barrel and swung the gun in a smooth lateral motion. Although there was no way he could see them, the muzzle was pointed in the direction of their hiding place. They ducked down lower.

"I recognize some of the men from Avalon," Ariel whispered. "Uncles from outside the compound."

"They're with Guy now?" Hannah said. Somehow, she'd moved up next to them without D even hearing her.

"Choosing sides, I guess."

"We've got to get to the compound ahead of them."

"If they catch us, we're dead."

"Brave new world, ha!" Guy said. "Boom!" He mimed firing the gun and the other men laughed, gathering by the van, tossing beers to each other and handing out guns. A few of them were clustered around a large mirror set on top of the barbecue. Luke poured out more powder, chopped it, and snorted. "Get in line, boys," he yelled.

"Come on," whispered Ariel. "While they're distracted."

D started backing up again. Leaf mold filled her nose, and a hundred sharp twigs and brambles scratched her forearms, belly, and legs where her jeans had rucked up.

She wanted to rise to her feet and bolt but she forced herself to crawl, her world reduced to what was two inches from her nose. Down the incline, Spider a little in front, the soldiers flanking them both. It felt like miles. Her muscles were seizing up. Finally, Ariel spoke. "Get up. Run as quick and as quietly as you can."

They raced into the woods in a tight huddle, only stopping once the sound of the men had faded.

"We're gonna have to go the long way round. Can't risk running into any of them," Ariel said. She peered at the sky. "Still got a few hours before sunrise."

"Can't believe that Guy has turned traitor," Diana said. "Trying to take Big Daddy out!"

Hannah's eyes were huge and her hands trembled on her rifle. "We've got to warn them," she said.

"Let's backtrack to the fire road, then cut straight across the woods," Ariel said.

"Faster to get the car?" Hannah said.

Ariel paused. She seemed to be arguing with herself. "No, crow flies is shortest. Under an hour if we run like hell. Slip in at the back. My secret way."

"Wait a minute. Those guys are armed, and messed up on drugs. They're planning on killing people. We need to call the cops again," Spider said, yanking her phone out of her pocket. She groaned. "Damn cheap-ass battery. D?"

D shook her head. "Mine too."

It was as if none of the girls were listening. They had their heads together. All of them had taken their guns off safety.

"Who's got more firepower?" Ariel said.

"Seriously, that's the conversation we're having?" Spider asked.

"We're Big Daddy's soldiers. We've got to stand by him," Diana said curtly. "Theirs are newer. But I think we outgun them still. The fence and the towers give us some kind of advantage. We can hold it for days, pick them off one by one. And we can always hole up in the bunker."

Spider goggled at her. Diana gave her a quick dismissive look.

"Let's go. Fast as we can. Forget about slow and quiet. See something, shoot," Diana said. Her scowl had deepened. Her voice rang with authority.

"Aaron," Ariel said, biting her lip. She seemed shrunken down, her real age now, although D wondered when she'd ever appeared bigger or older. It was uncertainty and pain that weighed down Ariel's voice, she realized. Ariel felt the same way about this boy as they did about Min. She had as much at stake.

"Not our number one priority anymore," Diana said.

THIRTY-FIVE

— Spider —

DIANA WAS MORE MUSCULAR than the others but she moved like a whisper. Flitting from tree to tree, invisible except for when a trickle of moonlight caught the dull black gleam of her gun.

Not that Spider was in any mood to appreciate Diana's ninja stealth.

Her calves were knots of pain. She was sweating heavily, thirstier than she'd ever been in her life, and it felt as if an entire colony of tiny, itchy, bitey insects had set up shop on her skin. Under her skin.

Ariel had suggested that they take deer trails rather than risk being spotted on the track. Diana, leading, seemed to have no trouble finding her way, but Spider couldn't see any kind of a trail anywhere. She knew that Hannah and Ariel had ranged out a dozen feet on either side of them, but other than the occasional crunch of a leaf or branch, she had no idea where they were.

"Drop," Diana hissed, pumping her fist.

Spider collapsed with a barely contained groan.

Ariel ran over, kneeled and trained her gun at a point in the brush twenty feet ahead.

"What is it?" breathed Diana.

"Something's in the woods."

"Guy's men?"

"No."

"I can smell it," said Diana, fumbling with her gun. Her voice shook, and that, more than anything, scared the crap out of Spider.

"Wild," Hannah said.

Wild what?

"What do we do?" D asked.

"Stay down. Don't move. Wait." Ariel, Diana, and Hannah, guns shouldered, duck-walked a few yards and fanned out, taking left, right, and center positions. The woods swallowed them up.

In the dirt, D's fingers found hers. "I smell it too." And Spider realized so could she.

It was rancid, like the rotten hamburger she'd found at the back of the fridge once. Green mold had sprouted over it, emitting a gassy, sweet smell that crawled inside your nose. This smelled like that but punched up about a hundred levels. She tried to breathe through her mouth even though the thought of that slick, rotten odor coating her tongue almost made her heave.

"Something dead out there." Spider said.

"It's getting stronger."

"Not dead, then." She thought of the Monty Python sketch about the parrot. Mostly dead. It wasn't so funny.

Spider listened as hard as she could. Nothing. It was as if the two of them were in a vacuum.

"Where did they go?" D said.

"Can't see a thing." The shadows played dizzying tricks on her eyes. She strained to pick out something from the blackness.

A branch cracked like a rifle shot and goose bumps broke out all over Spider's back. She was on her feet before she realized it and D was next to her, breathing in great gasps.

More yells came from somewhere else. Behind them? In front? Spider couldn't tell. A piercing whistle shattered the air, the heavy thud of a rock against a trunk. Sounds were bouncing off of the mountain, she guessed. It was impossible to know where they were coming from.

Then silence again. Ominous. Branches cracking under pressure. Was it moving away? No, the trees were bending toward them.

"What is it?" whispered D. "What is it?"

"I can't see anything. Where are those crazy bitches?"

They clung to one another, crawling backwards until they were crouched by a bush.

"Bear!" yelled Diana. "Get down." She raced over to them and pushed them both flat against the ground. Spider felt her lips split against her teeth as her face smacked her knee.

"Just keep quiet and don't move. If it comes at you, play dead," Diana snapped, and then she was gone again.

"Can we crawl under this bush?" D said. They backed in as far as they could and heaped mounds of leaves in front of them. Spider tried not to think about how it would feel if the bear just scooped them out of their hiding place like oysters from a half shell.

"I can't see anything," D said. "Is it close?"

"They'll drive it off, or kill it," she said. The soldiers' voices were coming from several directions.

"Where you at, Di? Hannah?" Ariel shouted. A flashlight beam swung crazily. "Who's got eyes?"

A whuffing sound interspersed with clacking sent chills up Spider's spine. She'd never heard anything so strange. Branches snapped and cracked as the bear forced its way through.

"It's heading back toward us," Hannah cried. Her flashlight signaled her position. She was to Spider's right about a hundred yards.

"Can you get a shot?" Ariel shouted.

"Gun's clogged with mud. I fell."

"Diana? Position?" Ariel screamed. "Where is it?"

Diana slid to a stop next to them. She raised herself on her elbows, aimed her gun, called out, "With the girls. I got nothing."

"Two o'clock," yelled Hannah. "My two o'clock!"

"I got it," Ariel yelled.

"Stay down! Stay down!" A gun boomed. The bear bellowed. Ariel kept firing until her gun clicked. Empty.

And then, a shuddering impact as the bear hit the ground.

The silence that followed was heavy, as if the whole world was holding its breath. Flashlight beams crisscrossed as the three soldiers converged.

"Is it dead?" Hannah said.

"I killed it. I killed it," Ariel said, a note of triumph in her voice. D and Spider raised their heads. She stood next to a mountainous heap. Her flashlight beam illuminated the hollows of her face then narrowed as she focused the beam on the dead bear. A great, dark, shaggy coat, yellow teeth snagged on slimy jowls. She cautiously poked at the body with the barrel of her gun.

The rotten hamburger smell mixed with the rank odor of fresh blood and Spider felt her stomach churn.

Hannah and Diana drew near. "Is it the same bear? The one that attacked Aaron?" Hannah asked.

"I think so. Grizzled like an old man. See, its fur is all matted around the neck where I stabbed it with the spear. Look how its coat just hangs on its bones. It was starving. Poor old—" Ariel made a hiccupping sound and then threw up.

THIRTY-SIX

— *Min* —

MIN STARTLED AWAKE. In sleep, she and Kat had curled themselves around each other's bodies, trying to keep warm. Behind her head, the hens roused and settled again. How on earth she had managed to fall asleep, she didn't know. The hay was prickly, sticking sharp shafts through her clothes, and the stink of farmyard made her want to sneeze constantly. She sat up—still dark, so she couldn't have been out for more than an hour or two—and then sucked her breath in as her eyes made out the figure hunched in the doorway. It held something long and bulky in its hand.

"It's me," Ruth said. "I was going to wake you in a couple of minutes. It's close to dawn, all quiet. Now's as good a time as any."

Min pressed Kat's shoulder, waking her. "C'mon." Kat stretched. Her long hair was snarled and spiked with bits of straw. Min was sure she didn't look much better. When she stood, she staggered a little, overcome with hunger. "Don't suppose you have something to eat?"

"Got the bolt cutters," Ruth said, handing them to Min. "You could suck some raw eggs if you hurry."

Min didn't know if she was kidding or not. Kat met her eyes. "They're full of protein."

Once, back when they'd had the chickens, Min had cracked open a fertile egg and found a perfectly formed chick inside. Transparent beak, wispy golden feathers, curled talons.

"Taste a little like warm snot," Ruth said. "You get used to it."

Min decided to skip it.

The solar lighting had died along the paths but there was a grey glimmer beginning to show at the horizon and it was sufficient to see with. They followed Ruth's dark back as she darted from building to building, using them as cover, and then ran low and fast across the open area between the meeting hall and the gate. Lights blazed from inside the hall. Min wondered if the Uncles were strategizing. She held Kat's hand, helping her as much as she could, but the girl's old injury slowed her down, and Min was feeling weak. Every second in the open felt dangerous. There was a humming, not so much a sound but something Min felt through the bottom of her shoes. She looked up at the guard towers and saw no one. They were unmanned for now, but for how long?

"Switching the guards over," Ruth said. "Probably grabbing something to eat while they can."

Kat exclaimed and stopped suddenly. "Sorry, my ankle turned on a stone."

"Just a little farther," Min said, bracing her under the elbow as much as she could. The bolt cutters were getting heavier by the second and her grip was slippery with sweat.

Tucked against the fence, Ruth crouched down, slung her gun across her back. Her eyes darted in all directions and then she was moving again, leading them to the stairs below the platform.

"We'll be totally visible once we reach the top," she said, "so you'll have duck down and be prepared to move fast."

At the top, it was amazing how everything opened up. Min could see sections of the mountain road that wound past their campsite. In the other direction were dense woods, a silver thread that might be a river, and the steep flanks of the mountain. They must have been about twenty-five feet up, and the drop over the side seemed even higher. And there were rolls of razor wire to contend with as well, far bulkier than she'd imagined they would be. Min's heart sank.

"I can't," says Kat. "I'm sorry. I just can't."

"We'll find a way," Min said, though she didn't know how. She glanced at Kat's arms surreptitiously. Her elbows protruded, wrists as narrow as Min's, bird-boned. Could she climb? Min wasn't sure she could do it either. Falling from such a height would surely break her legs. But still, it was the only way.

"Keep a look out," Ruth said sharply. Her face was without pity. The scorn felt like a slap to Min and she knew Kat felt it too. She was conscious of a fierce desire to protect Kat from all harm.

"Those men come you won't have a choice," Ruth continued. "They'll stick you in that cell forever. And I'm telling you right now, I won't take the blame for you. I'll say I caught the two of you out here. If you climb, jump, fall, it's all the same to me. Faster the better."

With dread, Min glanced at Kat, but to her surprise the girl was standing taller and there was a firmness around her mouth, a new fierce light in her dark brown eyes.

Ruth unhooked the coiled rope from her belt and handed it over. "Once we get rid of the wire, we'll attach this here on the bracket. You ever cliff-climb before?"

Min blinked at her. "I did the fitness rope-climb in gym," she said, glossing over the fact that no one in the class, including herself, had managed to get higher than halfway. It didn't matter; Ruth stared at her uncomprehendingly. Climbing down, though, had to be easier than climbing up.

Stashing her rifle, the girl took the bolt cutters from Min. And set the blades to the wire.

At the same instant, Min suddenly realized what the persistent humming was. "No, wait!" she yelled, but it was too late. There was a crackle, a flash of blinding light, and Ruth was thrown backward. Her head struck a wooden beam with a resounding thud. The bolt cutters flew over the side of the fence.

Min and Kat traded wide-eyed looks.

"Shit. They've electrified it," Min said. "The generator's on. I should have realized but I wasn't thinking. Is she alive?"

Kat kneeled to check on her. "She's breathing. Just knocked out. Can we get her down before anyone notices?"

Min hesitated. Should they abandon Ruth here? Run and hide? What was their best shot? She was still arguing with herself when the alarm started to sound.

THIRTY-SEVEN

— Spider —

HALFWAY UNDER THE FENCE in mid-crawl, Spider raised her head. She'd heard something—an explosion, like a transformer blowing. "What the hell was that?" she whispered. "Is it gun fire?"

"Nah," Ariel said, crouching down next to her head. She seemed to have recovered in the hour since killing the bear. "Guns don't sound like that. Get a move on though. Something is going down. People are mobbing."

"C'mon, c'mon, move," said Diana from the other side, kicking at Spider's feet.

Spider gritted her teeth. Her split lip twinged.

It was a shallow trench, dug out for willowy types like Ariel, and in the last rains it had collected water. Spider had to get right down in it to clear the bottom of the fence, and although she kept her mouth and eyes closed, she still felt gritty sludge dripping over her face and down her chest. Just another layer of filth.

"Keep up against the fence," Ariel hissed as Spider emerged, spitting mud out of her mouth, cold and wet, her braids leaking rank ditchwater. D was in equally bad shape, but somehow Diana, hot on Spider's heels—so hot if almost felt as if she'd clamber over Spider's prone body—had made it through relatively untouched.

Hannah, who'd gone first, was scouting just a little way ahead, poised on the balls of her feet, her gun ready in her hands. She raced back. "Meeting hall is all lit up like a bonfire," she said. "People milling about like headless chickens." The words were hardly out of her mouth before a strident alarm pierced the quiet.

"What the heck?" said Ariel. "We never had one of those before. It must be Guy and his thugs already. Trust that jacked-up bastard to get impatient."

"We probably drew him out when we fired on the bear," Diana said.

"No help for that," Ariel muttered.

Diana was almost buzzing with excitement, eyes glittering. "All kind of shit's going down. We've got to warn Big Daddy."

"Can we get closer?" Spider said, exchanging looks with D. "We have to find Min and get her out."

"If we cut around past the dog yard there, in between some of the huts, we can come up right next to the hall," Diana said. "See what's going on before we decide our next move?" She checked in with Ariel, who nodded. Seemed like killing the bear had put Ariel back on top, Spider thought.

"If an Uncle stops us, keep your heads down, and stay in the back," Ariel said. "Hannah, Diana, stick near them. If we run into anyone, grab them by the arm like they're prisoners."

They quickly fell in behind her, keeping to the shadows as much as possible, although there was no real need. All the action was centered near the hall. Panicked people gathering, running everywhere, and over it all the clang of the alarm. Suddenly it cut off, the strident noise replaced by dozens of people yelling. A tall, muscular man tried to make himself heard, waving his arms. "Back in your homes," he yelled, but no one was listening. Every second saw more people arriving, kids in tow, some carrying babies, all converging on the square. This was a far bigger settlement than Spider had imagined, although judging from the circumference and height of the fence she should have guessed. Rows of small cabins, sheds, and outbuildings, large areas devoted to plantings. It sprawled over an area as large as their high school campus. As they approached the big round building, a group of men in khaki military garb muscled their way through the crowd. "What's going on?" D said, trying to see over the heads of the crowd. Spider stood on tiptoe, making the most of her two inches on D. "They've got a girl. One man is carrying her. She's hurt, passed out, I think."

She felt the pinch of D's nails as she grasped her elbow. "Is it Min?"

"No, I don't recognize her. She's dressed all in black like Ariel. Dark-haired, small, but not Min."

The crowd parted a little and they got a clearer view.

"Ruth," Hannah said, pushing past them. "It's Ruth." She ran over to the man, laid her hand briefly on Ruth's face, and then helped to support her limp form.

"Hannah, where are your sisters?" a deep voice barked. Diana jolted to attention. "Big Daddy," she said.

With a surge of panic, Spider recognized the speaker who'd just exited the meeting hall. Compact, broadly built, it was Art, the man from the gas station. He was wearing a camouflage shirt and pants, and black boots, same as the rest of them. D inhaled sharply beside her. Ariel was in front of them suddenly, ineffectually shielding them with her slight body, eyes round with alarm. "Get back in the shadows before he spots you!"

Diana was next to him now, speaking in his ear. Was she ratting them out? She pointed to the gates, her voice raised in excitement, the words tumbling out. They caught snatches of her warning: "Guy's got guns and men. Coming here at sunrise. Got to be ready."

"Out of sight. Now," Ariel hissed.

Spider moved back immediately, letting the crowd close around her, but D was rooted in place. Spider grabbed hold of her sleeve and yanked her backward into the shadows thrown by the pitched roof of a shed. "I see Min," D cried, her voice almost swallowed by the crowd's excited chatter. Spider craned her head around Ariel, catching a glimpse of bright blue-dyed hair. Min and another girl, both wearing dirty white shifts, were being dragged away from the fence by two gun-wielding men. As they watched, Min stumbled and almost fell. She seemed woozy. A second man ran up and supported her on the other side. Her body slumped between them.

"What have they done to her?" Spider said.

"Oh shit, oh shit," D breathed in her ear. "What are we going to do?"

Ariel was next to them again, her eyes darting in every direction. Her hand squeezed Spider's arm.

"Here, get behind this stuff," she said, hauling and pushing first Spider and then D toward a small hut. Grain barrels, some hay bales, and chicken-wire crates were tumbled next to its walls. Ariel kicked aside a couple of boxes and shoved Spider into the muddy space. D was pushed to her knees next to her, and then Ariel was piling the crates around them both.

"Stay down," she said. "Wait for me. I'll bring her to you."
She ran back to where Min was.

"She's here. She's here," D said. "I almost can't believe it."

D's jeans had torn on something. Her knees were grazed and bloody. Spider popped her head up, peering through the chicken wire at the crowd. D sneezed multiple times into her hand. "Tell me what you can see," she said.

"Bunch of people milling around. Lost sight of Min . . ."

Someone shot a gun in the air. It was shockingly loud and the noise ceased instantly.

"Go back to your homes now, comfort your children," Big Daddy shouted.

Slowly the crowd began to disperse, hurried along by the Uncles.

"Oh my god! Where's Min?" D asked.

"Those men are taking her to that round building." Spider raised herself up and then ducked back down. "Big Daddy . . . Art . . . has her." She clenched her fingers, trying to put on a comforting face for D, who was rocking a little in place. She shifted a couple of crates to give herself a narrow field of vision. "Diana and Ariel are sticking close. They won't let anything happen to her."

Art had leaned in to speak to Min. He tilted her face upward, his fingers spanning her jaw. She tried to turn away but he held her tight. Her wrists were bandaged and Spider felt her anger rise. Art switched his attention to the other girl who drooped between two Uncles, long, stringy hair draping her face.

A volley of shots came from the fence. A man came running up. "ATVs in the woods!" he yelled. "They're firing at us."

Spider hunched down but kept her eye pressed to her spy hole. It was hard to see much.

"Ariel, take these two back to the cells," Big Daddy shouted, "and then rejoin us. I need all my soldiers. Diana, come with me. And the rest of you spread out around the gates."

They ran off.

Suddenly Ariel was leaning over their hiding place, kicking crates away. "Get a move on," she said. Min was with her, swaying and blinking with exhaustion. A shallow wound near her ear streaked her neck with blood.

"Min!" said D, struggling to her feet. Spider followed her, pulling Min into a hug, and then all three of them were clinging to each other.

"There's no time for this," Ariel hissed. "We need to find a better place to hide you." She pointed down a narrow alley between two buildings. "Get down there and then wait for me," she said, pushing them in front of her. Min staggered, almost fell, and Spider half-dragged, half-carried her to the alcove of a doorway. Ariel raced back the way they'd come.

"What the hell is she doing?" Spider said. Ariel was struggling with the other girl, yanking her forward by her arm. Spider had forgotten all about her. The girl struck at Ariel with her fingers clawed, but Ariel was too strong for her. She dragged her inexorably forward and now they could hear their raised voices.

"No!" she said.

"Don't be stupid, Ghost," Ariel snapped.

The girl still held back.

"I'm not going back to the cells," she said clearly, fighting to free herself. "Let me go. Let me just disappear."

That voice.

"Goddammit," Ariel swore. "I'm not taking you back there. You have to trust me."

She grabbed the girl's arm, twisting it behind her back, and frog-marched her toward the others.

The hairs stood up on Spider's body. She turned disbelieving eyes toward D and watched as all the color drained from her face. D folded, dropping to her knees, and Spider blindly thrust out her hand to steady her, struggling to hold Min up at the same time. Her blood surged, pounding in her eardrums, wave after wave. Hot and cold shivers radiated throughout the length of her body. That voice.

Min's face bobbed in front of her, the tears tracking down her face. Her mouth was open, saying words, but all Spider could hear was that precious voice and the blood crashing in her head.

And then D had dashed forward, yelling "Kat, Kat!"

And their two bodies melted together, dark heads pressed so tight it was impossible to tell where one began and the other ended, and Spider felt as if her heart was swelling, too full, too full. It was pain like she'd never felt. It was joy, pure and incandescent, and it hurt so bad she thought she might die from it.

Min's blood-streaked face swam up in front of her eyes again and her mouth was still opening and closing, and then, like a volume switch suddenly turned up high, Spider heard her, "Please Spider, help me, we have to get to safety," and felt her hand on her sleeve pulling at her. There were other much louder sounds, the rapid fire of many guns and the roar of vehicles, and people shouting and screaming, but all Spider could focus on for the moment was Min's pale heart-shaped face. Somehow D and Kat—*Kat!*—and Ariel were in front of her running, and she let Min clasp her hand and together they hobbled forward. There was a tremendous crashing sound. The shriek of metal and the snapping of lumber.

"They're trying to smash through the gate," Ariel yelled over her shoulder. She dodged around a low rectangular building. Stopped short, and ran back. The structure was built on a raised foundation. There was a crawl space underneath it, maybe two feet above the ground, walled in with a combination of sheets of plain plywood and lattice board. Using her knife, she jimmied a panel loose. "Get under there. Quick, quick," as she grabbed them one after the other and basically hurled them through the narrow opening.

They scuttled in, crunching through dead leaves and brushing past thick cobwebs.

"Take this." Ariel tossed a flashlight to D.

"Aren't you coming?" D asked. Ariel shook her head and let the panel swing into place. "I'll be back. With Aaron." She put a finger to her lips. "Quiet as mice now."

Spider's head was still spinning. The only thing anchoring her to the earth was Min's cold hand, tight around her fingers. A thousand questions were lodged just behind her tongue but she couldn't formulate the words.

D was crying softly. Or perhaps it was Kat. They sounded the same, though Kat had never been a crier. Instead, she had raged and broken things.

Min had curled up into a ball. Spider rubbed her back in small circles. "What's wrong?" she whispered, but Min said nothing. "Did you fall?" she asked, thinking of the head wound.

Min made a small whimper of pain, and moved closer, pressing her face against Spider's shoulder.

They huddled in the gloom, panting in ragged gasps, peering through the lattice. Spider remembered the hot summer days when they all used to play under her porch, spying on the neighborhood kids, having dusty picnics of sherbet sticks, soda, and pilfered peanut butter cookies.

Time stopped.

She was afraid to move in case it shattered this fragile moment. Kat, herself, occupying the same space, breathing the same air. It was something she'd thought would never happen again.

"Is it true? Is this real?" she whispered.

Min pressed her hand. And then D said *yes*. And Kat said *yes* one millisecond later. Spider exhaled. For now it had to be enough. Spider couldn't let herself get any more open. If she did, she was afraid she'd split at the seams and it would all come pouring out. Everything she'd spent the last two years denying. The stone laid on her heart would lift.

THIRTY-EIGHT

- Ariel -

I RACE TO CATCH UP WITH DIANA and the others. Hannah has returned from the sick shed, her gun cleaned. We squat down, guns on our knees. We check our rifles quickly, count out and share extra bullets. I can't quite catch my breath. This feels different. All that talk about preparing us for war? I don't feel prepared at all.

Until this is under control, I won't be able to get Aaron out of here safely. I'm antsy and worried.

There's a lull. It feels as if time has ground to a halt and it unnerves me. I inspect my hands. They're shaking. I sit on them and try to calm my nerves. Guy has something up his sleeve. What could it be? Maybe he's got some men sneaking around the back fence? What's he gonna do? Knock until we let him in?

"Ruth?" I ask Hannah, trying to ignore Diana huffing and puffing right next to my ear.

"She came to pretty quick after we got her on the bed. Has some burns on her hands and elbows but Nana Esme bandaged her up. She's resting now."

"What do you think she was doing?" Diana says. "Up there with those two?"

"Maybe she was trying to stop them escaping?" I say. Now that we're back home, Diana is in full soldier mode. She'll report straight to Big Daddy. I decide to keep my own counsel for a while. "And how about Aaron?" I ask, avoiding Diana's judgmental expression.

"Faith's caring for him." Hannah ducks her eyes. "Nana says he's been burning up all night. Nothing is bringing the fever down. He's stopped taking any liquids." Dread like a cold knot of metal seizes my heart.

And then the gunshots start up again. They must have tons of ammo because they're spraying it all over the place. Uncles Clive and Ronald are hunkered down on the towers returning fire. One, maybe two shots for every ten Guy's boys direct at them. That's the difference between a rifle and a semiautomatic. My gun seems like little more than a pea-shooter now.

Ronald silently signals to Big Daddy, moving his hand from the right to the left. I know what it means—he's low on ammo.

We fall back.

"You four, get down to the arsenal and bring us all the rounds you can carry, and the assault rifles," Big Daddy says, pointing at me, Diana, Randall, and Monroe. Uncle Monroe is one of Nana Esme's brothers. He lives way up the mountain usually. He smells like someone who treats water like a stranger; his army-green surplus clothing is so filthy it could stand up by itself, and his black dirt-clumped hair is longer than mine. I try to keep upwind of him. Big Daddy tosses Randall the key.

We hunch-run our way to the supply shed and race down the stairs.

"Should we check on the prisoners while we're down here?" Diana asks. She's all suited up for combat. Camouflage pants and jacket over her black hoodie.

For a moment, I don't know who she's talking about, and then I remember she thinks I locked Min and Kat in the cells.

"No time for that," Randall says, fortunately.

He unlocks the padlock, pulls the heavy chain free. Laying down our rifles, we head for the back wall, past the tall, stacked shelves of canned food and barrels of potatoes and apples. Plasterboard paneling covers the wooden struts and we hack at it with our knives and then pull great chunks of it away to reveal the boxes of ammunition and the gleaming black pistols and semiautomatic rifles that are hidden there. Randall and Monroe pick through them, making piles of boxed bullets that go with the correct weapons. Nearby in an open crate are a bunch of bulletproof vests.

I raise my eyebrow at Diana and slip one on over my hoodie. It's bulky but not weighty. I thrust one into her hands and she puts it on. Can we carry a couple more for Faith and Hannah? I slip on another, wearing it back to front. I feel like I'm cocooned; I can barely move my arms.

"You're as fat as a cow," Diana says with a sneer.

I think about shutting her down, reclaiming my authority, wiping that smirk off her face.

She spies a couple of handguns and raises an eyebrow. We could slip them into our waistbands but I'm worried about not being able to run if I'm too weighted down.

Monroe barks at us to line up and the opportunity is gone.

Randall loads me and Diana up with the heavy boxes of clips, piling them to our chins. He and Monroe grab three or four guns each, load a couple of handguns, and strap the rest across their backs.

From above our heads we hear a thunderous smashing sound. Then wheels spinning and an engine revving, followed by another crash. A volley of shots rings out, more hollering and hooting.

Diana and I look at the ceiling, half-expecting to see cracks appear. It's hard to move fast when I can hardly see above the tower of boxes, but desperation gives me a boost.

"Move, move, move," Monroe yells, snapping at our heels. We stop at the bottom of the stairwell while Randall scopes out the area ahead.

"You got this?" I ask Diana, putting my boxes down for a second. I check my gun, make sure a bullet is chambered and the safety is off. It's an automatic gesture but how can I shoot when my hands are encumbered? My heart is beating a million miles a minute and I'm so jacked full of adrenaline I feel sick.

"I'm pumped."

Her cheeks are red and her eyes are glistening.

"This is what we've been waiting for. What we trained for."

It's different though. It's real. Real bullets, real guns. Those aren't targets we're aiming for. "They're not outsiders," I say.

She's looking at me like I'm nuts, and I know I'm looking at her the same way. "He betrayed us," Diana says.

I stare at her steadily.

"What happened to you?" she asks.

I shrug. And something clicks off in her eyes. I have no trouble reading her expression. She's thinking, *Weak. This here is weakness.* But I let her have it because it means so much to her.

If I'm honest, I know what happened. That kind boy in the sick bay happened. And those girls and the love they have for each other. Did we ever have that? Me and her? The other soldiers? Are we really sisters? Or are we all crabs in a bucket, willing to climb all over each other to get to the top, all jostling for Big Daddy's favor? They love their homes like we do, but did they ever have to fight to protect theirs? Or is that where their safety lies? Home. Family. Those should be good, true things.

Randall appears at the top of the stairs and gives the clear signal. Monroe pumps his fist twice and I load up, then we climb as fast as we can. Once up top, we race through the supply shed and burst into the night air right behind him and Randall. Right into a gun fight.

The Uncles zig and zag and I'm trying to stay behind them and keep up. My hands are sweating and my forearms scream with the pain of holding all those heavy boxes but I've got the bullets and they've got the guns and one without the other is no good at all. I hold my head down and I make sure that Randall's wide back is in front of me. From what I can tell, the gunfire is coming from in front, so at least I'm not gonna catch a bullet to the back of my head.

Randall ducks down behind a small building made out of cinder blocks. I hit the ground with an *oof* as the air is knocked out of my body—no graceful way to do it with the vests bulking me up, but at least I keep hold of the boxes enough that they don't spill open. I flatten myself up against the wall. Should be better protection than the wooden huts but I wrinkle my nose at the stench coming from it. It's an outhouse and it smells even worse than Uncle Monroe. Diana hurls herself down beside me and now for the first time I can scan around and suss out the situation. I can't see Big Daddy. He's moved from his position near the hall but I can see where shots are being returned from. Looks like the Uncles are spread out covering the gates, which are smashed and hang from their hinges.

The van, doors open, riddled with bullet holes, just sits there like a black toad. Not sure where the tweakers have gotten to and that's making me even more jumpy. My eyes dart to every shadowed recess, to the trees, back to the gate. Sharp bursts of light coming from the woods tell me where they are. They are everywhere.

Monroe and Randall load the guns. Two figures in camouflage wriggle up behind us. I take my finger off the trigger when I recognize them.

"Can't believe Guy had the brains or the guts to attempt something like this," Uncle Ronald says.

"He made a deal with those fiends," Big Daddy says, reloading. "Knew he wasn't to be trusted. This evens things out a bit." He sends Randall and Monroe out to distribute more guns and ammo. Tells Ronald to cut around by the supply building. He slides a pistol into a holster on his hip.

We kneel near him. He's directing the Uncles silently with the complicated hand gestures they've worked out. They lurk in dark pockets alongside the huts and sheds between the hall and the gates. There's a couple of shooters on the nearby roofs, Uncles lying flat on their bellies, concealed, but I catch the gleam on their gun barrels. They've cut the juice to the generator, leaving a lot of the compound in shadow, which gives us an advantage over Guy's tweaker friends who don't know the layout here.

Big Daddy crouches low. He gives us a quick smile. "Hold position. You know what to do," he says, and then he's gone, melting into the gloom.

I count heads quickly, guessing who's been called down from the mountain. Give or take a couple, there's maybe twenty, including us soldiers. Ruth is out for the count though, Faith is in sick bay, and I haven't seen Hannah for a while now. If I remember correctly, Guy's crew looked to be about ten or twelve strong. And they've got more of the big guns. I should try to get to Hannah, give her the spare vest.

"What the hell are they playing at?" Diana frets. She's checked and rechecked her gun a bunch of times. "They blow the gate, then what? Lay low?"

I peek around to the gate.

I can hear the ATVs idling just beyond the fence. I try to strategize, figure out what Guy is going to do next. We're wide open now; cracked in the middle like a crayfish, soft belly exposed. I hope those girls have the sense to stay put.

Then a bunch of things happen all at the same time. The ATVs rev and charge forward, streaming through the opening with their guns blazing. I see Monroe stand up, run. A gun blasts and he goes down in a sprawl of limbs. Something explodes in a shower of glass and flames against the roof of the neighboring building. Monroe is up again, limping as he ducks for cover. Pretty sure his kneecap is shattered.

"Molotov cocktail," Diana says. "Meth lab chemicals." Another smashes to the ground. And then another ignites the roof of a hut. Bob and Norbert take out the driver of one of the ATVs, which crashes into the fence, and in turn are gunned down. Norbert falls not ten feet away. His brown eyes are half-open, a trickle of blood worming into his thick black beard. Where'd he get shot? I don't know but he sure seems dead. Like that bear. It could have been me so easily. This all comes down to a matter of inches.

He's providing cover. I flatten myself against the sandy soil and try to look in every direction at once.

I haven't taken a shot yet. I can't seem to unfreeze my finger. I track bodies, prepared to squeeze one off, but something stops me every time. I can't replace the faces with the targets I'm used to shooting at.

I recognize the different sounds the bullets make on impact. The hollow thunk when they hit wood, the soft smushed sound as they explode in the dirt, and the punch like walloping a pillow when they strike a body. That sound, both dense and soft at the same time, finished with a shriek of pain or dead silence, makes me pant with fear.

Next to me, Diana is on her belly too. Each time she fires, it jerks her body back. Through it all, she's got this wild smile on her face. She tracks her gun right and says, "Dammit, can't get a clear shot." I follow her gaze.

Guy stands on the roof of the van as if he's invincible. He holds his semiautomatic at his hip like he's some kind of cowboy, shoots off short bursts that spray up the dirt clods. In between rounds he taunts Big Daddy, like he's playing. "Come out, old man. We can end this right now. On the battlefield. What are you always saying? A toothless dog's no good for anything?"

Behind the glow of the fire, I can see the deeper reds and pinks of sunrise. Two ATVs peel off, careening around the edge of the compound. Men hanging from the sides and off the back blast their guns and throw more of the fire bombs. People are leaving their homes, running, screaming. A woman with two children pressed to her chest runs right through my line of sight. I move my finger away from the trigger. I could have shot her so easily. I force myself to fire. It goes nowhere. I just want to put my head down. My stomach is churning and there's a foul taste in my mouth.

"Isn't this the best?!" Diana yells. She stares at me and then shoves her gun in my direction. "Reload mine and hand yours over if you're just going to lie there." The scorn in her voice stings my cheeks but I tell myself I don't care.

I load, reload, try to see through the grit clogging my eyes. It feels like hours have passed but it's only been minutes.

"You two, get everyone out. Bring them to the hall," Big Daddy yells. And to the Uncles, "Fall back. Get ready." We crane our necks to see. They're taking to the roofs. Clambering up on top of any flat platform, laying down the first line of defense.

Diana nods to me and takes off.

For the next half hour, I'm focused on two things: dodging bullets, and helping the families get to safety. The dog pen is hit with a flaming bottle and goes up like a torch. Nicky barely gets out alive. He freaks out, kicking and head butting me until I am able to pin his arms, hold him close long enough that he recognizes my voice. The dogs—Biter and her pups, Tooth and Claw—run wild, sinking their teeth into anyone they can find.

Once Nicky calms down, the dogs follow him into the hall. I've lost contact with Diana. The air is full of heat and ash.

I lean against a wall, choking, trying to get my breath back. My hands are too weary to hold my gun. I can't see more than five feet in front of me.

Big Daddy appears, wreathed in smoke like the fog on the Grey Sisters. Not for the first time, I think he is made from the same stuff—hard granite. That he will outlast and outlive everything.

His eyebrows bunch. "Are you alone?" His gun is held ready. I make myself pick mine up and try to control the quiver in my fingers.

"Diana and I split up so we could get people to safety," I tell him.

"You should have your sister's back."

"She . . ." I can't tell him how she ran off whooping with excitement. How I had to reload her gun a dozen times. How she killed a man. Maybe two. Not because he will be angry but because he will be pleased and he will know that I am lacking in fortitude.

His eyes bore into me. I straighten my back. "She is nearby."

"This is the testing, Ariel," Big Daddy says. "Do not waver."

The enemy is so clear to him. Not so to me. Not now. It is all muddled in my head and it makes my bones heavy and my muscles tired.

Guy, those men. Are they the enemy we've been waiting for all this time? A threat from within? This is not the glorious war of my imagining. This is not what Big Daddy promised to us.

"Find her. Stand and fight at her side."

He waits for my response. And in that moment I find strength, but not where he would expect me to find it. I think of those outsider girls, the chance to save Aaron, and I answer honestly.

"I am fighting for what I believe in."

THIRTY-NINE

— D —

SMOKE LIES THICK ON THE GROUND, or maybe it's fog. D
can't tell. Her eyes are stinging and her lungs feel congested. For
a while she tried to follow what was happening, but all she can
see are legs, booted feet, ATV wheels spinning. A man, not in
combat gear, was shot, fell just outside their hiding place. She
can see his face. His eyes are open but he's not blinking. Someone out of sight drags him slowly away. She's transfixed by his
cheek scraping against the rough gravel, his eyes still open.

She hides her face in her hands but it doesn't help much.

There's a terrible smell. Like bleach mixed with rotten eggs.
It reminds her of the meth trailer. Through the diamond-shaped
opening in the slats, a building burns like a torch. What if their
hut catches fire and collapses around them?

It feels like the end of the world but they have no choice. Out
there is chaos and gunfire. At least in here they are hidden.

Kat lies next to her, shivering. Min on the other side pressed
up tight. She's no longer moaning, and when D briefly shone
the flashlight on her wound, it seemed to have stopped bleeding. D has her arms around both of them. Spider is the farthest
away. She hasn't said anything for a long while.

"Spider," she calls.

After a silence so thick she can sense it, she hears, "I'm fine. I'm good. I'm okay." She doesn't sound like she's any of those things. She's unrecognizable. The Spider D knows is strong in herself, stubborn beyond belief; this one is in pieces.

She's relieved when Min crawls over, wrapping Spider in her embrace.

D moves even closer to Kat and tries to warm her.

It's dark in the crawl space but beyond, lights are flaring and D can see Kat's ashen face. She presses the length of her body against her sister. Cradles her head against her shoulder, strokes her hair, feeling how matted it is. She's scared but the dark, smothering wings in her head have vanished. Her heartbeat is fast but strong. And there's a new feeling, stronger than any other.

D realizes it is happiness. Even in the midst of this, she is so happy. Because they are together again, whatever happens next.

Feet are pounding closer. Something heavy hits with an impact that shakes the hut's walls.

Screaming. A woman. Just screaming and screaming and then abruptly the sound cuts off.

"Oh my god. They killed her," Min says.

An explosive hits the ground, sprays up rocks and grit. D can taste sand in her mouth. A volley of shots impacts the wood near where they cower. Spider yelps.

"Spider!"

D flicks on the flashlight again. A coil of dread tightens her ribcage.

"Are you hit?"

"I'm bleeding, I think. My face." Spider touches her cheek. Examines her fingertips.

D strives to keep the light on her. There's a red line across Spider's cheek as if someone painted it with a small brush. "It just grazed you," she says, feeling a burst of relief.

"They missed me," says Spider. There is a note of triumph in her voice.

"Someone is coming," Min says suddenly, gazing beyond the lattice. "There's a light behind you."

D flicks the flashlight off but it's too late.

A high-powered beam blazes, sweeping across their hiding place. A man hollers. The girls grind themselves down into the dirt. Inch backward until they're all the way against the back wall.

The beam is aimed in their direction. A large figure looms, casting a shadow over them. Then a screech as wood is jimmied loose. A man's face appears. Dirty, blood-streaked. His head is shaved smooth and an eagle tattoo spreads its wings across his neck.

D recognizes the smoking man from the trailer.

"Well, let's see what we have here," he says, smiling broadly. "Out you come." He rips the last of the wood away and crawls in, grabbing for D's feet.

She kicks at him, hollering, and feels Kat's hands on her arms holding on, but he's dragging her and her head hits the ground with a force hard enough to rattle her brains. Min is grabbing at her too and Spider is pummeling the man but he is so strong. D gives one last desperate kick, but she's out from under the building now. And his hands are reaching for her neck, and he's squatting over her, and even though Min is out and battering at him with clenched fists, he backhands her, sending her flying. His weight settles more solidly on top of her, crushing her lungs, and she can't breathe. She can't breathe, until suddenly he cries out and falls forward, crushing her under him, but she can breathe again. Min and Kat pull him off. He's still conscious but dazed. His lips curl. And he makes a wild grab at Kat. Spider holds the chunk of brick up and hits him across the head again. There is a ferocity in her eyes and D thinks she will keep hitting him but Kat throws her arms around Spider. "Spider, enough," she says, and they both sink to the ground shaking and crying. And the man just lies there with blood puddling around his head.

"There could be others," D says, drawing them back underneath. They pile up broken pieces of lattice to block the hole and cluster together at the far end, a heap of bricks near at hand.

FORTY

– Ariel –

I'VE LEFT THE DOORS AJAR in the huts I've evacuated, working in an ever-expanding circle from the middle out. I glance around; most of them seem to be open. Diana is still nowhere to be found. I feel a surge of anger toward her and pause to catch my breath. Under the two vests, I'm sweating. I can feel the wetness pooling around my waistband. The sick bay is across the compound at the far western side. I count my remaining bullets. I've still only fired one. Double-checking my periphery, I run for it, doubled over, tracking left and right.

I'm praying Faith is still inside. And Ruth. There's no way I can move Aaron to safety without their help.

I bolt through the door, breathing hard, clutching my ribs where a cramp seizes my muscles, and find myself looking down the barrel of a gun. Nana Esme is sitting in a rocking chair facing the door. Slowly, she lowers the rifle. "Girl, it's a wonder you're still alive, barging in here like that, looking all crazed."

"Big Daddy is moving everyone into the hall. I came to get you."

She sits back, starts rocking, jerks her head toward the bedroom. "Can't move Sally. She's too near her time."

"Guy's people have fire bombs. Some of the huts caught on fire."

"One thing I have enough of is water." She nods to the buckets lined up against the wall, the pot boiling on the stove. "Someone other comes through that door, I'll shoot them dead."

Faith emerges from the room, white-faced, black circles under her eyes, exhausted. Her sleeves are rolled up. "Maybe an hour yet," she tells Nana, then catches sight of me.

"And Aaron?" My breath rasps, my throat is bone dry. "Can we move him?"

Faith hesitates, looks to Esme.

Please please please. I'm desperate to hear but terrified in case the wrong words come out of Faith's mouth.

"She packed the wound with comfrey and plantain, gave him birch leaf for the pain and elderflower for the fever. Did better than I could have done," Nana Esme says, studying Faith with rare approval. It softens the hard lines of her face.

"Fever broke a couple of hours ago," Faith says. "He's weak as a baby chick, but he sat up, used the commode, even took some broth."

My legs feel trembly. I try to suppress the sob, choke on it, reach out blindly with my hand, and Faith is there, closing her fingers around mine. "Thank you," I whisper.

"He needs proper treatment," Nana says. "We can't give it to him here."

I stare at her. Is she giving me permission? She holds my eyes, nods.

"I've got a car. In the woods. Can you help me get him to it?" I ask Faith. "With some others? Where's Ruth?"

"She got up. Insisted on going back out there even though she's all dizzy still."

"You go, Faith," says Nana. "Pack some bandages, take that blanket there."

I hurry into the room. Aaron's lying on his back with his eyes closed, but when he hears me, he opens them. They are so big in his gaunt face, the lines of pain clearly etched across his brow, but they crinkle at the edges as he smiles at me. "Are we winning?" he asks. The tape binding his cheek doesn't quite conceal the ugly stitching. The edges of the wounds are red but they appear dry.

"We're holding our own," I tell him, unable to stop the grin spreading across my face. It's so big it hurts. "I'm taking you for a ride."

He grimaces and sits up. His torso is wrapped in clean gauze, his shirt unbuttoned and open around it. I help him into one of the bulletproof vests, trying not to press too hard on the wound. Still, he whitens and his teeth bite through his lip. I wipe the blood from his mouth with the tail of my shirt, linger with my hand there, feeling his cool skin.

"Where we going?"

"Big city."

I slip my arm under his, take as much of his weight as I can as he slides his legs around to the edge of the bed.

I find his boots and slip them on. There are black stains on them. I know it's his blood. And I flash back to it soaking the makeshift bandages I put on him out in the woods. I didn't think a body could hold so much. But here he is, awake, still himself shining out from those golden eyes.

"Ready?" I ask, easing my arm around his waist.

He stands, breathes in deeply, adjusts his feet, and finds his balance. We walk, oh so slow, but we walk together.

Faith has found a thick cane, cut from a piece of wood with a heavy burl fashioned into a handle.

She gives it to Aaron, and a little of the pressure on me subsides as he leans on it. I would carry him if I could. I strip off the other vest and make her put it on. "What about you?" she asks.

"Haven't taken a bullet yet. Maybe too skinny to see unless I'm standing square. Where's your gun?" I ask.

"Dunno. I put it down . . ." She grimaces. "Couldn't shoot it anyway."

"Yeah, me neither." We share a smile that's ashamed and understanding both.

Nana Esme has disappeared into the other room. I can hear panting, moans, her voice low and reassuring. Outside, the gunfire is sporadic, intermingled with the sound of glass smashing and a lot of hollering.

"I checked it out. Guy's people have the front of the hall covered. Big Daddy and everyone must be holed up in there. A bunch of the huts are burning," Faith says. "But it hasn't spread." *Yet.* I hear the unspoken word. I know she's torn. I am too.

"They can make a break out the back and barricade themselves in the basement if they have to," I remind her. "There's enough food and water there for everyone for weeks."

At the door, she peeks out, and then motions for us to join her.

"See anyone?"

"No," she says. Still, we keep close to the walls and move

as quickly as Aaron can manage. Faith carries a backpack and my gun.

A shot rings out, close enough to make my ears hum. Where did it come from? Faith drops the bag, raises the gun. Her hands are shaking so bad I'm afraid she might shoot us by accident. Another shot and she jumps back. We're in an alley between two shacks. I can't tell where the shooter is. Straight ahead is one of the outhouses. The walls are solid concrete blocks. If we can make it there, it's just a short run to the gates. From here I can see the van, and a couple of ATVs.

"Can you make it?" I ask Aaron. He presses his lips together. "As fast as we can." I catch Faith's eye, point. We move from the shelter of the hut. Shots pepper the ground around us. I stumble, barely catching myself, and Aaron falls with me. He cries out, clutching his ribs, and I pull him up. Have to keep moving. Faith is on his other side, bracing him, and we half-carry him, half-drag him. Where's the shooter? I can smell the acrid tang of burnt powder. He must be close by. I whip my head around searching for the flash but see nothing.

We keep moving. A bullet sinks into the wall of the build-ing beside me, and my arm is stung by wood splinters. Across Aaron's slumping body, I see Faith's scared expression. We're on a section of open ground. Nervous energy is pumping through my veins but my legs feel leaden. More shots. Is he on the fence? A roof? I can't stop to pinpoint him.

Suddenly a figure is in front of us. With relief, I recognize Diana. She grabs my arm, squeezing with a bruising force.

"Where were you?" she says, her face darkening. "You should be laying down covering fire. Not playing nursemaid."

"Diana! Who are we fighting? What is right?"

"Jesus, Ariel. What kind of soldier are you?" she snaps. "Follow your orders."

I wrench my arm away. She staggers. And at first I think it's because of my roughness, but she slumps, falls straight back, and that's when I see the round hole in her forehead. No blood. Just a perfect black hole and an expression of intense surprise on her face before the spark of her fades. Diana! God knows when the last time I ate was but the vinegary contents of my stomach rise up as I fall to my knees.

No kind of soldier. I'm no kind of soldier.

My head is buzzing. I've gone partially deaf from shock. There's more shots—but the bullets hitting sound like popcorn popping, and men yelling—more of them than there were before, but I can't figure that out right now—and I can't hear Faith or Aaron at all although they're both kneeling in front of me yelling and clawing at my arms. Just *pop pop pop* and a whirring in my ears, and way off, the familiar but unfamiliar sound of sirens. Dust billows up, wind catches at my clothes, a light brighter than the sun, the letters P O L I C E painted on the underside of it. I'm blinded, tasting grit in my mouth. Aaron's mouth makes words. My brain finally catches on. *Police. Helicopter.* Something explodes nearby, a cloud of white smoke, and now my eyes are tearing up, stinging, doubling my vision. And then Aaron and Faith are ripped away from me as something solid hurls me face down and I feel a crushing weight against the small of my back.

FORTY-ONE

— *Min* —

THE GUNFIRE AND SCREAMS and explosions blend together in Min's aching head. A cacophony that makes her want to break and run. She has to will her body to stay still. She has to believe that it'll be over soon.

"I think I killed him," Spider says. She hugs her knees. She's been shaking for half an hour. Her face is a mask of anguish. Min wants to tell her about Jonathan but she's afraid it will break her. What words should she use?

"He tried to hurt us," D says. "There was no choice."

"He was still bleeding," Min says. "I checked. A few minutes ago."

D glances at her questioningly.

"If he were dead, it would have stopped by now."

"We're being stupid. There's more like him. We need to get out of here. We can go through that hole in the fence. Escape through the woods," says Spider. "Just run." She looks pleadingly at Kat. "You can run, can't you?"

"Ariel said she'd come back for us," D says. "We have to trust her."

"Why wait for her? Kat is with us now. We should just go, escape out the back."

Min's stomach drops. "We can't leave yet," she says. And she hears Kat make a choking sound. Kat knows what Min is about to say.

"Why not?" says Spider.

Min places her fingers on Spider's arm. The muscles underneath jump. Spider looks from Min's hand to her eyes, and her breath catches in her throat. "What is it?"

And Min can't bring herself to speak the words.

"Aaron is Jonathan," Kat says. "He's here and he's injured. Ariel went to rescue him."

"Jonathan?" Spider shakes her head violently. She brushes Min's hand away. Her voice cracks, rises in pitch. "I have to find him." She crawls to the hole, scrambles out. They all pile after her and come to a sudden halt.

"The compound is burning," Kat says. The guard towers and a large section of the fence are on fire. Huts glow red, lit from within. Black smoke plumes the air.

D's hand bites into Min's arm. "So is the forest." Trees burst into flame like the tails of rockets.

"Where is he?" Spider yells, seemingly unaware of the chunks of flaming wood falling around them. "Take me there." Min grabs hold of her, trying to get her back under shelter, but she won't move.

Everything seems to erupt at once. Clods of dirt hit the sides of the building, sting their faces with gravel. A wind churns up, scattering grit and embers. "Get down, get down," Min screams. "They're shooting at us." Kat drops, D alongside, covering her sister's body with her own. Then Spider hits the ground next to her, wailing and cursing. A *pop-pop-pop* sound fills the air and Min sees a black canister roll toward her.

There are many of them, spraying acrid black fumes like ink. And then the air is filled with a smothering smoke that clouds her vision and snarls her lungs. Just before she is blinded, she sees the helicopters land, and an army of men and women in blue uniforms spill through the gate.

FORTY-TWO

– Ariel –

DIANA USED TO TAKE CARE of the baby chicks when they hatched. Hers was the first face they'd see, and afterward, they'd follow her around cheeping, clustering around her ankles like fluffy slippers as she walked. They ignored their own mother hen and adopted Diana as theirs. She named them. She wasn't supposed to, because they were meat-to-be, but she couldn't help herself. Although they all looked the same to me, she could tell the difference. "See here, this one is speckledy, so that's Freckles. And this one here feels like a seed puff—Dandelion. And this one is Minnie because she's so small."

A fox ate those chicks, all but Minnie. And then a week later, one of the Uncles stepped on it and crushed it to yellow pulp. Diana cried and cried. And then I never saw her cry again. Not even when she burned herself on the boiling kettle so bad it made giant blisters like half-inflated plastic bags all up and down her arm, or broke her ankle on the mountain. You could see the bone sticking up out of the skin.

They wrap her in a sheet and put her in an ambulance. They don't turn the siren on, so we know for sure that she's dead. Me and Faith are handcuffed and shoved in the back of a cop car. The doors lock and there's no way to open them from the inside. I kick with all the strength in my legs but they won't move. They took Aaron away already. The ambulance wailing down the hill. Sally too. We press our faces against the window trying to see. I spy Uncle Monroe and Uncle Bob kneeling on the ground with their hands behind their heads. The left side of Bob's face is a mask of gore. I see Guy shot in the legs as he tries to run and then wrestled down to the ground by five men in flak jackets. I see Uncle Clive's yellow head, legs and arms flung out like he tripped or is fooling, but he's not moving. And I see Big Daddy, his hands held out, palms up as if he's about to deliver a speech, and I see the police surround him, angry voices, warning him, a red light hovering over his heart, rifles poised until finally he unslings his gun and tosses it aside, and then topples and falls. It's like seeing a mighty tree come down in a storm. They send a big armored van for the men. And guards with guns ride in back with them.

At the hospital, our handcuffs are removed. There's a lady with a soft voice who asks questions we can't answer. Age? Not sure. Illness? I know the names of the plants that cured us but never knew the sicknesses. Family history?

We are Pembrokes, Faith says. But even she doesn't sound so sure. In my head, I replace it with *We are grey sisters*.

A few days later, they take her someplace else. Because she's too sick. I made the nurse write it down for me: *amebic dysentery*. I can't pronounce it but the nurse told me it means that there are worms in Faith's guts, from drinking bad water. I made her write down the name of the special hospital too, just in case I have to rescue Faith.

I am too skinny but there's nothing wrong with my guts. A stomach like iron. They feed me three times a day. Soft food.

White and brown and green and sometimes pink. At first, I kept something from each meal, wrapped in a napkin, hidden under my pillow, but the nurses found it when they changed the sheets.

I can sleep all the time if I want. Watch TV all day. The nurses tell me to call them Dawn and Jackie and Robert. I was scared of Robert at first. He has big arms and hands and looks like he could wrestle a bull. He brings me extra Jell-O: the raspberry, like soft red crystals that dance on my tongue. He said he would help me write a letter to Jonathan, but the words won't come now that I am away from Avalon. What would I say to him? What would he want to hear from me?

When the lady and the man come to see me, sitting next to my bed, all upright and uncomfortable-looking, they tell me that Faith will be fine after a few weeks of treatment, and that they will make sure I see her again.

She is small with hair the color of flames and he is big and bony with trimmed yellow hair and spectacles that make his eyes bulge out.

They tell me they run a place for kids like us. "When you are well, we will take you home. We will find you a family."

Family. I thought I knew what that was. The common blood that runs through our veins and binds us together. Guy was family and he betrayed us. Nana Esme was family and she cut us loose. She chose Ruth and Hannah to go with her when she escaped. Does that mean that she found me lacking? Diana was family and I loved her and I hated her oftentimes too but mostly I loved her.

I am comforted now but I am stifled too. Where is the want in these people's lives? The bed is too soft. There is clean water, hot and cold from a tap. Light and warmth at the touch of a button. There are gentle voices, and hushed silence, extra blankets, and books with pictures, and a TV right there on the wall and no need to do anything. But heal. That's what they tell me. There is so much care and concern that I am suffocating but still I want more. I am greedy for it and I am scared of it because what if it's taken away from me?

What if this is one of those tricks that Big Daddy used to speak of? The way *they* seduce you with things until you give strength to possessions and are enslaved. Until you are obsessed with needing to acquire more things. When you know the true value of nothing.

I dream about the mountain. My mountain.

They are the lost but we are the found, Big Daddy told us.

I don't know who speaks the truth anymore. I don't know if I am Ariel or just Jenny Pembroke, daughter of Arthur who was brother, father, uncle. Jenny was nothing and no one. Ariel is strong, fierce; she will survive.

FORTY-THREE

— D —

"MAMMA MADE CANNOLI FOR BREAKFAST," D said, handing the plate to Min, who took one and then passed it on to Spider. They sat lined up on the wooden porch steps facing the back garden. The three of them, plus Kat. Every so often D had to reach out, without her sister seeing, and just lightly touch the tip of her finger to Kat's shoulder, as if to reassure herself that she was really here.

"Most delicious thing ever," Min said, crunching through the golden pastry and licking the cream off her fingers.

"How about you?" Spider said to Kat, a tender note in her voice. Kat smiled and shook her head. D had noticed that the shyness went both ways. What had Spider said to her the other day? "I thought she was dead. I was so sure. I got used to loving this dead girl. It was so beautiful and so tragic. And now I don't know what to do."

And what had D said to Spider? "Don't make her wait any longer."

"She's already had three anyway," D said now, pretending she hadn't noticed that Spider had crept her hand toward Kat's and that there was barely a quarter-inch of space between their hips. They leaned into each other like flowers bending toward the sun.

"I only had two, in fact," said Kat. "But I asked her to save me some more for later."

When Mamma saw Kat eating with gusto, she'd had to go back into the kitchen and cry a little. They'd all pretended like they couldn't hear her.

"She's sending some home with you too, Spider. For Jonathan. Thinks he's too skinny."

Spider's expression darkened. "Well, he is. His clothes from two years ago still fit him." D knew that like her own mother, Spider's had kept all of Jonathan's belongings and just closed the bedroom door on the heartache.

"Luckily Maman's got him on a strict couch-plus-gumbo diet." She sighed theatrically, her eyes dancing. "Absolutely no concern about my well-being." Kat snorted out a tiny laugh, and Spider lit up.

The joy in her face was so naked it made D feel almost embarrassed, and she switched her attention to her sister. She'd mastered the skill of keeping an eye on Kat without her sister noticing too often.

Kat had her chin tilted up to the late August sun. Her freckles stood out against the paleness of her skin. She'd asked their mom to cut her hair to a shoulder-length bob, complaining that it was constantly bothering her in physio. Now it curled in tight ringlets, exploding from her scalp. Just barely visible near her left ear was the twisty scar from her head injury. It would fade, along with the new one on her leg, this one made by a surgeon's knife to repair the damage done to her hamstring.

"They used to cut that muscle to cripple people, you know? Prisoners, and criminals," Kat had informed her. "Just my bad luck that a piece of airplane shrapnel happened to hit me right there." The summer maxi dress she wore hung on Kat's gaunt frame, but D could see the brace covering her upper thigh almost to her knee. *My bad luck.* Kat had taken a weird kind of ownership over her ordeal, but D couldn't wait until she heard the words *my good luck* come out of her sister's mouth. So much hurt piled on hurt it was almost unbearable.

Focus on the now, Doctor Octavian told her. Told Kat too, probably, since she was also in therapy. And the now was cannoli and their feet, bare and basking in the sun. Hers so brown; Kat's pasty, scarred. Same long toes, the two next to the big toe branching from one trunk like some weird tree. Min probably knew the scientific term for it. Something Latin.

Their mother had it too, and Nonna, the cousins in Calabria. Family trait, Nonna had said, signifying good strong peasant stock. "Matrilineal," said Mamma. Was there strength in that commonality, D wondered, imagining all the mothers—a line of dark-haired women with weird feet stretching back and back and back. Lately she'd been thinking about genealogy charts, family trees, and arteries and hair and embroidery and blood and love and wondering if there was some way she could put it all together and make art. Maybe she'd start by photographing her sister's feet?

A delivery van pulled up in front of the house. D hopped up to meet it.

"Amandola?" said the brown-uniformed driver. She nodded. He'd butchered their last name but that was typical. Sometimes when their mother signed for a package, she just informed them her name was Smith.

She carried the parcel back to the porch. "It's for you," she told her sister. "Want me to open it?" Kat had been getting some weird mail. Bibles and book deal offers and scholarships to private colleges in Idaho. But also, long letters from people either praising or criticizing her. It was unbelievable how many blamed her for what had happened to her. Mamma burned all of them now without unsealing the envelopes.

This was a large plain padded envelope. D couldn't tell if it was going to be something nasty.

"No, it's addressed to me," Kat said. She turned it over between her fingers, tracing the hand-lettered name. Katerina Amandola. "My full name," she said. "It's from Abbotsford."

D sat down beside her, ready to snatch it away if necessary. Spider and Min leaned in.

Kat tugged on the strip tab and the envelope gaped. It was stuffed with white tissue paper. She bent over it, moved the tissue aside. Try as she could, D wasn't able to see the contents.

"Oh," Kat said, and leaned back for a moment. D searched her face. She sounded happy but sad too. Her sister turned to look at her, eyes brimming with tears as she pulled Floppy Monkey out.

"It's from Annie Wilbur. She sent him back to us."

FORTY-FOUR

-Kat-

IT WAS JONATHAN'S IDEA to visit their graves. Kat didn't tell Mamma or D what her plan for the day was, but Dr. Octavian said things didn't need to make sense to anyone else if it felt right to you. "You are in charge of your life," she said. And it did make sense. Her death had happened, to all intents and purposes. She just wanted to check it out.

She was a little nervous about driving She-Ra. Not because it had been two years since she'd been behind the wheel. She'd started taking lessons as soon as she turned fifteen and a half, and the instructor had told her she was a natural. And she'd borrowed D's license just in case she got pulled over. Total perk of being a twin!

No, it was her left leg that was worrying her the most. She could partially bend the knee now but it was still ungainly and awkward. Just moving it around was hard. She had to kind of fall into the front seat, which she had adjusted as far back as it would go, and then haul her leg into position.

"Okay," she said, wiping the sweat off her forehead. It felt as if she were wedged in like a foot in a too-small shoe.

"Want me to drive?" Jonathan asked. Kat was shocked that he'd noticed her difficulties at all.

"Can you?"

"On paper, yeah." He pushed his glasses up his nose.

"Thanks, but I'm in here now," she said, checking that she remembered where the turn indicators were, the lights, the hazards.

"*Allons-y*," he said, scratching furiously at his cheek. Kat was sure his mother would be having a fit if she could see him. She'd threatened to duct-tape gloves on him like a little kid with heat rash but he wasn't having it. His wounds had healed, although the scarred skin was knotted and very pink compared to the brown of his face. He didn't seem bothered that people stared. Kat, on the other hand, couldn't bear it.

She slipped an oversized pair of sunglasses on and rolled down the window, glancing up at the second floor. The curtain twitched and she knew D was watching, agonizing.

She sighed and backed out slowly. "What do only children do?"

Jonathan grinned at her. "We never have to think about that."

"Is it shitty to want a break from all that caring sometimes?"

"Not today."

Once beyond their neighborhood, she stuck to the small roads, not feeling secure enough to deal with the heavy traffic and loud noises of the highway. The route meandered through quiet neighborhoods, then pastureland, up and over small hills, completely unlike the harsh terrain of Pembroke Cross and the Grey Sisters. She tightened her fingers on the wheel. Her mother and D tried to shield her from the news as much as possible, but enough filtered through. She knew that Big—No!—that Arthur Pembroke was on the twenty-second day of a hunger strike. And that they still hadn't found any sign of Nana Esme, Ruth,

Hannah, or Randall. They'd disappeared into the heights. Guy and the surviving men were in prison awaiting trial.

"Jonathan, do you think about Ariel?" He raised his nose from the book he'd brought with him.

His cheeks were a little flushed. "Yeah, but you know." He stared out the windshield at some faraway spot. "I sent her a card. At the hospital. But she didn't write me back. Figured that meant . . . I mean, it's different now that we're not there. We're different, right?"

"Maybe," she said gently.

He shrugged like he was shaking something off, and retreated into his book.

She didn't mind the silence. It felt familiar, comforting like the landscape.

"It hasn't changed," she said as they drove by the white picket fence leading up to the small wooden church. They'd all gone to daycare here. She remembered the sound of the bell calling them in for lunch and the graveyard just behind, down a little path and next to a field that had been allowed to grow wild. They weren't supposed to play in the field—it ran down to a river—but they did anyway. She pulled over and they got out. A delicate wrought iron gate marked the entryway to the cemetery. There was no fence. Just the gate. Even though they could have gone around it, Jonathan lifted the latch and pushed through. It felt like a formal entry.

She followed and paused. "Is this weird? What they did?"

"You mean doing the whole burial ceremony thing? Without us?"

She nodded.

"Would have been weirder if they hadn't done anything. I

wish they hadn't buried my Stephen Hawking books though." He looked back over his shoulder at her. "Come on."

She shook herself. This wasn't just about her. "Wait a second," she said, stooping to pick a bunch of wildflowers. Purple owl clover and blue cornflowers.

"Know where we are?" she asked Jonathan once she'd caught up to him.

"Plots D 46 and D 84. It's set up on a grid. I'm actually just across the path from you. I researched it."

Kat swallowed. She was sure their families had done that on purpose.

It was pretty here. If that was a word you could use for a cemetery. The headstones were mostly plain white marble laid out on a velvety slope, groves of trees softened the lines, and pebbled paths wound around to the different plots. They had no trouble finding theirs. Kat traced her name, the dates of her birth and death. It was surreal. What would happen to the coffin now? Would it just lie there, empty, under five feet of earth, waiting for her? Or would they dig it up and store it somewhere?

Were there contingencies for do-overs?

She knelt down.

Her grandmother's grave was right next to hers. She removed the dry flowers in the vase and replaced them with her bouquet. "*Te amo, Nonna,*" she said, and pressed her fingers to her lips and then to the cold stone. Processing her nonna's death wasn't something she'd been able to do yet. It was too fresh. Too painful. It pissed her off. She'd been robbed of so much she would never get back.

Jonathan was sprawled out on the lawn, his feet up on his stone, as if he were laying claim to it. She settled down next to him with a groan and carefully stretched her legs out, feeling the pull around her left kneecap. "Most people don't get to experience this, you know?" he said, chewing on a stalk of grass. "Hanging out at their own gravesite. It's interesting."

"Interesting?" she said with a small laugh that surprised her considering where they were.

"Better than completely uninteresting."

"Do you ever think that we didn't fight hard enough? To get away?"

He stared at her injured leg for a second. His hand went up to his ribs. He seemed unconscious of it, spectacled gaze fixed on the neat rows of tombstones. She knew that the surgery on his wound had taken hours, and that he'd need more reconstruction if he ever wanted to go shirtless again.

"What I think about is when did that become normal and this become strange?" he said at last. "I almost felt like I dreamed this. It still feels like that sometimes."

"Same. That reality took over everything."

"It won't always be like that though. Tons of possibilities, a bunch of new realities."

Maybe. She could ground herself. In D, in Mamma and home, in Spider and her soft, hungry kisses and whatever came next.

"Maybe it's the surviving that matters," she said slowly.

"At the end of the day. Yeah." His mouth quirked. "We came back from the dead, Kat."

She exhaled, turned toward him, the tears pricking her eyes. "And that is something."

ACKNOWLEDGMENTS

Love and heartfelt thanks and hugs to my family and friends—you make my life so special; to my agent Ali McDonald—always in my corner; to the wonderful team at Penguin Teen Canada, most especially my editors—the indefatigable Lynne Missen and the perspicacious Peter Phillips. Also eagle-eyed Linda Pruessen and Sarah Howden; the fabulous sales team; my stalwart publicist, Evan Munday; Leah Springate for the wonderful cover design on this and my previous book; and everyone else behind the scenes who helps books find readers.

As always, my undying gratitude to booksellers, teachers, and librarians everywhere. And to the vibrant, diverse, and inspirational YA writing community who help me manage the crazy.

To my children, Milo and Lu—YOU are my everything.

Don't miss Jo Treggiari's *Blood Will Out*, a gripping
YA thriller in the vein of *Silence of the Lambs*!

Read on for an excerpt . . .

CHAPTER ONE

*S*omeone seemed to be shouting her name from far away—"Ari Sullivan!" She sat up and was instantly rocked by a wave of nausea and an excruciating pain that knifed through her head. She clutched her stomach and moaned. She was breathing too rapidly and she felt as if she were about to pass out. She forced herself to take deep breaths, counting between inhalations. Gradually the pain subsided to a throbbing ache and she peered around in shock. She could see nothing. Was she blind? She blinked rapidly but there was no difference.

It was dead quiet except for the thrum of blood in her ears. Pushing herself onto her knees, she crawled forward a few inches. She could feel earth under her fingers, smell the dank rooty cool of it. She ran shaking hands over her body. She was wearing jeans, a T-shirt, a sweatshirt and running shoes. She ached all over but nothing seemed broken, except for maybe her head. There was a lump at the back of her skull, but the worst injury originated just above her ear. She probed that area and felt a mushy spot. How had she hit her temple? She moved her head gingerly, half-afraid it might detach from her neck. Another crescendo of pain battered at her and she breathed through her nose, imagining that she was at the cool blue bottom of the pool. Take stock, she told herself, remembering the guidelines she'd learned in lifeguarding. Assess the injury. Her neck muscles were stiff but her spine was all right; her fingers wiggled, and she could feel her toes even though she couldn't see them.

Okay, so she'd live, probably. Now, where was she? Her brain cried in agony, as if all her nerve endings were centered in her skull, but she struggled to focus. Clearly she'd had an accident, fallen down the stairs to the cellar. But not her cellar, she decided, trying to pin down the muddied swirl of her thoughts. Her cellar was concrete-floored and brightly lit and smelled of laundry detergent and fabric softener. Not rotted leaves and swamp water. She was somewhere unknown.

"Mom, Dad?" she breathed, as if the sound of her voice might summon something terrible from the pitch black. All the horror movies she and Lynn had giggled over came back to her in a flood.

The darkness pressed down, a physical weight as if she were pinned under two tons of water. She held her eyelids open with her fingers and still there was nothing—not a flicker of light. This must be what it felt like to be buried alive. And with that thought, it seemed suddenly as if there were not enough air. She gulped, choked, desperate to fill her lungs, and felt the hysteria swell until it burst from her.

"Help! Help! Please!" Over and over until, propelled by rising panic, she was on her feet, unsteady and swaying, her voice ripping out of her throat. "Anyone!"

CHAPTER TWO

I am remembering the very first time. I am nine. My eyes follow Ma Cosloy's finger from the pigs to the knife as she tells me, "You tend to them. You tend to this too." Her work-rough hands are on her wide hips. She looks ten feet tall and not a hair straggles from the tight bun she wears from early morning to night. If I were to sketch her, it would be as something carved from granite, not flesh. She is unyielding. One couldn't call her expression kind, but it is not without compassion. Even so, I wouldn't dream of arguing.

The chosen piglet comes snuffling around my feet. He knows me. I bottle-raised him and his siblings and now, at near three months, he is the biggest. His rubbery snout prods, greedy and insistent. He is looking for acorns in my pockets. "None today, Ferdinand," I murmur, fondling his soft, pink ears, looking into his bright, curious eyes with their white lashes. Pigs are only slightly less intelligent than dolphins and apes. No one wants to hear that though, because we like to eat bacon so much. I named him after the gentle bull in the storybook: the one who wouldn't fight even when provoked. I scratch along his spine, feeling the stiff hairs. He leans and pushes against my side, his trotters scrabbling in the hay. I gather him up in my arms. He is a good weight but not impossible for me to lift for a short time. His whiskers brush my cheek in wet kisses. His breath smells sweet from the breakfast of hot bran mash and potato peelings he's just had. I put him down again and he frisks, puppy-like.

He trusts me and wants to be near. Even when I move over to the other end of the barn, with the big iron pot full of water bubbling over the fire pit, the knotted ropes and pulleys hanging from the blackened rafters like a simplified web, the razor-sharp knife lying ready on the table. Old stains spatter the floor; bluebottle flies buzz. He follows me there, making those grunting sounds that mean pure happiness. Smart as he is, he has no idea what is coming until he is hoisted into the air by his hind legs, and by then it is too late.

Later, when I have been scoured clean with the bristle brush and a bar of Ma Cosloy's gritty rosemary soap, which never lathers no matter how much you try, and my skin is sore and tingling, and I am alone again in the shed, I sit with my knees tucked close to my chest. My heart gallops. Ferdinand's squeals still ring in my ears; his blood is a cold slick of metal in my throat. The bath is an iron pot, similar to the one in the barn, and at first the water was scalding but now it has cooled, though it is still warmer than the frigid air around. I can see my breath and the small window is beaded with moisture, and my fingers and toes have pruned, but still I sit in the dirty water replaying it all in my mind. I barely recognize the emotion rushing through me. Exhilaration? Excitement?

My best shoes are cleaned and polished; my new clothes are folded neatly on the bench next to the rough towel. Ma Cosloy only finished sewing them last night. I know they will fit well, but the seams will scratch and the fresh-dyed cloth will feel stiff against my neck. My old clothes have been taken away to be soaked and scrubbed with lye, though I think the stains will never come out. I think about the colors I have just seen. So vivid and unlike the browns and grays and solemn blacks I am usually surrounded by, those I am clothed in.

It's as if Ma and Pa Cosloy and I live in an old photograph—mono-chromatic and yellowed, the house and barn timbers bleached by the sun, and the earth stripped of nutrients and turned to ashy dust. On occasion I look at my adoptive parents and wonder if their hearts are as shriveled and hard as the dry old potatoes I find sometimes after the fields have been plowed. My heart, though, feels as if it is swelling—plump, juicy, like a split ripe plum. It's as if I was blind before and now the colors are so bright in my mind that they hurt my eyes and fill my entire rib cage with wonder. That was life that spilled thickly over my hands. I can still smell it on me: rich as beef broth.

I think of a line from my favorite tale, "Black as Ebony, White as Snow, Red as Blood," and I trace an outline of Ferdinand on the glass, his body limp, his neck articulated, the new lines I made with the knife. I can't wait to capture it in my sketchbook.